"So, what is this Khosadam thing anyway?" Annja asked.

"She's a Siberian goddess," Bob replied.

"As in a deity?" Annja shook her head. "You realize how ludicrous that sounds. They actually think there's a goddess stalking them?"

"That would be my impression, yes."

"What—did she get bored with heaven or Olympus or wherever she was hanging out?"

"She was kicked out of heaven, actually," Bob said. "By her husband, of all people."

Annja grinned. "One step forward for women's rights."

"Don't misunderstand it. Ec banished her for being unfaithful. She liked to cavort with the lesser deities and sometimes even mortals. She has another name as well," Bob said, leading them into the nearby café.

A wall of heat slammed into Annja as she walked through the door. She could smell burned coffee and some other scents she didn't recognize. Despite her unease with the entire situation, her mouth watered and she realized she was ravenous. "What's her other name?" she asked.

"Eater of souls."

Titles in this series:

ROGUE Angel

Alex Archer

THE
SOUL STEALER

A GOLD EAGLE BOOK FROM
WORLDWIDE®

TORONTO • NEW YORK • LONDON
AMSTERDAM • PARIS • SYDNEY • HAMBURG
STOCKHOLM • ATHENS • TOKYO • MILAN
MADRID • WARSAW • BUDAPEST • AUCKLAND

First edition May 2008

ISBN-13: 978-0-373-62130-9
ISBN-10:   0-373-62130-2

THE SOUL STEALER

Special thanks and acknowledgment to
Jon Merz for his contribution to this work.

Printed in U.S.A.

The
LEGEND

...THE ENGLISH COMMANDER TOOK
JOAN'S SWORD AND RAISED IT HIGH.

The broadsword, plain and unadorned,
gleamed in the firelight. He put the tip against
the ground and his foot at the center of the blade.
The broadsword shattered, fragments falling
into the mud. The crowd surged forward,
peasant and soldier, and snatched the shards
from the trampled mud. The commander tossed
the hilt deep into the crowd.
Smoke almost obscured Joan, but she continued
praying till the end, until finally the flames climbed
her body and she sagged against the restraints.

Joan of Arc died that fateful day in France,
but her legend and sword are reborn....

1

She was being followed.

Again.

Annja Creed sighed with an almost nonchalant grin as she felt the familiar feeling wash over her. As many times and as many places as she'd been, she could tell—without even turning around to confirm it—that someone was taking more than a passing interest in her.

Even here, she thought. Even in this remote industrial complex where the concrete was as gray as the cold sky overhead, she hadn't managed to escape the eyes and ears of the locals.

The question, as always, was who was following her? Since arriving in Moscow and then taking the Siberian railroad to the northeast reaches of the former Soviet Union, Annja had kept what she thought was a low profile. She'd paid cash for her transactions. She'd used her new fake passport and booked her travels under a fake name. She'd even tossed her schedule out the window and lingered in several stops for far too long.

But it hadn't worked.

She ran down the list of people in her head who might wish her harm and then frowned. The list was long and growing longer. Every new adventure seemed to add dozens of names to the roster of folks who thought the world would be a better place if perhaps Annja Creed wasn't inhaling any more of its oxygen.

She passed the plate-glass windows of a department store advertising fashions so outdated that Annja wondered if anyone actually came in and requested them. She paused, however, and used the reflecting surface to look behind her.

Nothing.

She kept moving rather than give away the idea that she suspected she was being followed. No sense altering the hunters.

Annja knew that professionals never allowed themselves to be seen when they followed you. So the fact that she hadn't spotted anyone in the shop window might mean she wasn't dealing with amateurs.

On one level, that was good. Amateurs in this part of the world tended to be thugs and rapists who would brutalize you and then sell you off into some sexual-slavery den.

At least the professionals just killed you and got it done with.

She smirked at the thought. How my life has changed, she mused.

She turned a corner and strolled up a narrow street.

Ahead of her, she could make out an outdoor market area filled with a smattering of produce, imported electronics goods and bootleg DVDs. Annja knew the *mafiya* controlled these impromptu bazaars. But she hoped she could use them to lose her tail.

Unless, of course, he worked for the very same gangsters who ran the marketplace. She pondered that for a moment. But she couldn't worry about that for long. Not when she had a pressing appointment to keep with Robert Gulliver, known to his friends as Biker Bob and to the rest of the world as the cycling archaeologist.

Gulliver liked riding across the world on his favorite all-terrain bike. It was how he had scouted so many famous dig sites. Before he went in to any place with loads of equipment, he would casually assess the environment from the comfort of his bicycle. So far, Gulliver had crisscrossed the globe numerous times, although this was his first outing in Siberia.

Gulliver had sent Annja an e-mail from a cybercafé in a town just outside Minsk, asking if she would join him on a scouting mission. Annja, bored with her self-imposed exile back in Brooklyn, had jumped at the opportunity.

But even she was somewhat disgruntled by the location. So far, the dour city of Magadan had failed to impress her. The entire city was formed of cookie-cutter buildings set into neat rows. The streets were all evenly paved with ancient cars zooming down them at breakneck speeds, unconcerned if they hit pedestrians. In contrast, she occasionally spotted a sleek new Lincoln Town Car that proclaimed its driver as belonging to organized crime. Poverty was rampant, and Annja had already doled out some of her money to several children who looked closer to being scarecrows than human beings.

Gulliver had promised her a spectacular adventure, but Annja couldn't see it. Not in a city so utterly drab and awash in human misery.

Still, the fact that she had someone following her at least meant that there might be a little excitement before the day was done.

She ducked under the low awning and entered the marketplace. Immediately, her ears were accosted by the sounds of techno music infused with Russian street rap. Annja spoke a smattering of Russian, but she knew better than to try to translate the music lyrics that blasted out of the nearby speakers.

And she wasn't there to listen to music, anyway.

Ahead of her, the narrow corridor seemed to twist and turn. Elderly shoppers, their heads wrapped in heavy hats and scarves to ward off the first taste of winter in the air, pushed past her, intent on finding something valuable in the midst of chaos.

One of the vendors called out to her and held up an iPod. Annja smiled but shook her head no. She knew they made the cheap knockoffs in China and shipped them north through Mongolia before they ended up here.

Besides, Annja had her own iPod back at the hotel.

She frowned. Unless someone had broken in and stolen it, she thought. She glanced back at the iPod hawker but he was already gone.

Her unpredictable turn had prompted a man thirty feet back to stop awkwardly and turn his head.

Annja smiled.

First mistake. Maybe she wasn't dealing with professionals after all.

She hurried on, aware of a pungent stench of rotting fish assailing her nostrils. Three stalls of dead fish bedded on ice bracketed the next turn. Annja glanced at them. Even the fish were gray.

She had a decision to make. She could allow her tail to continue his surveillance, or she could turn the tables on him and find out who he was. The first choice was annoying because it meant she'd never be alone. The second choice was the more dangerous of the two. Confronting a tail was always a risk. He might be following her because he wanted to harm her. Possibly, he might even kill her.

Annja closed her eyes for the briefest of moments, confirming that Joan of Arc's sword—her sword— was accessible. She could see it in her mind's eye, hovering as it always seemed to. All she had to do was reach out and grab it.

She ducked under a low-hanging portal filled with cheap polyester tapestries done up in gaudy golds and bright reds. She could see the fraying edges and knew that the quality of the material only looked good to those who knew no better and had never had anything better in their lives. To some in this remote outback of Russia, polyester was the fabric of dreams.

She risked a glance back and saw the man clearly. He had no interest in any of the wares being hawked by the vendors. His face was as dour as the rest of the city. But Annja could see the deep lines etched in his face and knew that he had a past—probably that of a hired killer. She knew finding one in this part of the world was easy. And they were always competent.

If they weren't, they simply didn't survive.

Annja made her decision. She rushed ahead and instantly heard the yells behind her as her pursuer bumped into one of the fish stalls. Ice slid everywhere and the dead fish followed, causing several shoppers to fall.

Annja ran.

More voices joined the fray. If her pursuer was with the *mafiya,* most likely he'd be able to enlist some help. But if he wasn't, then he was risking their wrath by upsetting one of the chief places they made their protection money.

Annja spotted an exit and took it. Fresh air smacked into her face and she saw the narrow alley ahead of her. Grateful that she'd worn her hiking boots instead of her sneakers, Annja raced down the asphalt street.

Behind her, footsteps pounded the pavement. He was close.

Annja skidded into the alley and saw that it was filled with trash. The smell of urine hung heavy in the air. She could smell cheap vodka and the aroma of body odor. Makeshift corrugated-cardboard-box homes dotted the edges of the alley. Annja had entered a town of sorts for homeless people.

She pressed on, dodging the clotheslines that hung between two buildings. Bits of spattered cloth, remnants of winter coats and shirts hung from the lines. Steam from several grates issued forth with a sharp hiss.

The entire alley seemed eerily quiet. Behind her, at the entrance of the alley, the footsteps stopped.

This was where it would get hairy.

Annja ducked low, aware that her vision was being compromised by the crowded nature of the alley. The steam, trapped by the many laundry lines and the clothes they held, seemed to hug closer to the ground, making the alley feel more like a moor drowning in early-morning fog.

Her pursuer would have moved into the alley by now. But he'd move slowly, aware that any one of the boxes might conceal his prey. He might walk right past her. Or she might ambush him.

Annja glanced ahead. Bricks. She frowned. A dead end.

Her heart hammered in her chest. She closed her eyes and tried to reach for the sword. But when she opened her eyes, it wasn't in her hands. She tried again and then it hit her.

The alley was too narrow to swing a sword.

She almost yelped when the disembodied hand grabbed her around the ankle. She yanked her leg away and shot a kick into the hand. Someone on the ground grunted and she saw the hand retreat.

This was not a place she wanted to stay any longer than necessary.

The air around her grew heavy. Annja could feel his presence now, looming and drawing down the distance between them. She ducked down by the closest cardboard box and waited.

The steam played tricks with her eyes. She thought she could see his body parting the mist like some ship on the sea. And then she saw his feet.

Without even thinking about it, Annja launched

herself at him, screaming as she did so. She collided with him, knocking him to the ground. He grunted and Annja felt a breath of air come out of his mouth as the wind was knocked out of him.

She winced. Judging by the smell, he was a fan of onion bagels.

He brought his hands up and twisted, trying to push her off him. She could see his left hand reaching for something in his coat. Annja chopped down with her fist onto his forearm, hoping his coat wasn't thick enough to dull the blow.

He grunted again and rolled.

Annja slipped off him and scrambled to her feet, her hands held up high.

As he came up, Annja lashed out with a round-house kick aimed at his temple. He ducked under it and punched up into the underside of her thigh. Annja jerked back, surprised that he seemed so nimble after being knocked to the ground. Again, he reached inside his coat. Annja ducked her head and flew at him, tackling him around the waist. Using her momentum, she brought them both back down to the ground.

He was better prepared this time and as she landed, his hands were already trying to work the nerve clusters in her neck with his fingers. Annja could feel the sharp twinges as he dug his fingertips into the area under her ear.

She slid away and got to her feet.

"Stop!" the man shouted.

Annja braced herself. The man got to his feet and held his hands up as if he was surrendering. "I mean you no harm," he said.

Annja frowned. "Really?"

He gestured at his pocket. "Do you mind? I will prove that I am no threat to you."

"Go slow," Annja said. "If I think you're pulling a gun—"

"No gun. Just a note," he said.

Annja watched as he fished a slip of paper out of his pocket, unfolded it and gingerly handed it to her. She took it and glanced down quickly at the words written on it.

Annja, welcome to Magadan. Please follow Gregor.
He will bring you to me.
Regards,
Bob

Annja looked back up. "Gregor?"

The man smiled. *"Da."*

Annja smiled. "Nice to meet you."

2

Annja followed Gregor out of the alley and back into the open air of the city. He turned and wiped his brow with a smile. "Robert told me you might not be an easy woman to track down. He did not say anything about you not being easy to *take* down, however."

"You got the two-for-one deal," Annja said. "I'm sorry if I hurt you."

Gregor stiffened. "You did not…hurt me."

"Of course," Annja replied quickly.

"You always react this way to people who are behind you?" Gregor asked.

Annja grinned. "Past experience has taught me it's better to go on the attack than wait for an ambush."

"You must have some sort of peculiar background for that to be your normal method of behavior."

"Nothing about my life has ever been normal," Annja said. "Now, where's Biker Bob?"

Gregor nodded. "He waits for us nearby. A libation

establishment that he prefers to occupy during his awake time."

"Never heard a bar called that before." Annja smiled again. "Lead the way. I'll follow you this time."

"Perhaps that would be best," Gregor said. He walked ahead of Annja, navigating the twisting streets and the throngs of people who bustled here and there. Horns sounded as the afternoon turned into early evening and commuters rushed from factories and offices to head home.

"This place gets busy in the evening, huh?" Annja noted.

"This city is not a wonderful place to be at night. Most people go home quickly to their families and dream of a time when they might leave."

"How depressing."

Gregor stopped and looked at her. "Have you not noticed how sad this city is? How sad its inhabitants are, as well?"

"It's kind of hard not to notice," Annja said. "What's the problem? The weather?"

Gregor shook his head. "This is the gateway to hell."

"That's a bit extreme. Even some of the grungiest places on Earth have something to look forward to," Annja said.

Gregor shook his head and gestured at the concrete high-rises that surrounded them. "It is not my name for this place, but rather the people who lived here who called it that. There was a time when this truly was the gateway to hell. Millions of people came here first before journeying to the slave camps outside of the city to mine for gold under the Stalin regime. They say three million died in the mines at Kolyma."

"This was where the mine workers first came?"

"*Da.* Criminals, intellectuals, the poor—under Stalin, it did not matter what you were. If you were perceived as a threat, then you were shipped here to mine for gold. They used the railway to herd workers here first before dropping them off the face of the planet and into the very depths of hell itself."

"Amazing." Annja sighed. "Good thing we don't have Stalin to worry about any longer."

"The scars of those times will take a very long while to heal," Gregor said. "My grandparents died in the mines. It is for me a very painful topic. One that is very close to my heart."

"Maybe they should have destroyed the city when the mines shut down," Annja said.

Gregor shook his head. "The mines are not shut down. They are under private companies now. The goal is the same—to provide wealth for the Russian government and the investors of the mine."

"But they don't use slave labor anymore, do they?"

Gregor shrugged. "Depends on your definition of slave labor, I would suppose. Some would argue that the wages paid to the workers are not much better than what the original laborers received."

A light drizzle fell from the sky, spattering Annja's face as she saw the lines around Gregor's eyes deepen. He sniffed the air and shook his head. "Death on the wind is never washed away, no matter how many times God cries."

Annja said nothing, but felt a cold breeze whip

along the sidewalk. Gregor tugged her arm. "I apologize. Sometimes, I reminisce too much. You have a meeting to attend and I am supposed to make sure you arrive there intact."

"Intact?" Annja asked, alarmed.

Gregor frowned. "In one piece? Is that better?"

"Either one works. I'm just curious as to why you chose those words instead of saying something, I don't know, less dangerous sounding."

Gregor smiled. "Robert told me something about you. He said trouble seems attracted to you. It was his wish I guide you along so that trouble this time keeps its distance."

"Damned thoughtful of him," Annja said. "Now, where's the bar?"

Gregor led her down the street, passing a Mercedes dealership. Gregor nodded at it. "Russian *mafiya* likes flashy cars. They have the money to buy, so the dealerships come to supply them with their wants."

"Are there a lot of gangsters around?"

Gregor sniffed. "Russia is run by gangsters now. Some of them wear suits, some wear army uniforms. All of them are dangerous men."

"Lovely," Annja muttered.

At the next block, Gregor turned right and the streets narrowed. Farther on, Annja could make out a blinking neon sign in red Cyrillic letters. Gregor nodded. "That is the place."

When they stepped inside, the heat and the smell of alcohol hit her at the same time. Smoke hung in the air, belched out by a hundred cheap cigarettes all bucking for room in the crowded joint.

Gregor nudged Annja ahead. "Robert waits in the back," he said.

Annja shouldered her way through the rough crowd. Some of them looked like greased pompadour playboys while others had the look of hunted men and women, all trying to scratch out some type of existence in a place that seemed to reek of death and haunting memories.

Annja spied a couple of Naugahyde booths in back and headed for them.

"Annja Creed!"

Rising out of one of the booths like a tall, rail-thin weed, Robert Gulliver rushed to hug Annja. To Annja it felt as if she were hugging herself, so lean was Biker Bob's body. Still, she knew that despite his lack of weight, he was lithe and sinewy, with a great deal of strength from all the cycling he did.

"Nice to see you, Bob," she said.

He hurried them back to the booth. Annja noticed that Gregor did not sit with them but lounged near the bar where anyone who wanted to get to the booth section would have to pass.

"Gregor's not joining us?" she asked.

"Hmm? Uh, no. Gregor will keep an eye out so we aren't disturbed," Gulliver said.

Annja frowned. "And he said you think I'm the one who attracts trouble."

"We can get into that later, if you don't mind." Gulliver leaned back and helped himself to the pitcher of beer on the table. "I've got a glass all ready for you, m'lady. Can I pour you one?"

"Sure," Annja said.

She watched Bob's hands grip the pitcher and pour the beer into her glass. Blue veins in his hand snaked their way up his forearm, twisting around bands of thin muscle. "I see you still haven't porked up any," she said with a laugh.

"It's genetics, I think. I was born this way and damned if I can eat enough to gain an ounce," he replied.

"That and all the biking."

"Well, sure, but then again, if not for my bike, we never would have met."

Annja smiled. She and Gulliver had met on the set of *Chasing History's Monsters* a few years previously. Biker Bob had arrived on the set each day riding a candy-apple-red 1950s five-speed bike complete with a playing card striking the spokes for the required sound effects. Over lunches and quick dinners, Annja had learned that he possessed an uncanny intelligence and sense for finding unique dig sites. While his methodology was unorthodox, his research and passion were undeniable. Annja had quickly realized Bob had the makings of a true friend.

"So what's so special that you dragged me all the way over here? I mean, Siberia? That's a bit of a stretch even for you, isn't it?"

"You know how much history is locked into this part of the world? We're in the regions where the Mongol hordes got their start. The legends that exist here are spectacular. And now, with the old Soviet guard finally dismantled, we can actually begin to explore this area like never before," Gulliver said.

Annja sipped her beer. "And it will look ever so

exciting as we tape bouncing along the roads on a bike. Is that it?"

Bob fixed her with a stare. "You know I never call for my video team until I have something to really show the world. This is more of an excursion. I've been fascinated with Siberia for years. And when I decided to bike across the northern part of the continent, I thought it would finally be a good time to see what could be seen."

"And you called me."

"Of course! Why not share this with the one person I know at least respects my work? I thoroughly enjoyed the time we spent together on set and thought this would be a magnificent way to continue our friendship."

"I suppose it is." Annja shivered. "It's just this part of Russia leaves a bit to be desired."

"You referring to the poverty, the gangs or the somber mood?"

"Is there an option for all three?" she asked.

Gulliver laughed. "Definitely. I won't pretend this is a pretty part of the country, because it's not. But we aren't staying here, anyway."

"We're not?" Annja asked, intrigued.

"No way. Our destination lies farther north. A road that winds its way through some very old places on the way to Yakutsk."

"Never heard of it," Annja said.

Gulliver downed his beer and poured himself another. "Remote doesn't begin to describe it. I hear that when the Soviets ran things, even they didn't dispatch much in the way of bureaucratic might to the area. Even to those guys, there were places in their own country that they deemed better left untouched."

"I wonder why?" Annja asked.

He clapped her on the arm. "That's what you and I are going to find out!"

Annja shrugged. "Well, as I was just lying around my loft feeling bored and restless, this is, I suppose, a great way to relieve the boredom."

Gulliver nodded. "That's the spirit I know and love."

Annja glanced at Gregor, who was paying more attention to the wood of the bar and very little to the small drink he had in front of him. "Gregor's not very social," she observed.

Gulliver smiled. "He'll nurse that vodka for hours if we let him. But he's just doing his job."

"Which is?"

"Well, one part was making sure you got here intact."

"And why wouldn't I?"

Gulliver sighed. "Don't take this the wrong way, but you're young and very attractive. And while I know that you're more than capable of handling yourself and any trouble that comes your way, the rest of this part of the world does not."

Annja grinned. "Sounds like you're protecting *them* from *me*."

"Well, using Gregor to ward off any unwanted attention is a smart move. He knows the ins and outs of this region better than anyone else."

"How so?"

"Born and raised here. He was an enforcer for one of the local syndicates but he went freelance a few years back."

"And they let him?" Annja asked.

"You might have gotten the impression it's not wise to say no to him."

"He is imposing."

"They thought so, too. He still does errands for them on occasion, but nowadays, he looks out for numero uno."

Annja sipped her beer. "And you trust him?"

"I saved his life," Bob said. "There's nothing he won't do for me."

"Now, there's a story I want to hear," Annja said.

"Later. I suspect he might be embarrassed if he knew I was telling you. And embarrassing these guys is never a wise move," Gulliver advised her.

Annja finished her beer. "What time are we leaving tomorrow?"

"Six in the morning."

"That early?"

"Sure." Bob's eyes twinkled with glee. "I even got you a bike."

"It's not candy-apple-red, is it?"

He laughed. "No, but it does have racing stripes."

"You wouldn't—"

"I'm kidding." He rose from the booth. "Now let's see if we can scare up one final good dinner before we head off into the great unknown."

3

By the time dawn poked its head over the gray horizon and lit up Magadan to more of a beige hue, Annja had already been up for two hours. She'd slept fitfully, tossing and turning until some time after three in the morning. She'd finally rolled out of bed and started working on her yoga asanas. Before she knew it, she was relaxed and sweaty, and she felt better than she had in bed.

She showered quickly, not for fear of being late, but because the hotel—if you could call it that—didn't have any hot water. Shivering as she stepped into her clothes, Annja warmed herself up by doing some deep breaths and jumping up and down to increase her heartbeat.

Downstairs, she wolfed down a cup of steaming black coffee and something that was supposed to resemble a muffin. Then she stepped outside and found Biker Bob already there, casually drinking from a Thermos as he looked to the northwest.

When he saw Annja, he took the Thermos away from his lips and smiled. "Good morning!"

Annja waved. "Hi, Bob."

He offered her the Thermos, but Annja declined as she saw the two bicycles Gulliver had arranged. "What in the world are those?"

He turned and bowed low, spreading his hand out as he did so with a flourish. "Those, m'lady, are our transportation."

"They look like two-wheeled moon buggies," Annja said.

Gulliver straightened himself. "NASA should be so lucky as to have such fine chariots as these." He waved Annja over. "Allow me to introduce you to the very noble and very rugged Yeti 575 Carbon Enduro. The 2006 model. In turquoise, because they don't have pink with polka dots."

Annja pursed her lips. "And because you know I would have kicked the snot out of you if you'd shown up with a pink bike for me."

"There's that, yes," he admitted.

Annja ran her hands over the bike's frame. She could see the front and rear shock absorbers. "It's good, I assume, for what you have in mind for us?"

"One of the best. And fortunately for me, Gregor was able to get his hands on them for our travels. These bikes retail for about three thousand dollars. And I only had to pay five thousand for these."

"You paid a two-thousand-dollar markup?" Annja asked, shocked.

Gulliver shrugged. "Cost of doing business in this part of the world, Annja. And besides, it's tax deductible once I get a dig going on the site we're heading for. Five grand, ten grand, it makes no difference."

"Must be nice having all that cash."

Gulliver smiled. "I'm not ashamed of being a trust-fund baby, Annja. At least I spend my money relatively wisely. I could be like those other idiots and charter three-hundred-foot yachts in the Mediterranean for the better part of a million each week. End up on VH-1 and all that ridiculousness."

"Your quest is noble, Bob. I've never held your family's money against you," Annja said.

Gulliver nodded. "That is precisely why you're along on this trip. Among other reasons." He pointed at her bike. "You want to try it out?"

Annja nodded and climbed onto the seat. The first thing she noticed was how comfortable it felt. "This isn't like the last time we went riding."

"They've made a lot of improvements since then," Bob said. "Comfort and practicality are key. Especially for bikes like this, which are made for all-day touring, mountain climbing and traversing various obstacles."

"So, you're saying my ass won't feel like a pincushion by the time we end our ride each day?"

Gulliver grinned. "I have no idea how your ass will feel. I can confidently assure you, however, that my own posterior has never felt the slightest bit injured after a full day's riding on these miraculous machines."

Annja bounced once in the seat. "It's got a fair amount of give."

"They call it travel now. The amount of movement

the suspension gives the rider. On this model, it's almost six inches, which is a good amount of give."

Annja pointed. "You took the black one for yourself?"

Bob shrugged. "I always ride a black bicycle. It's part of my marketing strategy for myself. The world has come to know me as always riding a black bicycle. What would they think if I showed up riding a red one?" He winked at her.

"Heaven forbid," Annja said. "So, where are we heading, anyway?"

Gulliver took a folded map out of his pocket and handed it to Annja. "Northwest of here. Out into the Siberian wilderness."

Annja glanced at the map and handed it back. She looked around the city, now just starting to percolate with signs of life. "As long as we're getting out of here, that's fine with me."

Gulliver nodded. "I understand. There are parts of this city that have a certain amount of charm, but I suppose there's no denying the awful past of this place. It's ingrained everywhere. Unavoidable. Perhaps I should have chosen a better staging area."

"This is the closest city?"

"Yes."

"Then there really was no other option," Annja said. "And don't worry too much about it. I've seen my share of horrible places."

Gulliver smiled. "We should be off, then."

Annja tested her feet on her pedals and found she could reach them easily enough. Gulliver had estimated her height correctly and ensured she had the right-size bicycle. As she leaned down to see if her water bottle was filled, she heard a sound behind them and looked up quickly.

Gregor skidded to a halt on his own bicycle. Annja glanced at Bob. "He's coming with us?"

"A trusted comrade is always a welcome thing out in the backwaters of a potentially unfriendly environment," Gulliver said.

Gregor smiled at Annja. "Good morning."

Annja nodded. "How are you feeling today?"

Gregor pointed at his ribs. "They have a nice blue to them. You have done very well in marking me up. But nothing that vodka and aspirin cannot handle."

"Sorry about that," Annja said sheepishly.

Gregor shrugged. "I was not careful. Not your fault. You were just defending yourself. As I would have done in your spot."

Annja turned around and saw Gulliver tightening the straps on the dual bags that hung over the back of his bike. Annja saw that she had two bags of her own. "You packed for me, too?"

"Gregor did some shopping. Just the necessities, I'm afraid. This won't be a glamorous event for any of us. Just a recon as it were."

"As long as the clothes are warm," Annja said.

"They are."

Annja looked at Gregor again. "Thanks."

"My pleasure," he said quietly.

Annja removed a playing card from her jacket pocket and slid it against the spokes of Gulliver's bike. He was too involved in his map and didn't notice. Finally, he folded the map and looked back. "Are we ready?"

Annja smiled. "Let's roll."

Gulliver turned, mounted his bike and started pedaling. Instantly, from the back of his bike came the telltale sound as the spokes slid over the playing card.

Annja smiled. Behind her, she heard Gregor chuckle. "He will not notice that for at least three miles," he said.

GREGOR'S ESTIMATION WAS correct. They pedaled for three miles on the paved highway leading out of Magadan. The road gradually waned from sleek asphalt to pockmarked concrete rife with potholes and bits of wire jutting out of the ground along its edges. More and more, they had to wind their way around obstacles.

Gulliver signaled a halt and they pulled over to the side of the road. He frowned and leaned back, removing the playing card from his spokes. "This your idea of a funny?" he asked.

Annja shrugged. "Yep," she said.

Gulliver took a swig of water from his bottle and then replaced it. "The road ahead goes from this to more of a hard mud track. It should be easier once we hit it."

"Less obstructions," Gregor said from behind them.

"They don't believe in road repair in these parts, huh?" Annja looked around them. Anything short of a combat tank would have flat tires in seconds.

"Is not they don't believe in it," Gregor said. "Just that the officials all have their hands out ready for a little grease. By the time the money filters down to the workers who must actually repair the road, there is none left."

"Wonderful," Annja said.

Gulliver waved them on. "I want to at least reach a way point by tonight. And that's thirty miles away."

Annja sighed. A thirty-miler wasn't the best way she imagined to ease back into the bicycling frame of mind, but she knew that once Gulliver had his mind fixed on something, he wasn't going to budge for anything short of a life in danger.

Gregor sped past her and then overtook Gulliver. He pedaled ahead. Annja marveled at how easily he rode his bicycle.

Bob glanced back at her. "He's a former military guy. Did I mention that?"

"No," Annja said.

"He's used to driving himself hard. One of those guys who measures himself based on how difficult something is. The bigger the obstacle, the better he feels about himself when he masters it."

Annja nodded. "I know someone just like that."

Bob grinned. "I thought you might find that a familiar sentiment."

They pedaled along for another hour. Magadan's outskirts disappeared quickly as the stark countryside reclaimed the edges of the road for itself. Annja saw the twisted, bent and hooked branches of the spindly trees reaching in for them. She saw little animal life and only a few birds cruised the skies.

"Is it always like this?" she eventually asked.

"Like what?"

"Devoid of life."

Gulliver shrugged. "Winter's coming. And soon. Most of the animals have already wandered off to their various hibernation areas. Birds have flown south. And the landscape just seems to be settling down for the harsh snows."

"We've got time, though, right?" Annja asked.

"Yes. Timing was crucial. I'm glad you were able to get out here. With luck, we should find something before we get snowbound."

"What happened with Gregor, anyway?" Annja could barely make out his bicycle far ahead of them.

"He likes taking point on these things. Takes his job of protecting me very seriously. Says there are far too many threats out here for a man to travel alone. He insists on driving on ahead to spot anything that looks a bit off."

"Does he cost a lot?"

Gulliver shrugged. "Not by our standards. But he makes a decent wage. Plus, it gets him away from the *mafiya*. And anytime he can do that, he's far happier than he is otherwise."

Annja dropped behind Bob as the road narrowed drastically. From two lanes, the hard-packed mud and gravel withered to barely a single lane. On her right side, the edge of the road fell away as they ascended what looked to be a fairly significant hill.

"Mind yourself," Bob said. "We're corkscrewing up the hill. It's a long way down."

"Why don't we use the left side?"

"Anything coming at us from the other way will crush us against the side of the hill. They won't see us coming."

"Makes sense." Annja kept pedaling. Her breathing was coming harder as her lungs got their first taste of serious exertion. She kept herself hunched low, trying to reduce her wind resistance as she climbed the hill. The bike seemed built for a wide variety of terrain and handled the ascent pretty well.

It didn't make the strain of the pedaling any easier for Annja, though.

Ahead of her, Bob seemed in his element. He used long, steady pedaling to carve his way up the hill. Annja tried to emulate him, but knew that as her body responded to the stress of serious biking for the first time in years, she was going to have a harder time than Bob or Gregor, for that matter.

She settled her breathing and tried to relax.

She heard a sudden sound. She turned in her seat and saw the large truck rumbling up the hill behind her.

She frowned. "Bob!"

He turned and saw the truck. "Oh, crap! Pedal faster, Annja!"

Annja drove her feet into the pedals. The truck sounded its horn. The sharp wail cut through the cold air and sliced into Annja's back. She looked back, but rather than slow down as another truck might be expected to do when it was climbing an incline, this truck seemed to be accelerating.

And it was headed straight for Annja.

4

Annja pumped her pedals harder, desperately trying to outpace the truck streaming up the hillside road behind her. Her breathing felt shallow, as if she couldn't get enough oxygen into her lungs to power her legs. Sweat broke out along her hairline and ran down her face. She knew the signs of adrenaline rush and this certainly qualified.

"Annja!"

Bob's voice broke through the rural air, and Annja heard him above the grinding roar of the truck. She glanced back over her shoulder. She guessed the truck was a two-and-a-half-ton truck used by militaries all over the world as supply trucks and to convey troops from one region to another.

There was a nasty gash across the radiator grille that gave the front end an almost comical toothy appearance. It looked as if the truck could simply overtake her and eat her alive.

Annja looked ahead and kept jamming her feet against the pedals as hard as she could. She huffed as her lungs worked like bellows. Her breath stained the air with steam and mixed with the sweat pouring down her face.

Ahead of her, Bob was pedaling fast, as well.

The road sloped at a severe angle. The increase meant Annja would have to pedal even harder and she didn't know if she had it in her.

Keep pedaling, she told herself. She could see the crest of the hill. If she could just manage to make it—

The truck horn blared behind her, jarring her. She glanced back and saw that it was even closer than before. It showed no signs of easing back or slowing down. Whoever was driving that rig was having a lot of fun at her expense.

She couldn't see through the windshield. For one thing, the entire panel of glass seemed to have a jagged line scored through it. She could see the buildup of bug guts and dirt had stained it so much that being able to determine who was driving was an impossibility.

Her legs felt like lead weights. She wanted to vomit.

Keep going!

She pedaled harder. She could hear the gravel underneath her tires kicking away from the wheels as she sped her way up the hillside.

Fifty yards to the top.

The truck horn blared again.

Annja turned and saw the bumper closing in on her bicycle. There was only twenty feet or so separating them.

He really means to run me over, she thought.

She felt herself growing angry. Furious even. Who the hell would want to kill her like this? Why were they so determined? She hadn't even been in Russia long enough to annoy that many people.

Annja gave one last, monumental effort, her lungs straining to their capacity. She drove her heels into the pedals and the bike shot forward.

Along the side of the hill, she could see the sheer drop-off, plunging hundreds of feet to the ground far below.

The truck nudged her.

Annja lost control.

"Bob!"

She jerked the handlebars of the bike to the right and then to the left. The truck nudged her again, and Annja headed straight off the edge of the hill.

She was falling.

Annja had the briefest sensation of being weightless—suspended in midair—before gravity exerted its pull on her body and jerked her back down toward the earth.

She hit the side of the hill and tumbled, rolled and somersaulted over jagged rocks, tree roots, upturned branches and forest debris. Somewhere she heard her bicycle doing a passable imitation of her own body as it caromed down the hillside.

Annja tried to relax herself as she bounced her way down the slope.

And then suddenly, she came to a stop.

Blackness came for her.

"Annja!"

Her head pounded.

"Not so loud. I believe she has a concussion."

"Annja." The first voice was softer now.

Annja blinked, saw the bright light of the gray sky and closed her eyes again, groaning as she did so.

"Annja. Can you hear me?" Bob's voice sounded as if he might break out sobbing at any moment.

"Unfortunately," she mumbled.

She heard Gregor chuckle. "Is good sign. She has sense of humor. That tells me she is not too badly broken."

Annja opened her eyes again. "Speak for yourself. I feel like crap."

Gulliver shook his head. "My God, when you went over the side of the hill…I thought you were a goner."

"So did I," she said.

Gregor frowned. "You should be dead."

Annja smirked. "That was subtle."

He held up his hands. "Forgive me, it's just that you fell so far it is truly a marvel that you are still alive."

Bob moved away and nodded for Gregor to move in closer. "Check her for broken bones, will you?"

"Hey—" Annja protested.

Bob held up his hand. "Annja, please. Humor me, will you? Gregor has some medical training and knows how to look for these things."

Annja felt Gregor put his hands behind her neck and then feel his way down the center of her back, pause briefly at her buttocks, and then continue down her legs. Then he ran his hands down her arms and finally peered into her eyes.

"Having fun?" she asked.

He shook his head. "No broken bones."

Gulliver whistled. "That'll be one hell of a way to start this show off. A dramatic reenactment of you tumbling over the side of the cliff and then emerging unscathed."

Annja tried to sit up, but Gregor held her down. "Not yet. Too soon. You rest a few minutes." He held a water bottle to her lips and Annja took a sip of the cold liquid.

As soon as she swallowed it, she turned and vomited.

She wiped her mouth. "Sorry about that, guys."

Gregor only nodded. "Concussion." He looked at Gulliver. "She cannot move too much yet."

Gulliver frowned. "As long as she's not seriously hurt."

Gregor shrugged. "We will see. If she falls asleep and never wakes up again, then that is bad sign."

Annja sighed. "You don't say."

Gulliver looked around. "Can we make this into a campsite?"

Gregor nodded. "It will suffice for our needs."

Annja threw some pine needles over the small pool of vomit. "Sorry about the smell."

Gregor shook his head. "No need. It will dissipate soon enough. You should rest now. I will make the camp."

He moved off and Bob knelt in close. "You okay? Seriously?"

Annja touched her head. "Aside from a raging headache, yeah, I guess so. But what the hell happened up there?"

Gulliver shook his head. "No idea. One minute

everything was fine and the next that monster truck was bearing down on you. I crested the hill and got into a small niche up there for safety. And Gregor was already ahead of me in the safe zone. There was nothing I could do. I felt totally helpless."

"You weren't the only one."

He sighed. "I'm terribly sorry to have gotten you into this mess. Christ, you were almost killed! It's all my fault."

Annja tried to smile. "Forget it. Our profession has its share of risks. I'm well aware of what these things entail."

"Yeah, but being driven off the side of the hill by a truck isn't usually one of them, is it?" Bob asked.

Annja grinned. "You got me there."

Gulliver sat back on his haunches and sighed again. "We couldn't even get a good look at the maniac driving the rig. I was so concerned about you when I saw you go over the side of the cliff. My God, Annja, I thought you were dead."

"So did I," she said. "I guess I had some lucky bounces."

Gregor returned, hauling Annja's bike with him. Annja was surprised. "You found it?"

"Farther down the slope. It is a little banged up, but otherwise okay. Like its owner, I would say."

Annja nodded. "Hell of a bike."

Gregor vanished into the woods again. Annja looked at Bob. "You guys rappelled down here?"

"Gregor always carries rope with him on these trips. He claims it's one of the most important survival tools you can have. After what happened today, I'm inclined to agree with him."

"How long was I out?" Annja asked.

Gulliver shrugged. "Gregor's been working on you for almost an hour."

"That's some hired hand you got yourself there, Bob. Guy seems like he can do everything."

"Short of stopping a truck," Bob said with a small smile.

Gregor returned, his arms laden with branches. He dropped them close to Annja's feet and then sat down on the ground. Using a large flat stone, he scraped away a portion of the earth and then lined the pit with more rocks. On top of these, he rested a small pile of tinder. Over that, he built a tepee of small twigs for his kindling. When he was satisfied, he stooped low, struck a single match and lit the tinder.

Flames erupted instantly as the fire ate into the dry tinder and kindling. Gregor added some thicker branches.

Annja felt the warmth of the fire and sighed once. "A fire is a very nice thing indeed."

Gregor smiled. "Warmth. Comfort. And food. These things will make you feel better quicker than anything else."

Gulliver opened his hands over the flames and then rubbed them together. "I'm afraid I didn't pack a tent for this journey. I figured we'd reach our destination and find board there. This side trip has certainly been unexpected."

Gregor looked at the sky. "We will need shelter. Tonight it will rain. Possibly it will also snow."

"Already?" Bob looked nervous. "I didn't expect the winter to come down quite so fast."

Gregor nodded. "One thing about Siberia. It is impossible to predict her moods. If she wishes to snow, then she will snow. She cares little about the whims of man." He turned to leave.

Annja cleared her throat. "Where are you going?"

Gregor looked back at her and then pointed at Bob. "He says he has not brought a tent. Neither have I. Since we have not brought a shelter, it will be necessary to make one. Otherwise, you will have hypothermia before morning."

He vanished into the woods again. Annja glanced at Bob. "Tell me again where exactly you found this guy?"

"Moscow. He was looking for work and answered my ad for a hired hand. He's pretty close-lipped about his past. Just what I told you before."

"He seems to have a lot of skills for a *mafiya* enforcer."

"Military. He never told me what he did, but I'm guessing special operations. Spetsnaz most likely. Those guys never talk about their past."

"Lucky for us, I guess," Annja said.

Gulliver pointed overhead. "I'd say so."

Annja looked at the sky. Dark clouds were moving in fast. It looked very much as if Siberia was getting ready to unleash a blizzard on them.

5

By the time the first flakes were drifting down to the earth from the dark clouds overhead, Gregor had constructed a working camp. He'd added a great deal of wood to the fire, which now threw heat and light across the shadow-filled landscape. He'd also laid in a tremendous store of firewood to get them through the night.

"Venturing into the snowy night will get us killed," he'd said simply.

Annja rested inside the large lean-to Gregor had built from thick saplings and pine boughs. She lay on a raised floor of more branches and boughs filled with huge amounts of pine needles. The scent reminded her of Christmas, even though it was a few months away yet.

"This is actually pretty comfortable," Bob said. He was lying next to her. "I never thought pine needles could be quite so luxurious."

Annja smiled through the pain that was still lancing her skull. "It's not the Four Seasons, but it will certainly do."

Gregor poked his head through the opening. "Dinner."

Annja glanced at Bob, who shrugged. "I had him pack some military rations. It's not the best stuff, but it will do."

Annja frowned. "That doesn't smell like rations."

She ducked out through the lean-to slowly. Gregor helped her to a log he'd situated near the fire. Annja looked around and saw two rabbits cooking on spits over the fire. "You got fresh food?" she marveled.

Gregor shrugged. "Have you ever had Russian rations?"

"No," she said.

"Then be thankful you do not have to have them tonight. I eat them for four years of my life. I say I will never eat them again."

Bob sat down next to Annja. "Told you he was worth his weight in gold."

Gregor said nothing but used a large knife to serve them up the fresh rabbit meat on sticks. Annja took hers and ate it like a kabob. She'd never liked rabbit much, but as the first bit hit her tongue, her saliva flowed and she realized then how very hungry she was. She bit into the meat and chewed it.

Gregor smiled. "Not so fast for you. You are still recovering from your head trauma."

Annja chewed slowly and swallowed. "Believe me when I tell you, this is really fantastic. It tastes wonderful."

Bob murmured his own appreciation. "Never had rabbit before."

Gregor helped himself to some and chewed it for a moment before passing judgment. "It could use some seasonings. My mother, she used to make a stew with the rabbits. It was very nice thing."

Annja watched his eyes dance for a moment before he concentrated on eating again. Had she just glimpsed something Gregor didn't want anyone to see?

She turned back to her own food and finished the skewer. Gregor sliced her off some more, and she devoured that, as well. She washed it down with some of the pine-needle tea Gregor had made.

"This will help you, too," he said.

Annja yawned. "I didn't realize how tired I was."

"I set a pretty grueling pace today," Bob said. "I'm sorry about that. I should have given you some more time to acclimate to the environment and the exertion. It's just that we can reach Yakutsk pretty quick and I'm not much for waiting. It's a fault of mine, I know. I hope you can forgive me."

Annja smiled. "Relax, Bob. You're forgiven. I know what it's like to be impatient."

He nodded. "Curse of doing what we do."

"There's always the risk of someone else finding it first. But in my defense, I didn't think I was going to feel quite so taxed today," she said.

She stared into the fire. Ever since she'd discovered the sword that Roux had pieced together, Annja had been physically tested again and again. As a result she was the fittest person she knew. But for some reason, it seemed as though her strength was deserting her thus far on the trip.

She yawned again.

Gregor chuckled. "I see we are boring our companion." He fished around in one of his pockets and came out with a small flashlight. He scooted over to Annja and looked at her.

Annja frowned. "What?"

"I need to look into your eyes."

"With that?" she asked.

Gregor held up the flashlight. "I'm afraid so. To check for concussion, which I know you have, but I wish to see if things are improving or not."

"And the flashlight will help?"

He nodded. "Many times a concussion will result in your pupils not dilating properly. This was how you were earlier today when we find you. I am hoping to see this is better now that you have rested."

"My head still hurts," she said.

"And it probably will for some time. You took many nasty falls which may have left you with some bumps and bruises for a long time."

"That flashlight's not going to make my head feel any better," she said.

Gregor sighed. "Please. It is just for a moment. I will not hold the light on you any longer than is absolutely necessary."

"All right." Annja brought her head forward. She felt Gregor's left hand grasp her around the back of her head. She could feel the immense strength resonating from his hand. It almost pulsed as he touched her.

She heard the click and then her head exploded in

pain as Gregor flashed the light into one eye and then the other. Tears ran down her cheeks.

The light vanished and Annja slumped forward, cradling her head. "Damn."

"You are getting better," Gregor said. "Sip some more of the tea."

Annja wanted to throw up again, but fought back the rising bile in her throat. Instead, she took the tea and drank it slowly. The hot liquid flowed down her throat and seemed to settle her stomach.

"Thanks," she mumbled.

"I am sorry I had to do that," Gregor said.

"It's okay."

Gregor moved back to his seat and nodded to Bob. "She will be okay tomorrow. But our pace must be less than it was today."

"We should have no problem reaching Yakutsk by sometime tomorrow, anyway. We might have even done it today if that maniac with the truck hadn't intervened."

Gregor frowned. "Perhaps we will meet up with that person at some time in the future."

Annja sipped some more tea. "And what will you do to him?"

Gregor's smile was anything but friendly. "I will engage him in discussion about the error of his ways."

The last vestiges of daylight had vanished as they talked. The deepening shadows of the forest seemed to reach toward the firelight like long, crooked fingers. Annja shivered as a breeze twisted around them, and the snowflakes stuck to her face before melting.

Far off in the distance, a howl punctured the serenity of the coming night. Gregor seemed unfazed by it. "Wolves," he said simply.

"You have a lot of them around here?" Annja asked.

"Siberia is full of them," Gregor said. "But they keep their distance. This time of year they are still not that hungry. If this was February, then we might have a problem. For now, no problem."

"Small comfort," Bob said. "That howl just brought back memories of those old horror movies I used to watch."

Annja grinned. "Doesn't help that it's close to Halloween."

Gregor let a genuine smile escape. "You think maybe these woods are haunted? That perhaps there are creatures living here who would do us harm?"

Annja looked at him. The firelight made shadows jump across his face, contorting his features and making him look almost comically terrifying. "I think I've seen a lot of things in my life that defy explanation."

Bob said nothing, but seemed to be searching the darkness for something.

Gregor held up one hand. "I come from this area, Annja. I am no stranger to legends. Or to being scared in the woods like this."

"I'm not scared," she said.

He smiled. "Of course not. But here we are, in the snow and dark, with just the fire to keep the evil away. Many other people, they would find this intimidating."

"Like me," Bob said. "I think my mind is getting the better of me."

Annja rubbed her hands together. "I guess this wouldn't be a good time to tell ghost stories, then, huh?"

"Ghost stories are a way of life for those who live in Siberia," Gregor said. "But perhaps Bob would prefer it if we did not talk about such things while his mind is busy replaying movies from his youth."

"I can't help it," Bob said. "I've got visions of the werewolf running through my head." He looked at Annja. "You have to admit, it fits the situation pretty well."

"Just because we're in the woods?" she asked.

"I was talking about that howl we heard."

Another howl sounded in the night air. Bob jumped. Annja and Gregor both laughed.

Bob pointed a finger at Annja. "No one finds out about my fear when we get back to civilization. I just don't think I ever outgrew those crazy flicks I used to watch as a kid."

"I used to watch them, too," Annja said. "I just think it's great that a guy like you who is so accomplished and relatively fearless—I mean, you bike and camp everywhere—gets freaked out by the woods at night."

"Yeah, well, my therapist suggested I confront my fears as much as possible. So I make a point of camping out whenever I can," he grumbled.

"But you don't like it," Annja said, laughing.

"I hate it."

Gregor laid a hand on Bob's shoulder. "I tell you the truth—I don't like it, either. I have to do it in the military and since then at a few times when I am on job. But I do not like being out in the dark, either. I always feel like someone else is out there watching me. No matter how much I am hidden or how concealed I make myself, it always seems like someone out there knows."

"You feel vulnerable," Annja said.

"Yes."

"It's probably a pretty common feeling. I know I've felt it during my life, as well," she admitted.

Bob sighed. "Doesn't make it any easier to deal with."

"I'd say you're dealing with it the best way you possibly can," Annja said. "At least you're not letting it paralyze you into inaction. I know of people so utterly paralyzed they let their fears dictate how they lead their lives. Most of them sit at home rocking back and forth afraid to do anything."

"Well," Bob said, "I couldn't do that. After all, as much as I dislike camping at night, I love cruising everywhere on my bike."

Annja smiled. "You see? You're successful even in spite of your fear. I think that's what makes us better human beings. Those of us who are able to take our fears and still generate a positive life despite the things that scare us. That's the mark of success. At least in my book."

Gregor nodded. "I agree with Annja. She is very wise, this woman. I appreciate her thoughtfulness in this matter."

"Thanks, Gregor," Annja said.

"Now we drink," Gregor stated.

Annja sat back. "What?"

Gregor produced a small flask from his jacket. He took their cups and emptied the pine-needle tea out of them. Unscrewing the flask top, he poured equal amounts of clear liquid into them and then handed the cups to Annja and Bob.

"Now." Gregor smiled at them both. He raised his glass then tilted his head back and threw the drink down his throat.

Annja glanced at Bob and then did the same. As the icy vodka hit her throat, it burned a path down her esophagus and then pooled in the pit of her stomach. Her head swam briefly but she managed to stifle the cough.

Bob, who had apparently been with Gregor enough times to have gone through this before, merely shot the drink down and then set his glass down. "Let everybody be healthy," he said.

Gregor smiled. "Now we have a trip to embark upon."

Annja was about to hand him her cup when another sound shattered the night.

But this time, it was no wolf howl.

It sounded like a human scream.

6

"What the hell was that?"

Annja peered out in the darkness. Gregor seemed poised to launch himself out into the woods.

Bob pulled them back to reality. "I don't know, but it's nothing nearby."

Annja glanced at him. "You sure about that?"

He nodded. "We're high up on a hill. Sound carries for quite a distance in these parts. That sound could have been twenty miles away from us. If we start thumping around in the pitch-black, we'll get lost and we'll all be injured before we find anything."

"Was not a sound," Gregor said. "Was a scream."

"A human scream," Annja said.

Gregor looked at her. She could see his eyes gleam in the dark as they caught the twinkling firelight. "Yes," he agreed.

Annja wanted to say something, but there didn't seem to be anything else to say. What could they do?

For his part, Gregor also looked concerned. The prospect of someone needing help seemed to stir something within him. Annja wondered if he might have an angel complex—a need to be a savior in order to feel good about himself.

But just as she thought she might have found something warm within his soul, Gregor cleared his throat and shook his head. "We can do nothing about it. We should get to sleep."

"Good idea," Bob said. He got up from his seat and helped Annja into the lean-to shelter.

As she lay down on the pine-needle bed, Annja felt the blanket of sleep come over her. Bob got two of the survival blankets from their gear and laid them on top of Annja and then himself.

Gregor poked his head into the shelter and dropped a pile of pine boughs on top of the blankets. "These will help preserve your warmth, as well."

Annja looked up, her eyes now heavy. "Aren't you sleeping?"

Gregor shook his head. "Not just yet. I will take first watch."

"First watch?"

Gregor looked at her. "We are in the woods. They are an old woods, filled with many stories and the potential for many dangers. It would be foolish of me to simply lie down to sleep. I might not ever wake up again."

Bob turned over. "Wake me when it's my turn to take over."

"I will." Gregor's head vanished.

Annja watched him resume his place on the log in

front of the fire. Even from there, she could feel some of the residual heat make its way into the shelter. More snow started to fall, giving the night an eerily quiet feeling, despite the strange noises they'd heard only minutes before.

She watched Gregor toss some more wood on the fire. And then, rather than stare into the flames, he turned himself around so that his back was to the fire and to the shelter. He stared off into the night.

Annja watched him for another few moments before her eyes drooped one final time and sleep finally overpowered her. The thought of her concussion made her briefly wonder if she might never wake again.

But she was sure that Gregor would not have permitted her to sleep if he thought she might die. Strange as he was, she couldn't quite shake the idea that he was deeply concerned about her well-being.

WHEN ANNJA'S EYES SLID OPEN, darkness still enveloped the entire campsite. Inside the shelter, Annja felt warm and snug. The pine boughs Gregor had placed over her earlier in the night had done their job. The scent of pine hung in the air.

Her head didn't seem to hurt anymore, much to her relief. Annja shifted and heard the dull snore of Bob snoozing nearby.

She knew hours must have passed, but what time was it? Why hadn't Gregor woken Bob to relieve him on guard duty?

Annja frowned and shifted again, working her way out from under the pile of boughs. The survival blanket made a noise like aluminum foil being crushed and Annja winced. The less noise she made, the better she felt. No sense waking Bob if she could get out of the shelter and give Gregor a break herself.

Annja poked her head out of the entrance of the lean-to and winced as the cold night air greeted her. There was a distinct bite to it and her skin, which had been warm inside, seemed to stretch taut against the cold.

Embers glowed a deep red in the campfire pit, but it appeared to have been some time since fresh wood had been added to it.

Gregor was nowhere to be seen.

Annja frowned. Had he abandoned them? She didn't think that made any sense. Why would he have gone through all the trouble of helping Annja with her concussion if he'd intended to desert them all along?

She moved out of the lean-to, hugging herself as she did so. The howl of wind broke the night, rustling the tall trees above her, making them strain as they leaned one way, then another. The sky overhead showed no stars, only the dark clouds of an approaching storm.

Annja's footsteps crunched into the fresh layer of snow that had covered the landscape while she slumbered. There was maybe an inch on the ground, but no more. Still, looking at the sky again, Annja sensed that there'd be more in the coming day.

That meant they needed to get to Yakutsk as soon as possible. Annja's run-in with the giant truck had cost them plenty of time. It couldn't have been helped, but Annja felt marginally responsible for slowing down the team.

She didn't like feeling hopeless. Or like some wounded puppy that couldn't hold its own. She knew

Bob would never say anything, even if he could be incredibly focused on sticking to a schedule.

They'd need to get going as soon as daylight broke.

But judging from the sky, it seemed that dawn was still a good way off.

Another blast of wind rattled some of the snow from branches high above, sending clumps of it down into the fire. The embers hissed as the snow melted into water that instantly sizzled and turned to steam.

Where was Gregor?

Annja turned and walked the perimeter of the camp. She didn't think he was the type of guy who would fall asleep while on guard duty. Not a man with all sorts of military and organized-crime experiences in his background.

So where had he gone?

She retraced her steps to the fire and knelt down by the log where she'd last seen him sitting. Annja felt the log and found it cold. He'd obviously been gone long enough for the log to lose the warmth his body would have left.

Her hands felt the muddy ground. She found the dull impressions left behind by his boots and followed them as they headed away from the fire in a straight line.

Ten feet from the fire, they vanished. Annja sighed. His footsteps were easy to find close to the fire because the ground was warmer there. Any snow that had fallen had melted into the ground, turning it muddy. As a result, Gregor had left tracks.

But farther away, the ground was cold and hard, and Gregor's tracks didn't show nearly as well as they had a few feet back.

Still, Annja felt the straight line leading away from the fire told her something important—whatever had attracted his attention, Gregor had headed straight for it.

There was little ambient light to work with. Seeing in the night was proving difficult for her, but what if Gregor was in trouble?

Annja stepped carefully through the snow, knowing that even a shallow layer could prove slippery. She didn't want to add a broken leg to her list of injuries.

The ground sloped down away from the camp. Annja closed her eyes and visualized the sword. It hovered there in front of her, ready for use. But did she really want to bring it out right now?

She opened her eyes. Which way to go?

Her instincts told her to move to the left.

She smiled, ignoring the pain for a brief moment. The decision had certainly come to her without hesitation. Maybe she was getting the hang of listening to her instincts a bit better.

She seemed to be walking parallel to the side of the mountain. To her left, the land sloped up, back the way she'd come. To her right, it leveled off for some distance and then seemed to disappear into the darkness.

The wind continued to howl all around her.

Annja crept forward, convinced that she was close to wherever Gregor had ended up.

A dull crack to her left made her pivot and squint into the darkness. She caught herself and then, instead of peering directly at the noise, she turned her head and tried to look out of the corner of her eyes, using

the natural structure of her eyesight to enable her to
see better.

Nothing.

She sighed. This was getting weird. She had the
distinct impression that she was being watched and
she didn't like it one bit.

Annja closed her eyes and visualized the sword
again.

Just as she was about to close her hands over it, a
hand slid over her mouth and she felt herself being
taken down from behind. Another hand kept her from
hitting the ground hard. And then she felt brute force
keeping her pinned, but without hurting her.

A voice hissed in her ear. "Quiet."

Gregor.

Annja relaxed some, trying to twist to see him and
ask what was going on. Instead of releasing the
pressure, Gregor pointed off to the right.

Annja could see that the ground fell away, forming
a steep cliff that dropped down into some sort of
valley. At the bottom of it, perhaps a half a mile away,
she could see a dim glow.

"Do not speak. It will hear us," Gregor whispered.

From half a mile away? Annja frowned. She'd
never heard of a person who could pick up a whisper
from that distance.

Gregor's breath felt hot against Annja's neck.

She strained her eyes to see what he was so interested in. But any detail seemed to elude her. She
could make out some kind of figure stooped over,
huddling in front of something.

A campfire?

No. The light would have been yellow or orange. This light was a pale shade of blue-green.

Gregor pulled her back away from the edge of the cliff. He released Annja, who rolled to face him. He held a finger to his lips. "Whisper only."

"Why did you sneak up on me?" she hissed.

Gregor pointed. "You would have fallen over the edge if you'd kept going."

Annja looked again. He was right. A few more steps ahead of her there was a shallow depression that gave way to a deep gorge. A pocket of snow inside it would have caused her to slide right over the edge.

"Thanks," she said.

He shrugged. "Your scream would have alerted that thing down there."

"Thing? Don't you mean person?" she asked.

Gregor looked at her. "Did you not see the color of it?"

"I don't know what I saw. It's too dark and I can't see that far."

Gregor nodded. "Perhaps we will find out when we reach Yakutsk later."

He stood and helped Annja to her feet. "We should return to camp. It will be light in a few hours."

"You haven't slept yet," Annja said.

"No."

"Why not?"

Gregor stopped and turned. "Because that thing back there was hunting earlier. And it was only by luck it did not stumble across us. Otherwise, we might not be having this talk."

"You're kidding me, right?" Annja asked.

Gregor leaned in close. "You should know one thing about me—I do not joke about life and death."

With that, Gregor turned and slid back into the night's embrace.

7

Bob was tending the fire when they returned, an anxious look plastered across his face. He jumped up when he saw Annja and Gregor come out of the darkness.

"Thank God! I was worried sick when I woke up and found you both gone." He tossed another stick into the fire. "I thought perhaps my snoring had driven you away, Annja."

She smiled. "No harm done. Although it's great to see your volume has increased since we last met."

Bob shrugged. "Can't figure it out. It's not like I'm carrying extra pounds or anything. And no matter how I sleep, I always carry on like that."

Gregor knelt in front of the fire. "I need to sleep," he said.

Bob looked at him. "You should have woken me sooner. I would have gladly taken your place."

Gregor looked up. "We might be dead if you had."

Bob's face grew pale. "What?"

Annja shrugged. "Gregor says there was something lurking in the darkness tonight. Something… that was hunting."

Bob looked at Gregor. "You're kidding?"

"No."

Bob glanced at Annja. "You saw it, too?"

Annja shrugged. "I'm not sure what I saw. At least not yet. It was too far to see and too dark to get any detail."

"But you saw something," Bob said.

"Yes."

He leaned back on his haunches. "I think we should get out of here as soon as possible."

Gregor cleared his throat. "At dawn. We will ride on. I think Annja is suitably mended enough to ride with us to Yakutsk." He crawled into the lean-to and within seconds, no more sound came from it.

Bob sat down on the log. Annja sat next to him. "Sorry we gave you a scare there," she said.

Bob grinned. "I thought maybe you and Gregor… you know—"

"What?" Annja said, shocked.

"You and him…" Bob shrugged. "It's not out of the realm of possibility. You're a beautiful woman. He's a good-looking guy."

Annja almost laughed. "You thought we hooked up?"

"Well, sure. I mean, the thought did pass through my mind."

"I woke up and saw he'd vanished. I went looking for him. He snuck up behind me and took me down, trying to keep me from alerting whatever it was to our presence. That's all."

Bob nodded. "He seems concerned."

"I think so, yes."

"He's never steered me wrong as long as I've known him. If he says we should be concerned, I suppose we should be, then."

"What if it puts your exploration in jeopardy?" Annja asked.

He grinned. "There was a time I might have thought there was nothing more important than achieving the glory of a new find over everything else. Those days are long behind me. I value my life and the lives of those I'm close to. If it looks like we're in danger, we'll head for Magadan and get the hell home."

Annja nodded. "I think I should get some more sleep, too. You okay here?"

"Yeah," Bob said.

Annja crawled back into the lean-to and burrowed under the bed of boughs and her blanket. She glanced once at Gregor, but he was already seemingly asleep. He breathed deeply, but made absolutely no noise.

Me and Gregor? Annja grinned. He was okay-looking, but she wasn't sure she could ever picture herself with a guy who could so easily sneak up behind her and catch her completely by surprise.

As she settled down and closed her eyes, she smiled once more.

Then again, who knew how things would turn out?

GREGOR NUDGED Annja awake just as the first tendrils of dawn crept over the horizon. Annja blinked her eyes a few times and then crawled out of the lean-to.

"Good morning." Bob handed her a cup of coffee and Annja drank it down, feeling the hot liquid warm her insides. Gregor accepted a cup, as well, and seemed to gulp it down.

Annja looked around the campsite. "You've been busy."

Most of the lean-to had been dismantled except for the portion covering the sleeping area. The fire had also been doused and the ashes scattered across the blanket of snow.

"Well, Gregor was kind enough to make it. I figured the least I could do was break it down."

"We can go now," Gregor said. "That is good."

Bob tore down the remaining bit of structure of the lean-to and threw the branches into the woods. Gregor got his bike and started pushing it up the hill, back toward the road.

Annja felt stronger and her head was clear. She got her bike and pushed it up the hill, feeling the strain in her legs as she did so. But it felt good to be exerting herself again.

They crested the mountain and got back onto the pockmarked road. Bob turned to Annja with a grin. "How about I bring up the rear this time? That way, if any more trucks come looking for someone to smoosh, they can have me."

"Wise guy," Annja remarked.

He smiled. "Just thought I'd offer."

Gregor slid onto his bike. "I will go ahead. Make sure the road is clear."

He pedaled off and Annja got on her own bike. "He's very serious this morning."

Bob nodded. "He was awake before you."

"Big surprise."

"We talked about last night. Gregor is of the belief that we will find trouble in Yakutsk. He is worried about you."

"I can watch after myself, thanks," Annja said with a smile. "Any head wounds notwithstanding."

"Oh, sure," Bob said. "We should get going. If Gregor's concerned, he'll pedal like the devil himself was after him."

Annja pushed off and found the going much easier. For several hours the road wound its way farther up the mountain, but then started to descend at a gradual pace.

About a half mile ahead, she could see Gregor working his way down the road. Nothing seemed to faze him. His legs worked easily and he kept glancing around the sides of the road.

Annja looked behind her and saw Bob just about to start the descent. He waved once and then leaned forward, anticipating that rush of downhill speed that all cyclists enjoy once they've finished a hard climb.

The descent took the better part of an hour, but at the end, the road evened out. They were in a heavily forested area, with tall pines and scraggly birch trunks dotting the landscape. Giant boulders thrown up from the depths of the earth bordered the road as they pedaled on. But Annja saw little to denote civilization.

Bob rode up next to her. "This part of the country is

remote. Even though we're still reasonably close to Magadan, it's like another planet out here. Weird, huh?"

"It doesn't feel cozy—that's for sure," Annja said. "And those woods seem anything but friendly. Even the trees seem to be leaning in on us."

"It is kind of claustrophobic, isn't it?" Bob asked.

"Just a bit."

"Gregor's stopped his bike."

Annja looked ahead. Sure enough, a quarter of a mile away, Gregor had stopped. They rode up and he spoke. "We are close."

Bob looked and smiled. "There."

Annja followed his gaze and saw the first indications of civilization she'd seen since they left Magadan. "Not exactly a bustling city, is it?"

Gregor shook his head. "Yakutsk is small. Just a few hundred people live there. But they are good souls." He handed out some energy bars.

"You've been there before?" Annja asked while eating.

Gregor shrugged. "I was attached to a military unit that operated in this area once. A long time ago."

"Any friends still left in these parts?" she asked.

"Everyone is friendly, once they get to know you. This part of my country is remote. Strangers are not a usual thing to see, so the people living here are somewhat suspicious. But having me with you is okay. They will be glad to meet you when they see me."

Bob nudged Annja. "Gregor's like a VIP ticket to any club back in the Big Apple."

"Handy guy to have around," Annja said.

Gregor grinned. "We ride now."

They got back on the bikes and pedaled on. The dirt road gave way to a cracked type of pavement that looked as if it might be all of fifty years old. Gregor pointed at it as they rode.

"Once this road was much sturdier. The Soviet army drove tanks all over the country."

"Guess it's been a while since they had any road-repair crews out here," Annja said.

"Money," Gregor said. "All comes back to money."

The woods fell behind them and muddy open fields dotted the countryside. Simple houses lined the roads, most with smoking chimneys. The air felt colder, and Annja could see there was a layer of fog moving in from the west.

The single road grew wider as they entered the town itself. Annja could pick out what looked to be a main all-purpose store and a small café. Aside from that, there was a loose cluster of homes and a church standing alone at the end of the road.

Gregor pointed at the church. "Father Jakob runs the church. He has been here since the dinosaurs."

Annja grinned. "Think he remembers you?"

Gregor looked at her. "Perhaps I made an indelible impression on him when I was much younger."

"How so?"

"He heard my confession. First time for me since I was only a boy. I think I may have scarred him," Gregor said with a laugh.

Bob pedaled past them. "Where is everyone?"

Annja glanced around. There seemed to be no one around the store or café. The streets looked deserted. There weren't even any dogs lounging around, which

Annja found very peculiar. She'd been around the world enough to know that even in the poorest places, you could always find a mutt or two mooching about.

She heard voices, though. "What's that?" she asked.

Gregor pointed to their right. "Over here."

They dismounted and walked between two houses, passing rusted drain pipes leaking water to the muddy ground. Annja caught a whiff of something that smelled quite disgusting and hoped they had some type of plumbing here at least.

They passed the houses and in front of them stood an open field. Annja shivered as they walked. Annja was sure the temperature must have dipped well below freezing.

As they approached the crowd of people milling around, Annja could see they were extremely agitated. Several women clutched at the few children present. The men all wore grim expressions.

Gregor strode up to them, but his gruff demeanor vanished as he approached. Annja heard him speaking with them. Next to her, Bob listened intently. As he did, he also frowned.

"What is it?" Annja asked.

Gregor looked back at her. "What we saw last night in the woods."

"That thing?"

Gregor shook his head. "It is not a thing. It is called Khosadam."

"Khosadam?" Annja glanced at Bob.

Gregor gestured for them to come closer. "It hunts. It stalks this village," he said.

Annja shook her head. "How do they know?"

Gregor pointed at the ground, and several of the villagers stepped back. Annja looked and there in the mud she saw the tracks of what looked to be human feet.

"So? Someone was out here walking around barefoot."

Gregor shook his head. "Look closer."

Annja knelt and studied the tracks. The footsteps showed six toes.

Gregor's voice was subdued. "You know many people that have six toes, Annja Creed?"

8

"This is insane," Annja said. "A couple of six-toed footprints and people are losing their minds? It doesn't make any sense."

Gregor led them back toward the town. "Then what would you call it? You said yourself you have never seen things like this before."

"I'd start by looking for someone who is suffering from frostbite," Annja said. "Walking around in subzero temperatures without shoes on might even get them gangrene."

Gregor stopped. "This is not a joking matter, Annja. These villagers take this very seriously. The idea that Khosadam is stalking this area has them very frightened. And rightfully so. Khosadam is not something to dismiss so easily."

"I'm not dismissing it per se," Annja said. She just didn't think that it was possible to get so upset over something so seemingly trivial. She'd seen plenty of things far worse and not been half as concerned as some of those villagers.

"And what about what we saw last night?" Gregor asked. "You are thinking that was nothing special, as well?"

"I don't know what I saw last night," Annja said. She looked at Bob. "Got anything to add to this craziness?"

Bob shrugged. "I told you last night that Gregor has never steered me wrong. If he says something is amiss, then we'd be fools to think otherwise."

Annja sighed. "So, what is this Khosadam thing, anyway?"

"She's a Siberian goddess," Bob said.

"As in a deity?"

"Yes."

Annja shook her head. "You realize this sounds even more ludicrous now. They actually think there's a goddess stalking them?"

"That would be my impression, yes," he replied.

"What—did she get bored with heaven or Olympus or wherever else she was hanging out?"

"She was kicked out of heaven, actually," Bob said. "By her husband, of all things."

Annja grinned. "One step forward for women's rights."

"Her husband, Ec—"

"His name was Ec?" Annja chuckled. "I would have left, too."

Bob shook his head. "Don't trivialize it. Ec banished her for being unfaithful to him. She liked to cavort with a lot of the lesser deities and sometimes even mortals."

"Okay," Annja said.

"She has another name, as well," Bob said, leading them into the nearby café.

A wall of heat slammed into Annja as she walked through the door. She could smell burned coffee and some other scents she didn't recognize. Despite her unease with the entire situation, her mouth watered and she realized she was ravenous.

"What's her other name?" Annja asked, distracted.

"Eater of souls," Bob said quietly.

"Sounds like a fun gal," Annja said. "What did she do to get a name like that?"

Gregor set down three cups of coffee in front of them. He spoke to the woman behind the counter, who nodded and began preparing something for them to eat.

Bob sipped his coffee. "Before she was kicked out of heaven, Ec had her fitted with something called a brank."

"I've heard of that," Annja said. "Some kind of torture device, right?"

"It's a metal insert, actually," Bob said. "It gets placed in the mouth of the victim, and a special hood goes over the head to keep the brank in place. It was used on women who spoke too much, but Ec apparently used it to keep his ex-wife from eating anything, figuring she would eventually wither away."

"Ec sounds like a real charmer." Annja sipped her coffee as fresh sounds streamed from the kitchen behind the counter. Whatever Gregor had requested, it seemed to be something special.

"When Khosadam couldn't eat in the normal mortal way, she had to resort to other methods to retain her vitality," Bob continued.

Annja looked at him. "Is this where the soul-eater part comes in?"

"Yes. Khosadam took to perching herself over fresh graves. When the soul of the departed rose toward heaven, she would ingest it."

"How?"

"The method is supposed to have been something like sniffing it up through her nose. Doing anything with her mouth would have been too painful for her to endure."

"Nice picture." Annja glanced at Gregor, who seemed to be paying rapt attention to Bob. "This is the thing the village thinks is stalking them?"

"Yes," Gregor said.

"A six-toed deity who has been kicked out of heaven."

The Russian shrugged. "I did not make this up, Annja. This is what they think. To them, it is painfully real."

Annja turned to Bob. "Does the legend say anything about six toes?"

Bob nodded. "Khosadam grew the extra toe to help her grip the tombstones of those she would eventually dine off of."

"Interesting." Annja watched the door to the kitchen burst open, and an old woman came out with a tray of bowls. She placed the tray in front of them and nodded toward Gregor, who thanked her.

Annja sniffed. "Smells…interesting."

Gregor pointed at the bowls. "Borscht. Most people in the West are familiar with it."

"Beets, right?" Annja asked.

"Yes."

Annja helped herself to a spoonful and found it surprisingly good, despite the deep red color that she didn't much like. It warmed her as she ate more of it. Gregor finished his bowl quickly, but Bob's sat untouched.

"I hate beets," he said. "A leftover from my childhood when my mother made me eat the things at a small orange table in the corner of my kitchen."

Annja cocked an eyebrow. "You may want to have an extended talk with your therapist about that one, Bob."

"I already have. It's taking me a while longer to work through it."

The old woman cleared the soup bowls and cast a disapproving glance at Bob. She brought out another tray and Annja took a whiff.

"Wow," she said, her mouth watering.

Gregor nodded at the plates. "Mashed potatoes and goulash."

"What's in the goulash?" Bob asked.

"Green peppers and roasted lamb, it would appear."

Annja helped herself to a heaping spoonful. "This is delicious."

Gregor translated and the old woman beamed at her. Then she cast another glance at Bob, who seemed to be picking his way through the green peppers. He saw the old woman's gaze and immediately took a big spoonful, chewing and smiling at the same time.

Her gaze softened, but only just. She left and Gregor leaned close to Bob. "I don't think she likes you."

"How is it," Annja said, "that a globe-trotting guy like you doesn't seem to like vegetables that much?"

"I like vegetables fine," Bob said. "Just not cooked ones."

"You must be putting your therapist's kids through school," Annja said. She dug back into her dish and washed down the spoonfuls with more thick coffee.

Gregor tore through his plate and leaned back. "This place is still run by the same woman who ran it when I was with the military. We came through here on exercise and she served my entire platoon. Her food, it is still as good as it ever was."

"She remembers you?" Annja asked.

Gregor nodded. "Yes."

The old woman returned and rested a hand on Gregor's shoulder. She spoke, her Russian thick around the false teeth she wore. Gregor smiled and seemed to almost blush. Annja smiled at the thought of such a big, tough guy blushing.

"What is she saying?" Annja asked.

Bob was smiling, too. "She says he is like her son. That when he came through many years ago, he helped her rescue her kitten from the roof when it got stuck. She says a man like Gregor is tough and gentle at the same time."

Gregor said something else to the old woman, who kissed him on the forehead and then gathered up the dishes.

"What did you say to her?" Annja asked.

"I told her that if this ever reached my friends, they would never let me live it down. I would be embarrassed."

"You're a big softie after all," Annja said.

Gregor shrugged. "Only when I have to be."

The old woman returned and this time served them a dark tea and plates of what looked like fruit slices.

"*Kissel*," Gregor said. "It is stewed fruit."

Annja popped a slice into her mouth and chewed, relishing the sweetness of the apricot slice she'd eaten. The tea reminded her of a dark black leaf tea she'd had once in China. "This was some lunch," she said.

Gregor smiled. "She loves to cook."

"But back to Khosadam," Annja said. "They really are taking this seriously, huh?"

"Yes," Bob said. He looked at Gregor. "What do they think will happen next?"

"They are concerned that she will hunt."

"But we didn't pass any cemeteries around here on the way in," Annja said. "Doesn't that kind of rule out the whole supernatural angle?"

"Just because you did not see the cemetery does not mean there is not one," Gregor said. "The last time I was here, the villagers buried their dead behind the church."

Annja nodded. "Down at the end of the street. Father Jakob, you mentioned."

"Yes. He is Eastern Orthodox."

"You think he's still here?"

Gregor spoke to the old woman, who had come out with the bill. She handed it immediately to Bob, who started fumbling around with his wallet.

When Gregor had finished speaking, the old woman nodded. Gregor looked back at Annja.

"She says he is still here and that he will be here until the wind sweeps his dust away."

"Colorful," Annja said, laughing.

Bob fished out a wad of money and handed it to the old woman. She grabbed the bundle of cash and leafed through it. Her eyes softened and she kissed Bob on the forehead before trundling off.

Annja shook her head. "Looks like you won her over."

"Money is the greatest facilitator of all," Bob said. "A little extra green makes everyone all lovey-dovey."

"I guess we should go and see Father Jakob," Annja said. "Maybe he'll be able to shed a little light on this whole situation."

Walking out of the café, Annja felt a funny sensation and turned back to see the old woman peering through the torn lace curtain framing the windows. Gregor didn't look back but steered Annja away.

"As I said, they are distrustful of strangers. Give them time and they will warm up to you."

"This business of the Khosadam has them spooked," Bob said. "Everyone is suspect."

Annja nodded. "Quite a place we've come to, Bob."

"It's about to get even weirder if that sky carries through on the promise of a blizzard," he said.

Annja looked up, and the thick, bloated clouds seemed as if they might fall out of the sky. "How long?"

"Soon," Bob said. "Another hour perhaps."

Annja looked at Gregor. "Is there a place we can stay here in town?"

Gregor pointed at a decrepit building that towered over the other buildings. "Yakutsk hotel. The only place in town."

It looked quite run-down, but any place would serve as long as it kept them warm and safe from the blizzard outside. Annja turned to Gregor again. "Has anyone in town died recently?"

"No."

"So, if no one has died lately, how is this Khosadam supposed to eat?"

Gregor frowned. "That is what has the villagers scared the most. It is said that when Khosadam cannot find a fresh grave, she will hunt the living."

"She'll kill?" Annja asked in disbelief.

"Yes. And when she kills, she will then wait for the dead person's soul to lift from the body."

"And then she eats it?"

Gregor nodded. "Yes."

The first flakes fell from the sky as they hurried toward the church. Already, the Siberian sky had darkened.

Annja wondered what the night might hold in store for them all.

9

By the time they reached the church, the air had grown thick with snow. A driving wind lashed snow at them almost sideways. The steps of the church were slippery, but Annja, Bob and Gregor crested them and stood in front of the thick wooden door.

Gregor pounded on it. The thunderous knocking seemed to vanish amid the howling wind and darkening skies.

Annja could see the faint glow of yellow through one of the glass windows facing the front of the church. It grew in size until at last they heard the latch sliding back.

The door opened and a withered, ancient face peered out at them. Gregor spoke loudly, trying to make himself heard over the coming storm.

The old priest squinted and then his eyes seemed to light up as he recognized Gregor. He waved them in and Annja gratefully followed Bob inside.

The air inside the church was still, but warmer than it was outside. Annja caught a vague scent of incense in the air. She closed her eyes and welcomed the air of holiness that surrounded the church. She always made a point to be thankful for her blessings whenever she ventured into any church or holy place, regardless of faith.

Father Jakob led them to a small room beyond the altar. The tiny kitchen had a coal-burning oven that radiated immense heat. Annja slid her coat off and rested it on the back of her chair.

Father Jakob busied himself preparing a pot of coffee while he and Gregor engaged in conversation.

Gregor looked at them. "Father Jakob has asked me if I have been good about going to confession since he last heard my sordid tales of debauchery."

"What did you tell him?" Annja asked.

Gregor smiled. "I told him I have been a saint and don't need to confess anything."

"Wow," Bob said. "He didn't believe you, did he?"

Father Jakob whacked Gregor on the back of his head. Then he looked at Bob and Annja. "No. I most certainly do not believe him."

"You speak English?" Annja said.

Father Jakob eyed her. "Of course. I speak it quite well. I haven't always lived in Yakutsk, after all. And there is a much bigger world out there." He set down four mugs and then removed the bubbling pot of coffee from the stove top. He poured them each a cup, replaced the pot on the stove and then sat down with them.

"So, what is it that brings you to this village?" the priest asked.

Bob took a sip of his coffee. "I'm researching dig sites in the area. I'm an archaeologist."

"And you think there are places around here that would be of interest to you?" Father Jakob shook his head. "I do not know what you hoped to find, but I don't think there would be much here worth exploring."

"This whole area is steeped in history. Siberia itself is awash in legends and folklore. But recent history might even be more fascinating. What with Magadan being so close by, relatively speaking," Bob said.

Father Jakob frowned. "We should not speak of that place. What Magadan was the gateway for, and how many people died as a result of those mines, it is a wound that should not be opened up again."

"But surely you'd agree that by understanding the past we can avoid the same mistakes in the future?" Annja asked.

Father Jakob looked at her. "You do not strike me as a naive woman. Surely you do not think that just because we look at the past that we learn all the lessons it contains?"

"It's a hope," Annja said.

Father Jakob frowned. "And we have so many examples of fools who have shown a complete disregard for history. They are more than happy to repeat the mistakes of the past time and time again. Why should this be any different?"

"There's no guarantee," Bob said. "But the history of Magadan and the mines is a story that more people need to know about. Three million deaths should never be covered up or left to fade away in the footnotes of history."

"Perhaps," Father Jakob said. "But perhaps my concern does not even matter much right now."

"What do you mean?" Bob asked.

"Yakutsk has other things to worry about."

Gregor nodded. "You have heard, then?"

"Certainly," the priest said.

"We didn't see you out in the field," Bob said. "We thought perhaps you had missed the hysteria."

Father Jakob smiled. "I live in a small village. I see and hear everything." He took a sip of his coffee and then set the mug down. "I was out there much earlier today. With the coming storm, however, I busied myself with preparations. As such, I was absent while you were there."

"What do you think of it?" Annja asked.

"There is much the world at large does not know," the old priest said. "There are still many remote regions. Many legends that do not have an easy way of dismissing them."

"You believe it?" Annja asked.

"I believe there is something out there. Yes."

"But the legend of Khosadam?" Annja shook her head. "It just doesn't seem possible to me."

"And you've never had anything in your life that seemed impossible?" Father Jakob peered closer at her. "I would have thought you would be more accepting of such things, my child."

Bob perked up. "Why so?"

Annja swallowed. Could the priest see that Annja had her own secrets to keep hidden away?

Father Jakob swallowed more coffee. "Just a thought."

Bob glanced at Annja, but she turned away. Gregor cleared his throat. "The villagers are quite worried."

"As they should be," Father Jakob said. "If the legends are true, then the beast will hunt one of them."

"Not you?" Annja asked.

"I am a holy man. I tend to think that perhaps my soul is not to the beast's liking."

"You sound pretty sure," Bob said.

Father Jakob spread his arms. "I do not have much material wealth being a lonely priest. But I do like to think that the wealth of God is with me. He will look after a kindly old servant long forgotten by the rest of the world. Perhaps I am presumptuous, but then perhaps I am allowed to be."

"You'll stay here tonight?" Gregor asked.

Father Jakob nodded. "It is my home."

Gregor finished his coffee. "We must go before the snow worsens."

Annja slid her coat back on. "Thank you for the coffee, Father."

Father Jakob bowed. "It was my pleasure to meet you. We get very few visitors in these parts."

Bob shook his hand and Father Jakob led them back to the church entrance. At the door, he stopped and turned to face them, the light from his candle illuminating the folds of skin under his eyes. "Do not go out after dark. That is when the beast will hunt," he said.

"I don't think anyone would venture outside in this weather," Annja said. "If they do, Khosadam is not the only thing they'd have to worry about."

Bob zipped up his jacket. "Everyone ready?"

Father Jakob pulled the door open, and a blast of cold, snowy air slammed into them. Annja leaned forward into the howling wind, following Gregor down the steps. Bob brought up the rear. Behind them, they heard the dull thud as the church door slammed shut. Darkness, punctured only by a few lights in the windows of nearby homes, seemed ready to swallow the town.

Bob leaned closer to Annja. "What did you think?"

"About what?"

"The priest."

"He seemed very willing to believe in the legend. His English was also quite good."

"Strange town," Bob said.

Annja looked at him, blinking away the snowflakes hitting her face. "You picked this place, pal. Not me."

"True enough. Father Jakob didn't seem too keen on me researching Magadan and the mines, though, did he?"

"No."

"I wonder why?"

Gregor's face materialized out of the blizzard. "Because what the mines represent is too painful for most. Now, if you two are done holding a conversation in the midst of blizzard, then we should get to the hotel before the owner decides to lock it up and not let us in. That would be bad, I think."

Bob hurried on and Annja followed. Already the snow was up to their shins, and wading through the drifts made Annja realize how tired she was from the day of pedaling.

She stopped then, aware of someone watching her.

She turned and saw the glow of a candle in the church window.

10

It took five minutes of banging on the front door of the hotel to get the innkeeper to open the door. As they did so, the snow and wind increased to gale force. Annja thought she might be standing in the midst of a hurricane, only with snow.

Gregor muttered and cursed while they waited, but at last the door cracked open and a terrified face peered out from within.

Gregor leaned in close and said three words. The innkeeper seemed to pale even more and then moved away from the door, letting it swing open. Bob, Annja and Gregor all rushed inside.

As soon as they had cleared the doorway, the innkeeper slammed the door shut behind them. From off to the side, he slid a giant plank into place that effectively barred the door. Annja noticed a sprig of herbs wrapped around the center of the thick plank and nodded at it.

"What is that?" she asked.

"A bundle of local herbs supposed to ward off evil spirits, I'd wager," Bob said.

"Yes," Gregor said. "People are obviously concerned about Khosadam walking around at night."

Annja glanced at the herbs and then at the plank. If there really was something supernatural stalking the area, she didn't know how effective some wood and plants were going to be at stopping it.

The temperature inside the hotel was warm, and they all shed their coats. The innkeeper seemed a little more friendly now that he had, at least in his own mind, protected his establishment and himself from whatever horrors lurked outside.

Bob removed some cash from one of the inner pockets of his parka and handed it to the innkeeper. The money disappeared faster than Annja could see, and the innkeeper grabbed their bags, leading them to a flight of old wooden stairs.

At the top of the steps, a long, narrow hallway flanked by doors on both sides showed that the inn was larger than Annja had first expected it to be. The innkeeper dutifully stopped at each door, ushering first Bob and then Gregor into their rooms.

Annja's room was in the middle of the corridor, and when he opened the door, Annja saw that the room was very small, but seemed pleasant enough. The fireplace was cold and dark, but sprang to life as soon as the innkeeper stuck a lit match into the pile of wood resting on the hearth. With the yellow-red flames licking their way through the dried logs, the room took on a nice glow and Annja thanked the innkeeper.

He stepped out of the room and closed the door, leaving Annja alone. She sat down on the bed for a moment, resting her legs, which by now were feeling exhausted. Annja could hear the wind lashing at the building outside, trying to sneak in under the eaves. But as seemingly decrepit as the building was from the outside, Annja sensed it would stand solid during the blizzard.

The pane of her lone window had frosted over with snow and ice. Annja peered out, trying to see anything outside, but the visibility was so limited, she could only see the flakes that seemed to shoot straight at the window. She let the curtain fall back and sighed. At least they weren't on the ground level.

She smirked. While the notion of a supernatural creature hunting the village didn't sit quite well with her, Annja wasn't so closed to the idea that she didn't appreciate what she considered to be small advantages in case there was some truth to the story.

The room grew warm from the fire and Annja sat in front of the flames, warming herself. Siberia during a blizzard. She shook her head. It wasn't even winter yet, but already Mother Nature seemed to have lashed out with startling ferocity. Annja wondered what the place was like in January.

A soft knock at her door caught her attention. She opened it and found Bob standing in the hallway.

"Everything okay with your room?"

Annja let him in. "Sure. It's small, but you know, it's comfy."

"You've got a fire going. Good." Bob peered out of her window. "I see our views are the same. Nothing."

Annja smiled. "But at least we're off the ground."

Bob looked at her. "Ah, I see that rough-and-tumble demeanor might just be falling for the local folklore. Is that it?"

"The higher ground always holds a strategic advantage," Annja said. "If something attacks this place, at least we have that small thing in our favor."

"I'll be sure to mention it while my soul is being sucked out of my body," Bob said. "You hungry?"

"You'd think after that lunch I wouldn't be, but I am."

"Gregor's downstairs arranging for a meal."

Annja walked to the door. "I suppose we should join him, then."

As they walked downstairs, Annja heard more than two voices. At the foot of the stairs, Gregor met them. "Dinner will be served soon."

Bob came up behind Annja and looked past Gregor's shoulder. "Who are they?"

Annja looked at the two men sitting by the fireplace in the main room of the inn.

Gregor nodded over his shoulder. "Two hikers driven indoors by the storm. Yuri and Oleg. They are from Georgia, exploring the country."

"Have they heard about what the locals think?" Bob asked.

Gregor nodded. "They do not strike me as being open to the idea of the supernatural. And there is something about them I do not trust, either."

"Why not?" Annja asked.

Gregor only shrugged before leading Annja and Bob over to meet the men.

As they approached, the first man leaned forward with a big smile. "Hello!"

He gripped Annja's hand and pumped it hard. Annja squeezed back and the man's smile broadened. Annja could see the thickness of his neck, but saw little movement when he moved. He was chiseled muscle with no fat.

"My name is Yuri."

"Annja."

"And now, we are friends."

Annja grinned. "Just like that?"

Yuri nodded. "We will drink later. Here is my friend Oleg."

Oleg was built the same way as Yuri. His handshake was only marginally less severe than Yuri's, but they both seemed friendly enough. Oleg's English was also less impressive than Yuri's. Annja found herself wondering why there seemed to be a fair number of people who spoke English in this remote part of Russia. It wasn't something she would have expected, but she did admit it made things easier.

The fire in the large hearth roared. Annja pointed to the small table between the two chairs that Yuri and Oleg occupied. "I see you've already found the liquor."

Yuri grunted. "Where are my manners? Would you like some?"

Annja nodded. "I'll try it, sure."

Yuri clapped his hands and the innkeeper appeared from the shadows bearing three more small glasses and a bucket of ice. He set them down and then disappeared again.

Yuri fished out two small ice cubes for each glass

and then poured a measure of vodka into each. Oleg handed a glass to Annja, Bob and then Gregor before hoisting his own.

All five of them clinked their glasses and Annja tilted her head back, tasting the fiery liquid as it raced down her throat, leaving an icy wake. When it hit her stomach, however, the ice blossomed into a raging fire.

Annja coughed. "Whoa."

Yuri roared with laughter. "Excellent, Annja. Excellent. You drink like a cossack!"

He poured Annja another drink. "Your friend does not seem to care much for it, however."

Annja glanced at Bob, who was nursing his drink. "He's more of a beer drinker."

Oleg made a face. Yuri waved his hands. "No matter. Before tonight, he will drink vodka like the fishes!"

The innkeeper returned and Gregor nudged Annja. "We eat."

They all sat at what appeared to be a picnic table only longer. The tabletop was made from rough-hewn planks covered with a threadbare tablecloth. Annja's nose detected a barrage of scents coming from the kitchen, and her mouth watered even as she felt the initial buzz from the vodka come over her.

The doors opened and the innkeeper's wife emerged bearing dishes. She set them down in front of the guests and Annja surveyed the scene.

Gregor pointed out some of them. "Sturgeon. Lamb. Potatoes. And *pelemi.*"

"Pelemi?" she asked.

"Like a folded pancake filled with ground meat and vegetables. Traditional Siberian dish. Usually there is much fanfare with their cooking. But tonight, the innkeeper is more worried than anything else."

"About Khosadam," Annja said.

"Yes."

"Eh? What is Khosadam?" Yuri asked from around a mouthful of potatoes.

Gregor explained it to him in fast Russian. Yuri and Oleg both stopped chewing their food long enough to take in the tale. When Gregor was done, they glanced at each other and then exploded in laughter, pounding the table with their meaty paws.

"Incredible!" Yuri said.

Oleg leaned toward Annja. "Do you believe this foolishness?"

Annja plopped one of the *pelemi* into her mouth. "I'm not sure what I believe. Most of my work deals with facts, not legends. And the supernatural and I aren't exactly on speaking terms if you know what I mean."

Oleg considered that for a moment and then leaned back and whispered something to Yuri, who nodded. "More drink!" they shouted.

Their glasses remained filled throughout dinner. Annja wondered just how much vodka the innkeeper had in stock because Yuri and Oleg seemed determined to drink him out of his supply.

For her part, Annja was careful. The substantial dinner helped ward off the effects, but it was only after she had worked her way through three plates of food that Annja at last felt content. She'd ridden hard for two days and suffered the concussion. Also, the stress of coming into town to find it in the clutches of some weird legend had certainly worn her out.

A sharp blast of wind outside plunged the inn into darkness. The glow of the fire from the main room provided enough ambient light for the innkeeper to light some candles and place them around the room.

Yuri swore. "It is good we are inside tonight."

"You and Oleg were hiking across the country-side?" Annja asked.

"*Da.* Is how we relax. We are businessmen in the south. Vacations are difficult to come by. Our wives do not share our zest for the outdoors, so they take our children to Europe and shop. Oleg and I come camping."

"Smart of you to come here, though. Given the weather and all," Annja said.

"We see the clouds today and think perhaps we should find shelter. Real shelter. Not the silly tents we bring with us for camping."

The innkeeper leaned in close to Gregor and said a few words. Gregor looked up. "The innkeeper wishes to close down for the night. He said we are welcome to stay up for as long as we want but begs us not to open the front door."

Bob smirked. "I don't think anyone has any intention of going outside in this weather."

"It's not us going out he is concerned about. It is someone coming in that worries him," Gregor said.

"But who would be out on a night like this?" Annja asked.

Gregor looked at her. "Exactly."

Yuri waved the innkeeper away. "Go. We do not need you anymore anyway. We have vodka. A fire. And friends. That is all anyone needs in life."

The innkeeper bowed once and then walked to the front door. He placed his hand over the wooden bar and the herb bundle. Annja saw his mouth move but heard no words. When he was done, he quickly climbed the stairs. His wife followed.

Annja nodded toward the door. "What did he say?"

Gregor shrugged. "Probably a prayer of some type."

"They're all superstitious around here," Bob said. "In case you missed that."

"Not a chance," Annja said. She looked at the door again and wondered if it really would help keep evil away. She tried to imagine something seemingly so insignificant wielding such power.

The candles on the table flickered. Shadows seemed to come alive in the dimly lit room. And as Annja watched Yuri converse with Bob and Oleg talk with Gregor, it seemed each man had two faces—one his own and a new one of dancing shadows courtesy of the candles.

Annja felt a wave of exhaustion come over her again. The combination of the day's travel, the excitement in the village, hearty meals and vodka was catching up with her.

Outside, the wind continued to blast the village as snow fell hard. Annja hoisted her glass again and wondered if Khosadam was already out in the midst of the blizzard.

And if so, would it come for them?

11

"I think," Annja said two hours later and after she'd consumed far too much of the icy vodka, "that I should go to bed."

At the far end of the table, Bob had slumped over in his chair, a line of drool strung from the corner of his mouth to his plate. Annja pointed at him. "And it looks like Bob is pretty much done, as well."

Outside the storm continued to rage. Annja looked at the old clock on the mantel and could just make out that it was fast approaching midnight. She stood and immediately gripped the edge of the table.

Gregor smiled. "You should go slow."

"You aren't kidding," Annja said.

Yuri seemed disappointed. "You're leaving now? But we were just getting started. Oleg knows some fantastic folk songs we can sing."

Oleg bowed his head and started to belt out a tune. Annja shushed him. "The innkeeper is asleep."

Yuri waved his hand and downed another shot of vodka. "We are his customers. We can do no wrong by him. He is happy to have our money in this remote outpost. He will not say a thing about it come morning."

"Nevertheless," Gregor said, "we should not take advantage of our status as guests. It would be rude."

Yuri sighed. "Very well. We will all go to bed now."

Gregor stood and helped Bob to his feet. Bob's head drooped and the cyclist mumbled something. Gregor took his weight and started climbing the stairs. "I have seen him like this before. Come morning, he will be fine."

Annja watched them ascend the stairs and turned back to see Yuri and Oleg clearing the table. "I thought you'd leave that for the innkeeper," she said.

Yuri shrugged. "I would have, but Gregor's comment about being rude sticks with me. He is a good man, that one. So, we will clear the table as our way of saying thanks."

"Want some help?" Annja asked.

Oleg held up his hand. "Is fine for us to do it."

Annja nodded. "All right. Good night, then."

"Good night."

Annja found her way to the railing and took the steps gingerly. As she did, her head swam, but she felt good and relaxed. Behind her, she could hear Yuri and Oleg engaged in hushed conversation. Strange how they don't seem particularly drunk after all of that drinking, she thought. Then again, perhaps they're used to it.

Annja certainly wasn't. Drinking vodka wasn't her normal habit. Still, she had to admit the drink was good and it seemed to have relaxed her to the point that she expected sleep to be absolute.

Provided Khosadam didn't come calling.

She smirked. Even the supernatural wouldn't venture out on a night like this.

Reaching the door to her room, she saw Gregor emerge from Bob's room.

"He is out," Gregor said.

"Thanks for getting him up the stairs," Annja said.

Gregor smiled. "Part of my job is looking after him." He seemed as if he wanted to say something more but then only smiled again. "Good night."

"Good night," Annja said.

Gregor disappeared into his room, leaving Annja alone in the dark hallway. At the end of the corridor there was a lone window. Annja could see the snow and wind battering it mercilessly, causing it to rattle in its frame.

She walked slowly to it and looked out into the snowy night. A lone streetlight glowed and showed the barrage of snow and ice streaking through the night. Apart from the howl of wind, which seemed to crest and fall every few seconds, and the sound of snow and ice hitting the inn, there was no other sound.

Annja found her way back to her room. Her fire had died since she'd gone to dinner, but there were enough embers left to restart a blaze in the hearth. She nursed it for a moment, warming herself before getting undressed.

When she took off her boots, her feet almost shouted for joy. She hadn't realized how they'd felt while her boots were on, but the sudden freedom caused them to feel utterly liberated. Annja leaned back on the bed, her head foggy from the vodka, and wiggled her toes until she heard the cracks and pops.

She got out of her sweater and pants, throwing on her favorite T-shirt before crawling into bed. As Spartan as the bed had seemed when she first saw the room earlier, it felt wonderful. There must have been at least six layers of blankets on the bed, and Annja snuggled under them before drawing the down comforter up to her chin.

The logs in the hearth sizzled, cracked and popped as the flames tore into them. Annja felt her feet get warmer.

She turned her head to look at the window. The panes were completely covered with snow, dampening the sounds from outside.

What a place, she thought. It feels so utterly cut off from the rest of the world.

Even her laptop, which Annja sometimes felt she couldn't live without, was safely tucked away back at her loft in Brooklyn. Who would have thought a girl like me would end up here? She grinned. Certainly not her. This wasn't the kind of life she'd envisioned for herself all those years ago back when she was still trying to figure things out as an orphan.

She'd felt shunned then. All alone in a big world with no meaning to her. She'd had no foundation. No one to call her family. Only a bunch of people who filtered in and out of her life with startling regularity.

She'd found solace in history. History couldn't be changed. The facts, the legends, the folklore and the artifacts were more real to her than anything she had in her life in the present.

Never mind what her future might look like.

Inevitably, Annja knew her future was all about the past. And while she had worked hard to get her career to the point it was, even she couldn't have predicted that one day the sword belonging to Joan of Arc would find its way into her possession.

She shook her head. *And here I am dismissing the idea of a supernatural entity lurking around a remote village in Siberia while I get to conjure a sword out of thin air.*

Yeah.

She sighed and closed her eyes, stretching her limbs out to the four corners of the bed, enjoying the feeling of lengthening her body. She felt the blanket of sleep lurking nearby and welcomed it in.

Her breathing deepened.

The fireplace crackled.

And her dreams came for her.

ANNJA OPENED HER EYES.

She first took stock of her room, wondering if perhaps there was an intruder. She didn't have far to look since her room was only twelve feet by twelve feet.

And aside from the bed, the fireplace and a lonely bureau, it was empty.

Annja frowned and sat up. *What's the problem?*

Outside, the storm continued to batter the inn. She could hear chunks of snow sliding off the roof as the weight became too much. Her windowpanes were still covered.

Annja slid out of the covers and felt the instant

chill come over her. She wanted nothing more than to crawl back into the warmth of her bed and fall back asleep.

But something wasn't right.

Annja crept closer to her door and put her ear against the wood. She heard a vague creak in the hallway outside. Someone or something was moving around.

Annja frowned. Bob? No, he'd stay in his room. Unless he needed to use the bathroom.

But there was something about the nature of these footsteps that didn't seem to jibe with someone intent on using the toilet.

Stealth.

Whoever was in the hall was purposefully being as quiet as possible. As if they didn't want anyone to hear them creeping around.

But why?

Annja sank to her knees and then put her face by the crack under her door and tried looking out. She saw only darkness. She closed her eyes and visualized her sword. It hovered there in front of her, ready to be drawn forth from the otherwhere.

Annja stood and placed one hand on the doorknob.

As she did so, a thunderous boom erupted from somewhere downstairs.

Annja grabbed the door handle and jerked it open. The hallway was empty. She raced downstairs. Behind her, she heard another door open, but she didn't stop to look back.

At the base of the stairs, she stopped. Another boom sounded.

Someone was trying to get into the inn.

Annja looked at the door. The heavy plank made an effective barrier. But she wondered if it would continue to hold back the assault coming from the other side.

"What is it?"

Annja turned. Gregor stood there in a pair of sweatpants and no shirt. Annja saw how chiseled his body was. She also saw lines of hideous scars scoring his body, reaching around to his back.

"The door. Someone is trying to get in," she said.

Gregor frowned. "What do we do?"

Annja shook her head. "I don't know. What if it's someone who needs help?"

"What if it's something else?"

Annja looked at him. "You really think it might be Khosadam?"

"I don't know."

The door shook again as whatever was outside tried to burst through it again. Annja stepped back unconsciously.

"Listen!" She could barely make it out over the din of the storm, but it sounded as if someone was crying outside. "Do you hear that?"

Gregor nodded, his face grim. "It sounds like a cry for help."

Annja looked at him. "We need to open that door."

Gregor paused but then nodded. "You know what will happen to us if we are wrong?"

"Yeah, we lose our souls," Annja said.

Gregor grinned. "You are okay with that?"

"Do we have any choice?"

"I suppose not."

Annja crept closer to the door. It thundered again. She could hear the wailing now from outside. Her stomach ached. Whoever was outside must be in danger. That was the only thing that made sense.

But what if she was wrong?

Annja glanced at Gregor. "Here's what we're going to do…."

Gregor came closer. Annja positioned him to the right side of the door. "When I say so, open the door and stand clear. I will handle whatever is there."

Gregor's eyes widened. "*You* will handle it?"

Annja closed her eyes for a moment. The sword was still there. "Yes. I will handle it."

Gregor shook his head. "If you say so."

"Are you ready?"

He nodded. "Yes."

Annja pointed at the plank. "When I say so, pull the plank back and then open the door."

Annja steeled herself. She could feel her heartbeat drumming fast. Adrenaline was coursing through her veins, and any remnants of the vodka she'd drunk earlier seemed a distant memory.

Annja half closed her eyes and could almost see the sword in front of her.

She extended her hands, ready to close them around the hilt of the sword and pull it forth.

"Ready?" she asked.

"*Da.*"

Annja nodded once.

Gregor started to pull the plank back.

"*Nyet!*"

Annja spun around. Gregor froze.

Behind them the innkeeper stood on the bottom step aiming a shotgun at them.

He did not look happy.

12

The innkeeper said something to Gregor, who moved his hand slowly. "He says we are to move away from the door."

Annja frowned. Someone needed help outside and she didn't feel right not going to them. But the shotgun in the innkeeper's hand was extremely persuasive.

Annja moved away from the door.

The innkeeper moved toward the door, keeping the shotgun trained on Annja and Gregor as he did so. Satisfied that the timber still kept the door barred, he moved away from the door just as another thunderous boom shook it on its hinges.

"Tell him there is someone outside who needs our help," Annja said. "We can't do nothing."

Gregor translated, but the innkeeper only shook his head and barked back at Gregor.

"He says Khosadam is adept at luring people to

open their doors. He said if he had not stopped us, we would have fallen for it and then we would all be dead."

Annja sighed. This was getting her nowhere. She briefly considered summoning the sword and disarming the innkeeper prior to yanking the door open, but reconsidered when Bob came downstairs followed by Yuri and Oleg.

"What in the world is going on here?"

"There's someone outside," Annja said. "Trying to get in."

Bob looked at Gregor. "Is this true?"

"Yes. But we do not know who it might be. We were about to see when the innkeeper stopped us."

"I see." Bob smiled at the innkeeper and said something to him in Russian. The innkeeper shook his head and gestured with the shotgun.

"So much for that."

Yuri cleared his throat. "Perhaps we should all go back to bed. This may be something that will have to wait until morning for us to explore."

The innkeeper nodded his head vigorously. Yuri and Oleg retreated with Bob on their heels. Gregor followed and Annja came up behind them all. When she reached the top of the steps, she turned around only to see the innkeeper still eyeing her. The barrel of his shotgun was still aimed directly at her.

"I hope he's satisfied if we find some corpse in the snow tomorrow," Annja said. "We should have been able to help."

"In his mind, he's doing the right thing," Gregor said. "We must respect that even if we do not agree with him."

"I suppose."

At the door to her room, Gregor stopped her again. "By the way, Annja, I would think twice about trying to go out of your bedroom window to see what the commotion outside is all about."

"Why?" Annja said.

"The windows are nailed shut," Gregor said.

"We're trapped here?"

Gregor smiled. "Only until dawn."

DESPITE HER ANGER over not being allowed to open the front door, Annja managed to fall back to sleep. The ache in her stomach vanished and the commotion outside drifted away.

Dawn broke with a bright but overcast light. Annja immediately hopped out of bed, grabbed a hot shower and dressed before anyone else. Refreshed and not feeling any effects from the vodka the night before, she walked downstairs.

If the innkeeper had been ready to shoot her a few hours previously, it certainly wasn't apparent this morning. Bright and cheery, he ushered her to her seat and placed a plate of sliced fruit, ham and eggs in front of her.

Gregor appeared a few moments later, followed by Bob.

"What the hell happened last night?" Bob asked.

Annja shook her head. "I don't know. But I aim to find out once we get some food down."

Gregor pointed at the door. "He has removed the plank of wood."

Annja glanced over. "The danger's gone now, is that it?"

Gregor asked the innkeeper, who nodded then spoke in broken English, "Eat, please. Please."

"I guess he's forgotten about shooting us," Bob said. "That's a good thing."

Annja drained her cup of coffee and found it instantly refilled. "Where are Yuri and Oleg? Still sleeping?"

Gregor shook his head. "I don't think so. Their rooms were empty when I went past."

"They're gone already?" Annja shook her head. "Talk about men on a mission."

"You get a weird vibe from them at all?" Bob asked. "Something about the way they carried themselves didn't sit all that well with me."

"How could you tell?" Annja asked. "You passed out pretty early on last night."

Bob shook his head. "Don't write me off that easily. I am extremely adept at acting stone drunk when in fact, I am observing the situation."

"Really," Annja said.

Bob shrugged. "Sometimes."

Gregor frowned. "If you were acting, you certainly did a good job letting me carry you all the way upstairs."

"Always nice to be carried," Bob said.

"Well, I don't know about Yuri and Oleg aside from the fact that they don't strike me as middle-aged businessmen. They're far too in shape to be sitting around a boardroom all day. Did you see the necks on those guys?" Annja asked.

Gregor nodded. "Yes. They are at the very least former military."

"Possibly more?" Annja asked.

"Possibly much more."

Annja pushed her plate away. "I want to get outside."

Gregor and Bob finished off their food and stood. Annja walked to the door and glanced back at the innkeeper first just to make sure there wasn't a gun trained on them.

There wasn't.

Annja opened the door and looked out. A few flakes drifted down in the morning light, but the brunt of the storm was over. Drifts of the white stuff towered at points along the main street, partially obscuring doorways and windows.

A pair of troughs led away from the hotel. They vanished farther down the street. Other than that, nothing looked unusual.

Annja frowned and pulled the zipper higher on her parka. "The snow took care of any prints around here. There's no telling what was banging on the door last night."

Bob peered out. "Well, at least there's no corpse. That's a good thing."

They stepped out into the deep snow, their breath staining the air in front of their faces. "It's freezing," Bob said. "But I guess that's a given."

Gregor pointed at the tracks. "Where do you suppose Yuri and Oleg have gone off to?"

"We could follow," Annja said.

"Nothing much else to do," Bob said. "I don't think the cruise director will have the shuffleboard up for at least an hour or so."

Annja smirked. "Always the joker."

They trudged off in the troughs left by Yuri and

Oleg. Even with the path through the snow, it was still tough going and took them over five minutes to reach the end of the main street.

Annja stopped. "And I thought biking was tough."

"You need to spend more time in the snow," Gregor said. "It will toughen you up."

"Gee, thanks." Annja shook her head. Gregor was nothing if not a master of the obvious.

Bob pointed ahead. "Looks like they went into the church."

Gregor turned around. "Do you hear that?"

Annja strained her ears. Someone was wailing. But the cries sounded nothing like what she had heard last night. "Come on."

They trudged back the way they'd come and then past the hotel another block. Outside one of the houses, they saw ten villagers standing around in a circle. As they drew abreast, the villagers looked at them with frowns.

"What's going on?" Annja asked.

Gregor pressed the villagers, who spoke rapidly at him. Gregor's face grew serious and he nodded repeatedly. He asked a few questions and then turned to Annja.

"One of the villagers is missing."

"Who?"

"The husband of this woman. He came out in the blizzard last night to get more wood for their fire. That was the last she saw of him."

"What time did he come out?" Annja asked.

"About the same time you heard the noise last night."

"You think it was him?"

"I do not know," Gregor said.

Bob looked around. "Any trail has been obliterated with all of these people here. There's not much to go on."

"What about police?" Annja asked. "Is there some type of constabulary around here? Maybe we could get their help."

Gregor shook his head. "Places like this are patrolled by a military police station a number of miles away. The odds are that even if we needed them desperately, they would not be able to get here until a few days from now."

"You don't consider this desperate?" Annja shook her head. "That woman's husband might be dead."

"He probably is," Gregor said. "And there is nothing we can do about it now. We can only try to make sure it does not happen again."

"And just how do you propose we do that?"

Gregor's eyes looked hard. "We find Khosadam."

"Just like that?" Annja shook her head. "If it was that easy, how come no one's done it so far?"

"Because they are frightened," Gregor said. "And you cannot blame them. They are but villagers of little worth in the world at large. Their lives are determined mostly by what they toil for. Nothing more. Something like this seems omnipotent to them. They feel powerless against it."

"Until we come in and rescue them," Annja said.

"If that is the way it has to be, then yes."

Bob nodded. "I'm good with that."

"You've never struck me much as the rescuing type," Annja said. "Are you sure you're up for this?"

Bob frowned. "Just because I'm on the thin side—"

"Like an anorexic starlet," Annja said.

"It's all muscle, I'll have you know."

Annja smiled. "I'm just giving you a hard time, Bob. If you're good with this, then fine, we'll do it."

Bob seemed relieved. "We'll need some supplies."

"We need more than that," Annja said. "We need a plan of attack. Just what do the legends say about this Khosadam, anyway?"

"I told you everything I know yesterday," Bob said. "Not sure what more you could want."

"I want plenty," Annja said. "Like specifically, where would a beast like this go during the daytime? Does it hide? Does it vanish into thin air or go somewhere in another dimension?"

Bob looked at her. "You seem a lot more accepting of the idea today than you were yesterday."

Annja shrugged. "Maybe listening to whatever it was outside the hotel last night gave me reason to reconsider."

Bob shook his head. "I don't really know much more about the legend than what I told you."

Annja looked at Gregor, who had remained quiet. "What about you, big guy? Got any information you can share with us?"

Gregor looked at them both. "We are serious about this quest?"

"Yes," Annja said.

He nodded. "Khosadam will hide during the daylight. It comes out to hunt only at night."

"So where does it hide?" Annja asked.

Gregor spread his arms toward the mountains bordering Yakutsk. "Anywhere in the mountains. Perhaps a cave. Perhaps a small shelter. I do not know exactly. But that is our best chance of finding it."

Annja nodded. "Then it looks like we're heading back into the mountains."

13

"You realize that it's basically insane for us to venture up into those mountains so soon after the snowfall?"

Annja glanced at Bob. "You said you were down with this."

"I am, I am, it's just that heading out now seems a little risky."

Gregor finished packing some supplies in his backpack. "When would you prefer to get started? Tomorrow? Perhaps after another person has gone missing?"

"I'm just saying we could get into trouble."

Annja smiled. "I thought that was the point."

Gregor nodded. "I am ready if you are."

Annja tucked a large hunting knife into her belt and shouldered her pack. "Too bad we can't use our bicycles. Might have made the trip out a bit easier to take."

Bob sighed and shouldered his own pack. "We'd

better get going, then. Night comes early around these parts, and it's already past noon."

"We'll just have to do the best we can," Annja said. She looked at Gregor. "Can we make it to the mountains before dark?"

He nodded. "It will be a tough march in the snow, but it is doable. We must hurry, though."

They headed out of the hotel and struck out on a path west out of town. Gregor volunteered to take point, and Annja and Bob were only too glad to let him plow his way through the high snowdrifts. They followed along in his wake.

Gregor drove them hard, but he also made sure they stopped every half hour and drank water. "Even though it is cold, you can still get dehydrated. We must always drink to replenish our fluids."

"Lucky for us, there's plenty of snow around here," Bob said. "All we have to do is melt it down and drink it."

Annja capped her water bottle and slid it back into her pack. Her legs were on fire from the march, but she was determined not to let it show on her face. The truth was, she would rather rest another day in her warm bed than slog through the snow in search of some mythical creature. But she figured she'd have an interesting story for *Chasing History's Monsters* at the very least if nothing else panned out. She knew the Khosadam story was the kind of thing her producer, Doug Morrell, would be thrilled to air on the show.

They moved across open fields. The footing tripped them up constantly. Unable to see what was beneath the heavy blanket of snow, they fumbled along over boulders and fence posts and bits of barbed wire a few times.

Annja unsnagged herself from some wire and looked at Gregor. "Good thing I got my tetanus shot."

He pointed. "We are almost at the foot of the mountains."

Bob came up behind Annja. "Good. I need a rest."

"I thought you were in excellent shape," Annja teased.

Bob shrugged. "I'm king of bikes, but marching across snow-packed fields is killing me."

Gregor led them up a shallow incline and stopped under the large canopy of a pine tree, its branches stretching out overhead like a giant umbrella. Under the canopy, there was hardly any snow at all.

"Nice place to camp," Annja said.

Gregor looked at her. "We cannot stay here."

"Why not?"

Gregor held his head up and sniffed the air. "Take a breath like I am doing."

Annja sniffed the air and blanched. "What in the world is that smell?"

Bob gagged.

Gregor knelt and studied the ground. Then he got up and crept around the back of the tree. When he reemerged a moment later, his face was grim. "I think I have found the missing villager."

Annja started to go see, but Gregor stopped her. "It is not something you want to look at."

Annja pushed his hand aside. "I'm a big girl. I can handle it."

She regretted saying it a second later when she

looked around the tree trunk and saw the disembow-
eled corpse on the ground. His limbs were out-
stretched and the ground around him was soaked with
blood and guts. A line of his intestines trailed away
from the open cavity of his abdomen.

Annja felt bile rise in the back of her throat and had
to clutch the tree trunk to keep from losing it.

She felt movement behind her and then heard Bob
retch twice before adding the contents of his stomach
to the mess already on the ground.

Annja ducked back around the trunk to where
Gregor waited for them. He handed her his water
bottle, and she readily accepted it. "Thanks."

Bob wiped his mouth as he came back. He took a
bit of his own water and then shook his head. "Is that
what this thing does to its victims? I can't imagine it.
I just can't imagine doing that to someone else. It's
utterly barbaric."

Gregor shook his head. "There is no reasoning for
such depravity. Only the foulest creatures of hell can
be capable of such things."

Annja frowned. "Nowhere in the legends you guys
told me did it say anything about this Khosadam thing
disemboweling anyone. Remember? She's supposed
to sit on tombstones and suck the souls out of people."

"Yeah, but she can also kill people and get their
souls that way," Bob said. "And it certainly looks like
that's what this beast has been doing."

"I don't know," Annja said.

"What is your concern?" Gregor asked.

"Just that it doesn't seem like the actions of a
supernatural creature to rip someone open like that.

I mean, short of a werewolf tearing into a person—
and we're not dealing with a werewolf here, are we?
It just doesn't seem like the kind of thing a deity
wearing some kind of torture device is going to do."

Gregor said nothing for a moment. Then he took
a sip of his water. "You may be right."

Bob looked up. "About what?"

Gregor pointed. "Perhaps there is no Khosadam,
after all."

"Just because she doesn't think it would kill like
that? Then what the hell *did* do that?" Bob asked.

Gregor smirked. "We replace one problem with
another. Maybe there's nothing supernatural about
this. But there is something hunting around here.
And killing."

"Wonderful," Bob said. "So, we're still in trouble."

Annja nodded. "But we love trouble."

"I love digs," Bob said. "And so far, this trip certainly hasn't lived up to my expectations."

"We should go," Gregor said. "We still have much
to climb before night."

Annja and Bob followed him farther up the slope.
Annja leaned into the hill, trying to carry the weight
of her pack on her lower back and upper thighs. She
was tired, but she knew she had to keep going. There
was no sense stopping yet, not when they needed a
better perspective than the one they had.

As they climbed, Annja looked around. The cold
mountain air wafted around them. A few lone bird
cries sounded high up in the trees. But otherwise,
there seemed nothing out of the ordinary. She felt
uneasy, though.

Bob came up behind her. "Am I the only one getting tired here?"

"We can't stop yet. Gregor will want to find a place with a good degree of protection. We need to be able to see from as many vantage points as possible," she said.

She glanced around again, studying the landscape and listening for anything unusual. She couldn't shake the feeling that something wasn't right. She looked back over her shoulder. "I'm getting the feeling that we're being watched," she said to the others.

Gregor's eyes narrowed. "For how long have you had this feeling?"

She thought about it. "Maybe forty minutes now."

Gregor waved them up behind some rocks. "I, too, have had the sensation that someone is watching us."

"You didn't say anything," Annja said.

"Neither did you."

The three hikers huddled behind the boulders. "This is a good place to watch the trail. If anything is coming, we will see it before it gets too close."

They didn't have long to wait. As they crouched behind the outcropping, Gregor suddenly pointed back down the mountain, his voice a harsh whisper. "There!"

Annja looked. Making their way up the trail were Yuri and Oleg.

Gone was any of the friendly demeanor they'd shown the night before over dinner and vodka. In its place, a cloak of lethal danger hung over them both.

"So much for being businessmen," Bob said.

Yuri and Oleg weren't carrying briefcases.

They carried AK-47s.

14

"So much for our new friends being vacationing businessmen," Annja said. "I can't remember the last time I saw that kind of firepower for a simple hike."

Gregor frowned and looked up the trail. "We need to put distance between us and them."

"You think they're after us?" Bob asked. "They could be out hunting."

Annja glared at him. "That gun fires 7.62 mm rounds, Bob. One of those hits you, it'll take an arm completely off. That's not the sort of gear hunters use."

"Well, maybe they're looking for Khosadam, too."

Gregor frowned. "I think it would be much better if we were not around when they get up here. I don't want to take the chance that they are after us. Guns like that do not leave a lot of room for talking."

Gregor scrambled up the trail, waving for Annja and Bob to follow. Annja crept up the trail carefully, trying not to make much noise. Bob was behind her and Annja could hear his breathing.

It seemed strange to her that someone like Bob, so used to adrenaline rushes at dig sites and riding his bike through remote areas, would suddenly turn so timid at the thought of danger. But she supposed facing armed gunmen was something new for a lot of people.

Unfortunately, it was all-too-familiar ground for Annja.

Ahead of her, Gregor turned right and motioned for her to follow. As she came up on his position, Annja could see that he had located a huge boulder jutting out of the side of the mountain. It appeared to sit flush against the mountain, but in reality, there was a small amount of space that would just hold the three of them if they squeezed in close. The wind had blown the snow off the trail, so there were no footprints to betray their hidden position.

"Here," Gregor said. "We will wait until they pass. Give them the trail and then move up behind them."

Annja got herself into the space and waited for Bob to join them. "But where are we going?" she asked.

Gregor pointed. "There."

Annja could just make out a dark patch hidden a few yards up the trail, covered almost entirely behind pine trees. "Is that what I think it is?"

Gregor nodded. "A cave."

Bob squeezed in. "You think that might be where Khosadam lives?"

Gregor smiled. "We'll find out."

Annja watched as he poked his head out from the side of the rock and then jerked it back in, holding a finger to his lips to quiet them both. Annja strained her ears and could hear bits of conversation as Yuri and Oleg made their way up the trail.

Gregor seemed to be listening intently. Annja watched his face crease into a frown.

He's probably thinking the same thing I am, she thought. Yuri and Oleg don't seem to be very concerned about things.

Their voices carried up the trail now. Annja pressed herself closer to the rock, willing Yuri and Oleg not to see them. She could feel Bob's body trembling next to her. Gregor remained completely still, and it reminded Annja of a pit viper she'd seen one time, coiled and ready to strike.

Annja closed her eyes and visualized her sword. It hovered in front of her, but when she tried to push her hands forward to grab it, she ran into a wall. She frowned. Stuck in such a tight, confined space, she didn't have enough room to pull the sword out. If they were discovered, she'd have to launch herself out of the space as fast as possible and then pull the sword free once she was clear.

The odds, she decided, were not good at being able to do so before Yuri and Oleg pumped her full of hot lead.

Bob's body continued to tremble. Gregor looked at Annja, and his eyes had a cold look that Annja had seen many times before. Whoever Gregor was, he knew how to kill and he'd done it before. That much Annja felt sure of. She was glad he was with them. But she wasn't sure how much she trusted him.

At least not yet.

Annja knew that Yuri and Oleg were within a few feet of them. They didn't slow down, and kept speaking at almost normal volume.

Why would they talk so freely? she wondered. If they were hunting us, wouldn't they try to be quiet? Wouldn't they want to catch us unawares?

The sounds of the conversation died away as they continued up the trail. Gregor waited another three minutes before risking a look out from their hiding place.

Annja halfway expected to hear Yuri shout, "Don't move!" as soon as he did so, but Gregor brought his head in and gave them the all-clear signal, although he still put a finger to his lips, warning them to stay silent.

Bob moved out of the hiding place after Gregor got out. Annja came out last, tapping Gregor on his shoulder as she did to let him know she was clear. Gregor moved off, crouched low and headed up the trail to the dark place hidden by pine trees.

Bob followed and Annja brought up the rear. Gregor crossed the trail and hunkered down near the pine trees, well concealed in their branches. He waved Bob across and the cyclist took three quick steps and sneaked into the branches, as well.

Annja checked up the trail, but all was silent.

Gregor waved her across.

Am I going to get drilled as I cross the trail? she wondered. But there was little choice. She had to get across and with Gregor waving her on, she sprinted the short distance and threaded her way into the grove of pine trees.

Bob leaned against a trunk, breathing deeply. He

looked terrified. Annja tried to reassure him with a grin, but Bob just shook his head.

Annja looked at the cave and then back at the trail. Their choice was Khosadam or Yuri and Oleg. Bob's day wasn't going to get any better.

Gregor ducked back inside the grove and then headed right for the cave opening. Pausing at the entrance, he tossed a rock inside and waited.

Nothing happened.

Gregor looked at Annja and nodded. She followed him into the inky darkness. Behind her, she heard Bob stumble once near the opening but then regain his footing.

The interior of the cave drooped and Annja could tell by the air that the ceiling would be low. She stayed in her crouch until Gregor signaled she could stand.

She hadn't noticed it before, but Gregor had a red-lensed flashlight in his hand that threw decent light around the cave without sacrificing the onset of their night vision.

Annja leaned in close. "Is it safe to speak?"

"I think so," Gregor said. "We're inside now and while we should not speak at regular volume, I believe we are able to whisper without worry."

Bob sighed. "I thought I was going to piss all over myself out there when they came past our hiding place."

Gregor nodded. "Everyone feels that way when they are hunted."

"You know what that's like?" Annja asked.

Gregor smiled as shadows danced across his face.

"When I was with the military, we had an exercise. Each one of us would go off on their own and there was a hunter force after us. For four weeks we had to elude them and survive on our own in the middle of winter. Horrible cold. Deep snows. And always, they had dogs." Gregor shook his head. "It was a challenge."

"There's an understatement," Annja said. "How did you do?"

Gregor shrugged. "I was only one not captured."

"Wow," Bob said. "You never told me that."

"Was not important," Gregor said. "Just another experience in life."

Annja watched him move deeper into the cave. "Real interesting guy you got yourself there, Bob."

Bob shook his head. "Sometimes I feel like I don't even know him."

Gregor led them down into the cave. Annja could hear the dripping of condensation higher up on the cave walls. Perhaps there were stalactites overhead. She couldn't tell since Gregor had the only flashlight and he was using it to light up the ground. A misstep could mean a broken bone.

And a possible audience with Yuri and Oleg.

As they moved deeper into the cave, Gregor pointed at places on the ground. "It is softer here. And there are depressions in the soil."

"What does that mean?" Bob asked.

Gregor looked back. "We are not the only ones to use this cave."

"Is it Khosadam?"

Gregor shrugged. "I do not know. There is water damage on the track and it is tough to feel the details."

Annja frowned. "Feel?"

"Yes. I can read tracks with just my hands. I do not need to see usually."

"Where did you learn that?"

Gregor shrugged. "An American Indian."

"In Russia?"

Gregor chuckled. "No. In Arizona."

Just what the hell kind of guy is this? Annja wondered. A trained killer who could track in the dark and seem as nonchalant as ever. Weird, she decided. Definitely weird. Still, she was glad he was on their side. At least as far as she could tell.

Gregor pointed ahead of them. "Do you see it?"

Annja came up next to him and then Bob stood next to her. "See what?" he asked.

"A fork. The cave branches into two different directions." Gregor sighed. "We could split up."

"No way," Bob said. "I'd much rather that we all stuck together. It's safer that way, anyway."

"We can cover more ground if we split up," Gregor said. "And if we encounter anything, we can always shout for help."

Annja wondered if she'd even be able to pull her sword out in the cave. She didn't think it would work.

"I don't know." Bob sighed. "What do you think, Annja?"

"Well, Gregor's right that we could cover more ground. But then again, if there's something in here, am I really crazy about confronting it alone? No way."

"You wouldn't be alone," said Gregor.

"I wouldn't?" Annja asked.

"No. Bob would be with you."

"And you're taking off? Fat chance of that." Annja glanced at Bob. "No offense, old friend, but Gregor here seems a bit more adept at handling adversity than you do."

"No offense taken," Bob said. "I'd rather have Gregor here, too."

The Russian sighed. "All right. If that is what you want. You are the boss. And I work for you."

"Thankfully," Bob said.

"We should continue on," Gregor said. "We just need to pick a direction." He smiled. "Annja, would you like to make the decision?"

"Why me?"

Gregor shrugged. "I trust your instincts."

"Thanks for the pressure," Annja said. She sighed and closed her eyes. How could Gregor trust her instincts when she wasn't sure she did? She knew she needed to trust her instincts. She imagined herself walking down the cave passageway that went to the left. She felt a dull ache in her stomach. She took a deep breath then she switched it and imagined herself walking down the right side instead. This time her stomach stayed relaxed.

Annja opened her eyes. "I think we should take the right passageway."

Gregor eyed her. "You're sure?"

"I think so," she said.

"All right, then. I will lead."

"You will stop," said a voice from the darkness.

They turned around. Yuri stood ten yards away. Oleg flanked him on the left. Both of them were aiming their assault rifles at the group.

Annja sighed again. "Great, more people crashing the party."

Yuri smiled, but there was nothing friendly about it. "Sit down, all of you. We have much to discuss. And if you try anything funny, we will shoot you dead and leave you here to rot in this cave as a sacrifice to Khosadam."

15

Oleg turned on a big black flashlight, which instantly bounced bright beams of light across the interior of the cave. Annja was grateful for the light since she could at least pick a safe spot to sit.

"You two," Yuri said, pointing at Bob and Gregor. "You sit over there away from the woman."

"Woman?" Annja scowled. "Last night we were on a first-name basis and now you're calling me woman?"

"Be quiet," Oleg said. "And listen."

Yuri shouldered his rifle and sat, as well, but he kept some distance from the group. "Why don't we start by having you tell us exactly what you're doing here and what you hope to achieve."

Bob looked at Annja and then back at Yuri. "We are archaeologists."

Yuri smiled. "Go on."

"There's nothing to go on about," Annja said. "Like we explained last night, Bob here rides around looking for cool places to research. I came along on this trip and we got caught up dealing with this whole Khosadam thing. That's it, plain and simple. No embellishments."

Oleg rattled off something quick in Russian.

Yuri nodded but Gregor shook his head. "They are not lying," he said.

"And why would we believe you?" Yuri asked.

Gregor shrugged. "I have nothing to hide."

"And just how long have you known about these two?"

"I was hired by Bob to act as a guide and protector of sorts. I have known him for a number of years."

"Of course you have," Yuri said. "You have been trying to recruit him."

Annja perked up. "What?"

Bob looked amazed. "Recruit me? For what?"

"For Russian intelligence," Yuri said. "Gregor is an agent with the SVR, what you used to know as the KGB."

Bob smirked. "You've got to be kidding me."

Yuri shrugged. "I have no reason to lie. Gregor, on the other hand, has every reason to. He is an experienced agent used to recruiting Americans to spy for the Russian government."

"So much for the Cold War being over," Annja said. "This stuff sounds more like it belongs in a movie somewhere else in time."

"Yeah, and why would he bother with me?" Bob asked. "I don't have any access to anything even remotely classified. What use am I to him?"

Yuri smiled. "You have a brother who works in the Department of Defense."

Bob frowned. "How'd you know that?"

Yuri shook his head. "There is nothing that money cannot buy. And we happen to have a very powerful boss. Someone with a lot of money who can make telephone calls and get whatever information we need."

"So, that makes you—what? More spies?" Annja asked.

"We work for the Georgian *mafiya*," Oleg said. "For a man by the name of Viktor Prezchenko."

"I know that name," Bob said. "He's a power broker in the natural gas and oil industries here in Russia."

Yuri nodded. "Yes. He is a man who knows how to get whatever he wants, by any means necessary."

"I suppose that means killing, maiming, torture and all the rest of that kind of stuff," Annja said.

"It means by any means necessary," Oleg replied.

"And those AKs are for what?" Bob asked.

"For you, if necessary," Yuri said. "But I honestly hope we do not have to use them. I dislike wasting ammunition on people."

"If you're here at the behest of Prezchenko," Bob said, "then that means you must be up to something highly illegal."

"Legalities do not bother us very much," Oleg admitted.

"So what's Prezchenko doing sending his henchmen out into Siberia? Is he looking for more coppers in his chest?" Bob asked.

Yuri smiled. "Stalin thought the richest region of Russia was Siberia and he was right," Yuri said. "This area in particular has a pool of oil that could turn

Russia into one of the biggest producers in the world. Our own dependence on oil imports would be zero. And Prezchenko could set himself up as the man in charge of exploiting these resources."

"What happens to the people who live here now?" Bob asked.

"They're in the way," Oleg said. "We need the land they own right now. That is why we are here."

Bob pointed. "So, it was you two."

Yuri frowned. "Us?"

"Who unleashed the story of Khosadam on these poor people. You tried to use the legends to your own advantage by scaring them away. And when they refused to leave, you took it one step further and started murdering people like the poor villager we found mutilated on the trail. You two are utterly barbaric," Bob said.

Oleg eyed Yuri and then looked at Bob. "We haven't killed anyone," he said flatly.

"Yet," Yuri added. "Although we might make an exception with you."

"You're lying," Bob said. "We found the body. You didn't hide it well enough."

Annja pursed her lips. "Bob."

He looked at her. "Don't stop me now, Annja. I've dealt with people like these guys before. I know how they operate. I was on a dig in Indonesia that some lumber magnate wanted for his own. So he sent in thugs and beat all the men in a single village to death. The rest of the village fled and he got what he wanted. They think they're above the law and it really disgusts me."

Annja wanted to grab him, but Oleg's rifle was still aimed right at her. "Bob, there's something you're forgetting."

"What?"

"Yuri and Oleg were with us inside the inn last night."

"So?"

"So, there's no way they could have killed that poor man."

Bob stopped. Then he frowned. "Damn, you're right."

Yuri smiled at Annja. "I should say thank you for clearing our names."

"But you won't. And don't bother, anyway. You and Oleg there are still two nasty pieces of work," Annja muttered.

"Perhaps."

"Perhaps nothing. Even if you haven't killed anyone *yet*, as you say, it still doesn't make you guys saints. Especially since you're looking to rape the land in this area."

Bob glanced at Gregor. "Is what they said about you true?"

Gregor smiled. "I am supposed to deny it, of course. That is standard procedure."

"So it is true," Bob said, stunned.

Gregor nodded. "For what it's worth, I think you are a noble man."

"But not so noble that you wouldn't consider not recruiting me."

Gregor shrugged. "I have a job to do. The needs of my country outweigh my personal desires."

Yuri laughed. "You are a fool, Gregor. You could

have come and worked with us when we offered you a job. But you turned us down. You turned down very good money. And that is why we know who you really are. No one turns down the kind of money we offer unless they are already working for someone else."

Oleg nodded. "So, we found out who you worked for."

"And lucky me," Gregor said. "I happen to run into you two again last night. Imagine my surprise."

Yuri chuckled. "I suppose you had that old stomach lurch when you saw us, eh?"

"Something like that."

"Maybe you hoped we wouldn't remember you?"

"I'm not that naive," Gregor said. "I knew my cover was blown. But for the sake of all of us, I kept it up."

Annja looked at Gregor. "You weren't planning to tell us?"

Gregor shrugged. "My plan was to take care of things without you or Bob knowing about it. I prefer things nice and clean. Without a whole lot of explanations. Surely you understand that."

"So everything you told us, the old tales and folklore and your stories about military maneuvers—that was all a bunch of lies?" Annja asked.

Gregor shook his head. "No. It was the truth."

"How can we believe you?"

"I'm not asking you to. But you should know better than most that a good lie is always based on the truth. So even though I was not honest about my real identity, the stories to support my identity are true. Take it for whatever you feel it is worth. I'm not interested in impressing you with my honesty."

"Oh, no," Bob said. "He's interested in exploiting me for his country's gain."

"We still have a problem, then," Yuri said.

"What's that?" Annja asked.

"If neither you nor us created Khosadam, then who did?"

Annja looked at Bob and then at Gregor. Could Gregor have fabricated the tale to get closer to Bob? Annja supposed it was possible, but didn't think it fit Gregor's professed modus operandi of choosing simple tactics to produce results.

Could Yuri and Oleg be lying to them? Sure, she reasoned, but did that make any sense? They had the guns, after all. And it didn't look as if they had any interest in lying about who they were now that everything was out in the open.

She could hear the drips of condensation echoing throughout the cave. The air was cold and everyone's breath came out as steam. Annja shivered slightly as she thought about the corpse they'd found earlier. What a grisly way to go. It didn't seem like something any of the three Russians would do.

"I don't know who is behind the story," Annja said. "But I'd like to find out."

"Maybe there's no one behind it," Bob said. "Maybe Khosadam is real."

Yuri laughed. "Ridiculous. One of the villagers has no doubt figured out that there are too many strangers in town lately. They are trying to drive us away. But we will get to the bottom of things and show them that they are the ones who should be frightened."

"Yeah, that should go well," Annja said. She glanced at Gregor. "Are you sure this creature isn't something your superiors cooked up to help you in your mission?"

"Yes," Gregor said. "In fact, I haven't had contact with my superiors for almost a week now."

"Is that normal?" Bob asked. "I thought you spies checked in every twenty-four hours or else they send the cavalry in."

Oleg laughed now. "There will be no cavalry for Gregor. Our intelligence services are virtually bankrupt. Manpower is limited. Most of the higher-ups are corrupt and on someone's payroll."

"This is true," Gregor said. "I am one of a few still committed to my job."

"So where does this leave us?" Annja asked. "If no one is able to come up with a reasonable explanation about where Khosadam is or how it was created, we're not left with much."

"Except for what Bob said," Gregor suggested.

Annja sighed. "You're going along with that, too?"

"Why not?"

She shrugged. "Just seems a little too, I don't know, old-fashioned for the likes of a superspy."

"I am not a superspy. Not by any stretch of the imagination."

Annja grinned. "You might be right. Your English is a lot better now than it was before."

"You see?" Gregor smiled at her and in spite of herself, Annja smiled back.

Yuri yawned and the groan seemed to bounce off the cave walls. "Well, this is all well and good, but

I'm afraid Oleg and I have much work to do before we head back to the village."

"What kind of work?"

Yuri looked at Annja. "Tidying-up work."

"They're going to kill us," Gregor said. "And then they will most likely dispose of our bodies where we won't be found until nature has had a chance to do its work on us."

"Well, that or Khosadam," Oleg said. "Either way works fine with us. We are not picky in that regard."

Yuri smiled. "It has been nice conversing with you all again."

Oleg ratcheted the slide on his AK. "Your time is up."

16

As soon as Annja saw Oleg rack the slide on his AK, she closed her eyes. Her sword was still out of reach. The cave was simply too confined to pull it out.

But she didn't care. If she couldn't use the sword, she'd use something else.

In the next split second, she launched herself from her seat and drove a heel-stomp kick right into Oleg's rifle. The gun slammed into his midsection and Annja thought she heard his ribs crack as the steel met bone.

Good, she thought. The sooner I put these guys down the better.

Oleg moaned and doubled over momentarily. Behind her, Annja sensed movement and she hoped that Gregor and Bob were taking care of Yuri.

A gunshot rang out. Then another. The rounds echoed off the cave walls, and Annja ducked instinctively as a ricocheting bullet flew past her ear.

"Dammit!"

Annja pivoted and saw Gregor and Yuri fighting it out. Gregor was on top of Yuri, but Annja couldn't see the assault rifle. It must have been between them.

"Bob! Help Gregor," she shouted.

She turned back and found Oleg on his feet without his weapon. Annja spotted it on the ground a few feet away. She'd broken part of the assembly with her kick, and the gun was useless. But she had a more immediate problem. Oleg held a wicked-looking knife in his hand. And judging by the way he held it, he knew exactly how best to use it.

"Shooting you would have been kind," Oleg said. "Now I will cut you open instead."

Annja frowned. *I can't believe we actually drank with these guys last night not knowing they were killers.* So much for her intuition. Maybe the alcohol had dulled her ability to perceive danger. She didn't know.

"Lucky me," Annja replied. She kept her eyes locked on Oleg. Rather than fixate on the knife as she knew many untrained people tended to do, she focused her eyes softly on Oleg's shoulders and hips. They would tell her where Oleg's attack would come from. One area or the other would telegraph any movement he made, and Annja would know immediately how to respond.

Oleg punched in with the knife aimed at her midsection.

Annja barely had time to react. She dropped her hips and jerked her body out of the way. Oleg's blade flew past her, but before she could punch down on the top of his arm, Oleg had already brought the blade in front of him. "I am not so easy to disarm," he said, sneering.

Annja kept breathing, trying to keep her vision from tunneling. She was aware of a frantic battle going on behind her. But all she could do was hope that between Bob and Gregor, they could contain Yuri.

Oleg kept the blade dancing in front of him. He kept his other arm positioned over his chest.

He's used to fighting other people armed with knives, Annja thought. She recognized the classic knife-fighting posture one of her old military buddies had once taught her.

But Annja didn't have a knife handy.

Oleg stabbed in at her again. He wasn't wasting time with a slash. He could have toyed with her if he'd wanted to but he wanted her dead. At least that was a small measure of respect, she thought. Oleg considered her too dangerous to toy with.

She knew she had to do something fast if she had any hope of surviving this fight.

Oleg's shoulders twitched and this time, as he stabbed in, Annja chopped down on his arm, directly into the vital point on top of his forearm muscle. She heard him grunt and then heard the blade clatter away.

But Annja was already following the chop with a backhand strike to Oleg's Adam's apple. Her hand sliced into his neck hard, and instantly Oleg's hands flew to his throat. He gagged and his knees buckled.

Annja watched him try to get air down his shattered trachea, but nothing would come. His gag reflex also seemed to be hyperactive. Nothing was getting in or out.

Before she knew it, Oleg slumped over onto the floor of the cave, facedown.

Annja took a breath and steadied herself.

She turned. In the midst of dealing with Oleg, she'd been unaware that the other fight had ended.

She could see two bodies on the floor of the cave. She rushed over.

"Bob!"

He lay on the ground clutching at his abdomen. His eyes looked unfocused and his face was pale. Annja knelt next to him. "What happened?"

Gregor's voice behind her was quiet. "He caught one of the bullets Yuri fired before I was able to kill him."

Annja looked at him. "Is there anything you can do?"

Gregor just stared at her. "I'll give you two a moment." He walked away.

Annja stared after him for a moment and then turned back to Bob. His hands were a deep crimson as his blood drained out of him.

He tried to smile. "Some dig, huh?"

Annja's eyes felt hot. She blinked hard. "You're going to be fine. Just hang on."

Bob tried to laugh, but it came out as more of a stuttering cough. "Don't. I've seen enough of the Military Channel to know this is…the end."

Tears rolled down Annja's face. "Don't say that!"

Bob shook his head. "And just two days ago, I was worried you might be close to death. Funny how fast things change, huh?"

Annja looked off into the cave. "Gregor! Please help!"

"There's nothing he can do for me now. He already tried to stop the bleeding. The bullet went too deep and high. I'm shredded on the inside," Bob said.

"Is there anything I can do for you?" Annja asked desperately.

Bob nodded. "When you get back, make sure they do something about this area. I'd like people to know the stories about our adventures here. It's a small thing, but maybe someone will enjoy reading about what we did. Or what we tried to do."

Annja nodded. "You've got it."

"There's a safe-deposit box at a bank in Geneva. It's got my will in it. Can you make sure it gets to my family? My important documents are with my things back at the hotel."

"I promise." Annja stripped off her jacket and laid it over him.

Bob shivered. "Never knew how it was going to end for me. I guess I always thought…" He paused. "Well, it was never like this."

Bob squeezed her hand one final time, and then Annja felt it go soft. Tears flowed down her face and fell to the cave floor below.

She felt a hand squeeze her shoulder.

"I'm sorry, Annja," Gregor said.

She looked at Bob and closed his eyes. "He was a dear friend."

"And a good man. Regardless of my motivations. He was a good man," Gregor said.

Annja saw Yuri's corpse nearby. His neck was bent at an odd angle. "Is he dead?"

"Very."

"Good."

She stood and bowed her head. She thought about the good times she and Bob had had in the past and prayed that he would find a wonderful home in whatever paradise he chose.

When she lifted her head, she saw that Gregor had bowed his head, as well. "Thank you," she whispered.

He looked up. "For what?"

"Helping him."

Gregor shook his head. "There wasn't anything I could do to save him. The bullet—"

"I know. But thank you anyway."

Gregor nodded. "We should get going. We'll need to organize a team to get up here and recover the bodies. He shouldn't be left like this."

Gregor started walking toward the front of the cave. Annja followed.

As they reached the entrance, Gregor stopped.

"What's the matter?" Annja asked.

But the sudden roar that echoed throughout the entire cave drowned out her question.

Something was inside with them.

17

Gregor pulled Annja down to the floor of the cave, his hand already starting to cover her mouth. Annja felt his body heat as they huddled together behind an outcropping.

Farther ahead, she thought she could see a shadowy form skulking through the cave. Was this the Khosadam she'd heard so much about? Was this really the supernatural demigoddess who ate people's souls?

She strained her eyes to look. She could hear the creature's feet shuffling along the rocky ground. Its breathing seemed raspy, as well.

And then as quickly as it seemed to fill the cave, the creature vanished.

Annja and Gregor waited there a few more moments, but Gregor gradually released his hold on her. He shot her a look that told her not to make any noise.

Slowly, Gregor peeled himself away from Annja and rose to a slight crouch. He lifted himself so he could peer over the outcropping, and Annja watched him remain almost motionless. She decided that he must be an expert at staying completely still from all of his years with Russian intelligence.

Gregor knelt back down beside her. Annja felt his warm breath tickle her ear. "It appears to have gone."

She turned and whispered in his ear, "Is it safe to get out of here?"

"I don't know. It could come back at any time."

"We can't stay here." Annja's eyes wandered back to Bob's body. There was no way she would ever leave him to rot on the floor of this cave.

Gregor seemed to follow her gaze and he nodded. "We'll try to make a break for it."

He rose again, taking Annja by the hand and pulling her along behind him. They moved slowly, knowing that if they moved too fast, they'd risk making noise and drawing the attention of whatever they'd just seen.

Annja's thighs screamed at her as the slow, low crouch took its toll on her already exhausted body. She closed her eyes briefly and pictured the sword. As soon as she did so, a slight surge of energy filled her body.

Ahead of her Gregor stopped every few feet, pausing and listening for any changes in the environment. Only after he was satisfied they hadn't made any noise did they continue on.

For Annja, they might as well have been walking to the moon. She hadn't realized that they'd come so deep into the cave when they first entered. And the quick dash for the entrance of the cave and the relative safety of the woods beyond now seemed to stretch interminably before them.

A groan to their left filled Annja with immediate dread.

Gregor froze.

But the groan seemed a fair way off, down another tunnel they hadn't noticed before.

Gregor shifted course. He drew Annja along with him, toward the groaning sound.

After a few minutes of feeling around, Gregor took Annja's hands and put them over the opening. She could feel the cool breeze coming from it. Was this the hideaway of Khosadam?

She could feel Gregor looking at her. Annja glanced at him and shook her head. There'd be time enough for exploring the lair later. She wanted Bob's body removed from any further harm. She owed him that.

Gregor seemed to sense her intention and nodded. Annja backed away and turned to head back in their original direction.

She heard Gregor slip behind her, jarring loose a chunk of stone. It skittered across the cave floor, causing a minor avalanche of small pebbles and gravel.

Annja and Gregor froze.

As the last pebble came to rest, Annja caught a breeze on her cheek.

And then heard the roar.

Something slammed into her, knocking her back and away. It felt as if a giant forearm had clotheslined her. She toppled back against the stones and immediately felt the rush of a giant form moving past her.

"Annja!" Gregor called out for her.

She took a step and then it felt as if everything were falling away from her.

She hit something hard with the back of her head and groaned.

The cave filled with another roar.

Annja heard the explosion of Gregor's gun once then twice, followed by another roar.

"Annja!" Gregor shouted again.

Annja tried to get to her feet, but was dazed. She felt the back of her head and her hand came away sticky. She could smell the coppery blood on her fingers.

She tried to call out, but her voice sounded weak. "Gregor."

She heard the beast roar again. Another gunshot sounded and then she heard the metallic clang of the gun knocking against some rocks. Had Khosadam disarmed Gregor?

She heard Gregor call out in Russian.

Annja's vision swam. Her head clouded. She felt nauseous.

Silence washed over her.

WHEN SHE CAME TO, Annja felt awful. For the second time in only a few days, she was sure she'd suffered a concussion.

If this keeps up, she thought, I'll need brain surgery to relieve all the pressure in my head.

She tried to ease herself into a sitting position, but moaned as she did. Her head ached and her stomach lurched horribly in protest. She wanted to vomit.

But she was also immediately aware of the pervasive silence of the cave.

She wasn't sure where she'd fallen, but it seemed she wasn't in the upper part of the cave anymore.

She couldn't be sure without light. And since she had none, she'd have to fumble her way along through the darkness.

She sighed and tried to get her bearings. The last thing she could remember was a huge form moving past her. The gunfire. Gregor shouting.

She frowned. Gregor. Where was he now?

Annja got to her feet again, slowly this time. Each movement seemed to hurt more and more. But she knew she had to get up.

Her hands palmed the cold, rough rocks around her, her fingers eventually finding sufficient purchase to support her weight as she tried to stand. She took a deep breath and pushed herself up. Her knees almost buckled twice, but then she finally got to her feet.

The motion was too much and she suddenly vomited.

She wiped her mouth on her jacket sleeve and paused to close her eyes and take a few more deep breaths. The last thing she wanted to do was move again. She just wanted to curl up into a ball and fall fast asleep. But she knew that would probably mean death.

And if Gregor was still alive, he might be searching for her.

Or he could just as easily be dead, too, she thought. Especially if Khosadam got its hands on him.

She had to find out for sure. And she had to make her way back to the cave entrance to get help. Now that it seemed pretty definite that this was where Khosadam or whatever it was hung out, maybe she could mount an assault with the villagers helping her. Surely some of them would own firearms and they'd be able to storm the cave and kill this thing.

She stopped.

What the hell was the matter with her? Had the fall taken its toll on her? Or was she simply reacting to the stress of the trip and then losing her dear friend?

It wasn't like Annja to want to kill something she knew nothing about. And Bob had made her promise to let others know about this place. In order to do so, she'd have to find out just what exactly this Khosadam thing was. If it was something supernatural at all.

She sighed. I've got to get out of here.

Annja turned and started moving her hands along the wall, searching for anything that might help her. As she moved around, she could tell she'd fallen into an almost circular pit that was much too deep to try to climb out of. Annja wasn't sure she had the strength to do so and the walls of the pit didn't seem to have enough handholds anyway.

She needed something else.

A sudden lancing pain in her head made her shut her eyes tight. In her mind's eye, she saw her sword hovering. As she looked at it, another burst of energy filled her body.

She opened her eyes and held the sword, hands extended toward the lip of the pit. She plunged the sword into the cave wall as high above her head as she could reach. It stuck fast.

Annja could still feel a vague pain in her head, but she shut it out and concentrated instead on pulling herself up. Her fingers ached, but then she was able to climb the wall carefully using handholds and the sword until she could draw one hand up and over the edge of the pit. She got her arms over and then finally, she hauled herself up.

She lay on the floor huffing for a moment, trying to flush more oxygen back into her system. She willed the sword back to the otherwhere.

When she felt better she got to her feet. She tried to make a mental note of where the pit was, hoping she wouldn't fall back down it again in the future. But without light, trying to fix its position seemed impossible.

Silence still blanketed the cave. Here and there an occasional drop of water would echo through the chambers. But otherwise, there seemed to be nothing moving anywhere in the cave itself.

Had Khosadam vanished again?

Annja frowned. She had to find her way to the hidden tunnel that Gregor had discovered. That was probably where the creature had gone. And maybe it had taken Gregor with it.

Annja shivered thinking about Gregor being eaten or worse by the creature. The sooner she could find her way back to where she'd started, the better.

Annja moved forward slowly and then stopped again. She brought her hands up and they touched the wall in front of her.

At least I didn't run face-first into that, she thought.

She shifted and realized the area felt familiar, even in the pitch-dark. Was this where we were when we were attacked?

She knelt and ran her hands along the floor of the cave. Her fingers brushed something smooth and small. She plucked it off the floor and held it closer to her face.

Annja could smell the cordite and knew she'd found one of the shell casings from Gregor's gun. The casing was cold. Annja figured that meant she might have been unconscious for some time back in the pit. But then again, a shell casing wouldn't hold its heat once it was on the ground.

She found three more casings but nothing else.

Gregor, as she'd feared, had vanished.

18

Annja considered her options. She had no light. Plus she had a concussion, although it did seem to be improving rapidly.

She looked around, not really seeing much of anything in the darkness. The general unfathomable depth of her surroundings unnerved her. She felt the outline of the hidden tunnel, tracing it all the way to the ground.

Well, she thought, I've got two choices—I can go down this tunnel and see if I can find Gregor and whatever took him. Or I can try to find my way out of here and back to the village.

She pondered her situation. There was no guarantee that any of the villagers would help her even in the daylight. She'd seen fear enough times to know they were all struck by it. The thought of hunting some unknown creature wouldn't sit well with them.

No, if she was to get to the bottom of this, she

would have to do it alone. There was nothing else she could do but press on.

Annja took a deep breath and moved into the opening. As she did, her boot rolled over something on the ground. Annja knelt and felt for it.

It was about four inches long and cylindrical. Her fingers felt along the cylinder and found a switch. She turned it on instinctively, and red light shot out of one end.

Gregor's flashlight!

Annja looked at it and smiled. He must have dropped it during the struggle with the creature. It was a good sign that he had definitely come this way.

Annja looked around. The cave walls seemed to shrink for about twenty feet and then beyond that, deeper darkness awaited her. She felt a cool breeze coming from somewhere down the tunnel.

Too bad he didn't drop me a gun, too, Annja thought.

Annja stepped down the tunnel and made sure she shielded the light as much as she could. No sense alerting the creature that she was coming.

The cave still seemed cloaked in silence. Annja's footsteps were as quiet as she could make them. She could hear the drips and drops that marked most of the caves she'd ever been in.

But beyond that, nothing.

She found it a little strange, actually, that with a creature like the one she and Gregor had encountered, there wasn't more noise. Surely it would have to hunker down somewhere close by and rest? And if it slept, might it not also snore?

Annja frowned. I'm being presumptuous. There was

no telling what the creature was like. And if it was supernatural in origin, then maybe it had simply disappeared into thin air. No, she thought. That's impossible.

She shook her head. Unless it's my sword.

She reached the end of the narrow part of the tunnel. Beyond the opening, the cave seemed to blossom into a much larger cavern. She could hear more drips now, falling into what sounded like a pool of water.

Annja stepped down and into the larger cavern. The air was warmer, and she relished the temperature change, suddenly aware of how much the cold had affected her.

She flashed the red beam of light over the cavern. She was dismayed by what she saw.

A dead end.

Annja frowned. That can't be. There must be something here that leads out. How else could the creature have gotten Gregor out of the cave?

Unless they went out of the front of the cave while I was unconscious.

Annja sighed and knew that she wouldn't have known if they had left or not. She squatted down and took a few deep breaths.

All around her, the walls of the cavern seemed to mock her. Nothing here but solid rock, they seemed to say. No way out except how you came in.

She flashed the light along the wall in front of her. There seemed to be nothing there but more solid rock. She moved closer and began tracing her hands over the rocky walls. She refused to give up.

It took her the better part of twenty minutes to locate a small opening close to the ground. She got

down on her hands and knees and put her face close
to the opening, trying to see beyond it.

She saw only darkness.

She turned her head and listened. She didn't hear
anything, either, but did feel a warmer breeze coming
from somewhere beyond.

She sat back. How do I get this open? She used the
flashlight to search for some kind of hidden catch
release, but she didn't find anything that looked un-
natural. This was the way she had to go, she had no
doubt, but getting through the portal was going to be
a challenge.

Annja's throat ached and she suddenly realized
how thirsty she was. She glanced back toward the
pool of water and listened to the drops falling from
the cave roof onto the water below.

She knew that survival experts always cautioned
you to boil water for several minutes to kill off any
bacteria in a pool of standing water. But she didn't
have anything to build a fire with. And worse, making
a fire might alert the creature to her presence.

Annja glanced up at the roof of the cave. There was
no telling how thick the rock was above her. There
was a fair chance that it had sufficiently filtered the
water dripping down and that pool was, in fact, quite
safe to drink from.

She stepped closer to the pool. It had been many
hours since she'd had anything to drink. Her lips
were dry and caked. The insides of her cheeks felt
mossy. Her tongue had thickened also. She knew she
was dehydrated.

She bent closer to the water and sniffed it. She was

aware of the risks. If the water was contaminated she'd know about it fairly quickly after she drank.

And then she'd be in no position to help anyone, least of all herself.

She touched her lips to the water and took a small sip. The instant the water crossed her tongue, she felt relief. The ice-cold liquid tasted incredibly delicious and she eagerly drank more.

After a minute of drinking, she leaned back and waited. If the water was tainted, her gut should have started acting up. But instead, she felt only a measure of contentment as her body processed the hydrating water. She licked her lips and felt her mouth fill with saliva.

After twenty more minutes, she felt confident enough to take another long draw from the pool. And with each swallow, she felt stronger and more rested.

Finally, she stood and moved back to the wall where the tiny opening was. Now, she felt better about looking for the release.

She was almost ready to admit defeat when she accidentally leaned on a section of the rock wall. She felt it give almost immediately, sinking farther into the wall with a low hiss.

It's mechanical? Annja frowned. A beast couldn't do that.

The wall slid back, revealing a narrow tunnel. The air beyond was much warmer, almost humid.

Annja closed her eyes and checked on her sword. It hung there, ready for her.

She stepped into the tunnel and shined the light around. The passage stretched in front of her for at least a hundred yards before it turned. Annja stepped into it and moved carefully along the tunnel.

The red light from Gregor's flashlight seemed to be waning. Annja took a final look ahead of her and then shut it off, trying to conserve some of its power. Who knew what might be ahead? She could very well need it desperately and since the way ahead of her looked okay for now, she could stumble along in the dark.

The warm air that surrounded her grew more humid and thick. Annja unzipped her jacket slowly, letting it flap open and shed some of her body heat.

The tunnel suddenly dipped down for about forty yards and Annja almost slipped twice, but kept her footing. Her stomach still showed no signs of reacting to the water, for which she was grateful. The mountain water had been a welcome relief for her, and if she could keep it down, it would help her with anything she had to do further on. Whatever it might be.

She noticed her footing felt different. Annja stopped and knelt down. She ran her fingers along the floor of the tunnel and smiled when she touched dirt.

Interesting.

She switched the flashlight on again and saw that the walls were changing, as well. Fewer rocks poked their way out of the walls. Roots seemed to stretch out like spindly tentacles from the hard-packed dirt walls.

Where is this tunnel going to lead me? she wondered.

She surveyed the area ahead and saw that the tunnel started to ascend again. She switched off the flashlight and kept walking.

Her thighs let her know when the angle of descent

increased. And Annja figured she must have walked at least a mile by now. Or at least, it certainly felt as if she had.

A sudden breeze washed over her and Annja froze.

It hadn't come from behind her, the way she'd come into the tunnel. It came from somewhere up ahead.

The tunnel was about eight feet across. And the distance between the sides of the walls wasn't big enough to permit many people in it at once.

A sound floated toward her that set her heart pounding. It sounded like a raspy cough.

Someone was in the tunnel with her.

Annja glanced behind her. To retrace her steps back to the cavern would take her too long. Plus, if she used the flashlight to see, she would alert whoever was behind her to her presence.

But where else could she go? The tunnel was too confined to hide anywhere.

Annja closed her eyes and tried to pull out her sword. Nothing. The tunnel was more narrow than the caves had been.

This is not good, she thought.

Another breeze washed over her. There was a scent on it that smelled like a rotting corpse. Annja blanched and clamped her hand over her mouth to keep from retching in the silence. She had to get out of there.

But where?

She pressed herself against the side of the tunnel, desperately looking for any kind of nook or cranny she could squeeze into. But all she found were the coarse, thin roots draping down from the walls like a mass of greasy hair.

Some of them were several inches thick, but others seemed as fine as thread.

Annja heard another sound and knew that whatever it was, it was getting closer. Was it Khosadam? Was it coming back to get her and finish the job? Had it already killed Gregor?

Whatever it was, it was coming straight for her.

19

The raspy moan couldn't have been more than twelve feet away.

Annja closed her eyes, visualizing the sword in front of her. I really need to be able to use this, she thought. If that thing sees me, I'm dead without the blade.

A breeze passed over her, and Annja kept her eyes shut tight and held her breath. Something passed her. Annja heard it continue down the tunnel and then silence returned.

She let out a breath that felt as if she'd been keeping it pent up for hours, careful not to let the whoosh of the exhale make any noise. All around her, the mass of roots draped over her.

Maybe it couldn't see me, she thought. Maybe its eyes are just as bad in the dark as mine are.

She eased out of the veil of roots and tried to look down the tunnel, but nothing but darkness met her eyes. She looked in the direction she'd been heading.

I need to keep moving. Wherever that thing went, I'm going in the opposite direction, she decided. She kept moving down the tunnel, intent on getting to wherever it ended before the creature came back.

Ahead of her, she thought she could see the barest amount of ambient light. The tunnel also started sloping down at an angle. The warm air grew more humid, as well, and the roots coming out of the walls grew more numerous.

At last, the tunnel seemed to end. Annja could make out the dim outline of what appeared to be a door. She pressed her head to the rough-hewn wood and listened.

Someone was on the other side.

Annja looked back down the tunnel. The creature could come back at any moment. She had to get past this door.

A thought occurred to her then. What if it wasn't just one creature? What if there were two of them? And what if one of them was asleep on the other side of the door?

She frowned. Back down the tunnel she knew for sure there was a creature—whatever it might have been. She didn't know what lay on the other side of the door.

She decided to find out.

There was no doorknob, so she pushed on the door. It didn't budge. Then, she felt around the jamb and found a lip of wood she could pull on.

The door opened.

Gray dim light seeped into the tunnel. Annja's eyes blinked a few times and then adjusted to the light, in spite of how little there was.

She stepped through the doorway.

It was a root cellar by the look of things. Old shelves contained bundles of drying herbs long since petrified and reduced to dust. Whoever owned the cellar hadn't used it for its original purpose in some time.

The furniture looked old, but used. Two heavy chairs sat by a table made from old planks of wood.

The air smelled of musty dirt and decay, and something else.

Blood.

Annja moved beyond the table, steeling herself for another creature.

Instead, she saw a body lying in a crumpled heap on the floor. Annja knelt and recognized Gregor's jacket. She nudged him. He moaned.

Her voice was a harsh whisper. "Gregor!"

He shifted slightly, his eyes barely able to open from the crusty blood that caked them. "Annja?"

"Yes, it's me."

"How did you find me?"

"I found the tunnel the creature took you down. It took me a while to find it, but I did."

Gregor's lips were caked with blood, as well. "Lucky for me."

"What happened to you?"

He tried to smile. "I fought it."

"Khosadam?"

He nodded and the motion made him groan again. "Yes. It toyed with me until it got tired and then left."

Annja looked him over. "Are you all right?"

"I was knocked unconscious."

"But otherwise?"

Gregor shifted and gritted his teeth. "Nothing feels broken, but the pain is immense."

"You've probably got plenty of bruises."

"No doubt."

Annja grinned. "Why did you fight it?"

"I don't believe in surrendering." He looked around as Annja helped him sit upright. "Did you kill it?" he asked.

"No."

"Why not? Where is it?"

"Gone. Back down the tunnel."

Gregor's face darkened. "You're sure?"

"It walked right past me."

"And didn't see you?"

"I guess not."

Gregor nodded. "You're a lucky woman, Annja Creed. I doubt many others would have been able to save themselves."

Annja looked around. "Maybe. We'll see how lucky I am once we get you out of here. Do you have any idea how to get out?"

"When the thing brought me here, it proceeded to beat me up fairly quickly. But I thought I saw another door against the far wall over there by the shelves."

Annja nodded and went to the wall. Whorls of dust spun into the air as she walked past them, causing her to stifle a sneeze.

"Stay quiet," Gregor said. "That thing could come back at any time and kill us both."

Annja shook her head. "I won't let that happen."

"You have no gun."

"You only left me the flashlight," she complained.

He grinned. "I was a bit preoccupied."

"I guess so." Annja turned back to the wall. She ran her hands over it until she got close to the shelves. "I think there's something here where the shelves connect with the wall."

"It's fake?" Gregor asked.

Annja nudged the shelves and saw a bit of space appear. "Yes. The shelves are built to conceal a door," she said.

Gregor got to his knees and then stood gingerly. "In that case, I suggest we leave."

Annja pulled on the shelves a bit more. "It's heavy."

Gregor appeared by her side and offered one of his hands. "I may not be much help."

Together they pulled and the doorway slowly opened before them. The dim light from the root cellar illuminated just a bit ahead of them, but there looked to be a smaller tunnel that led to a set of stairs at the far end.

Gregor looked at Annja. "That would appear to be our way out of here. I suggest we take it."

Annja smiled. "You want to lead—"

Gregor shushed her.

Annja stopped. "What?"

"Listen!"

From the far end of the root cellar, where Annja had entered from the tunnel, they heard a rising moan that filled the darkness and bled into the cellar. Annja looked at Gregor.

He nodded. "It's coming back. Probably to finish me off."

Annja ran back to the opening and peered back down the tunnel, listening.

She looked back at Gregor. "It's coming."

Another roar sounded.

Gregor's eyes widened. "It knows you're here."

"How?"

"Smell? Who knows? We have to get out of here," he said.

Annja closed the door to the tunnel and shoved the heavy table in front of it. Then she piled the chairs on top of the table.

From the other side of the door, she could hear the creature coming faster.

"Maybe that will slow it down," she said, not really believing it.

The creature roared again and crashed into the door. The frame shuddered and budged but seemed to hold.

"Annja!"

She hurried over to Gregor and they slid through the door into the side tunnel. The stairs were about a hundred feet away.

"Come on!" Annja got her arm around Gregor and they limped toward the stairs. Behind them, there was another crash and then silence.

"You think it got through?" Anna asked.

Gregor shook his head. "I don't know. We've got to get the hell out of here now."

They kept moving. And then Annja heard another crash.

But it wasn't behind them. It was in front of them.

Gregor stopped. "Annja."

To Annja's eyes, it looked as if part of the tunnel swung open about fifty feet in front of them. And then something moved out into the tunnel.

The creature.

"There was another way out!" Annja said.

Gregor grabbed her. "Now what?"

She made the decision in an instant. "Back to the root cellar. It's our only hope. We can't fight it in the tunnel."

They ran back to the cellar, ducking through the doorway. Annja shoved it closed just as Gregor cleared it. "Help me!" she said.

He leaned on it, while Annja tried to see if there was anything else she could use to seal it shut.

But there was nothing.

"I can't do this," Gregor said. "I'm spent."

"Get behind me," Annja said.

"What?"

"When it comes in," she said, "stay behind me. Do you understand?"

"Why? You can't handle that thing alone."

"Just do what I say. Stay back there and don't do anything unless I say so."

"You're crazy."

She eyed him. "We've got another choice?"

He shook his head.

The creature crashed against the secret door, rattling the shelves. A bit of space appeared between the wall and the shelves.

"It's coming," Gregor said.

Annja closed her eyes. The sword hung in front of her. She reached her hands out for the hilt of the sword.

She heard another crash in the root cellar, felt a breeze on her face. She opened her eyes.

The shelves exploded as Khosadam entered the root cellar.

20

The creature stood before her, and Annja's heart pounded against the inside of her chest like a sledgehammer. The thing stood over six feet tall, its head stooped to avoid the low roof of the root cellar. Annja could see the long cords of muscle snaking their way through its body like suspension cables. Worn leather leggings and a tunic scarcely covered its body, and Annja wondered how it could survive the cold.

On its face, however, was the most startling thing of all—a metallic half mask muzzled the creature's jaw.

It really was Khosadam.

If Annja couldn't see the dim outline of breasts beneath the tunic, she might have suspected the creature was a male, it appeared so utterly unfeminine. But she could tell that it might have once appeared more womanly.

Any trace of that was gone.

Khosadam roared and Annja felt the hot breath of

fetid air hit her face. It smelled as if the creature had been dining on fermenting garbage.

It regarded Annja for a moment, almost curious that its roar hadn't caused the intruder to move.

Behind her, Annja could feel anxiety bleeding off Gregor. "Are you sure this is such a good idea?"

She nodded. Khosadam weaved from side to side, like a slow metronome marking its time in hoary breaths. Annja stayed where she was and didn't move at all. If she did, she knew the creature might attack.

But then again, she suspected the creature would attack her soon enough anyway.

She closed her eyes. The sword hung there.

Khosadam roared.

Annja grabbed the sword and opened her eyes.

She barely had time to duck as a wicked-looking claw slashed through the air where her head had been a split second before. She felt the rush of air tousle her hair as the claw slashed empty space.

Annja stood and held the sword in front of her. Now she felt much better about taking the creature on. The blade gave off a dull bit of light, and Khosadam suddenly backed up when it saw the sword.

Behind her, Gregor gasped. "What on earth—?"

"I'll explain later," Annja said.

The creature's eyes narrowed as it regarded the sword. The appearance of the substantial blade seemed to give it a moment's pause. Annja nodded. That's right, she thought, this changes the game. Maybe you don't want to play now. Maybe you just want to run away and hide. And that'll be just fine.

Instead, Khosadam squatted lower and raised its

claws in front of it. Annja could see the curved, dark black nails that looked as sharp as her own blade. Khosadam clicked them together and Annja realized that the fight was on.

When it moved, Annja could hardly believe it. Khosadam came at her fast, its claws swiping at the air in front of it, trying to back Annja up against the wall.

Annja deflected the first two swipes with her blade, hoping she'd be able to cut the creature's hands off. But the sword only made contact with the nails, and most surprising, the nails didn't break under the steel assault.

"Annja!"

She ducked just as another swipe cut through the air. She'd been caught musing when she should have been concentrating on killing Khosadam. While she didn't want to kill it, Annja was hard-pressed to believe that there was any other way out of this.

Khosadam clearly meant to kill her.

Annja slashed out with her sword. Khosadam ducked away as the blade cut through the air. Then it immediately slashed back at Annja.

Annja pivoted as the claw came down, trying her best to retract the blade and get it back in front of her where it could offer the most protection.

Khosadam retreated again.

It's very smart, Annja thought. And clearly, it's used to fighting against skilled opponents.

How would she be able to defeat it?

Khosadam kicked at Annja's midsection, catching her right in the solar plexus. Annja toppled back, trying to gulp down air as her diaphragm spasmed. She rolled over and came back up with the sword in front of her just as Khosadam cut down at her again. The claws clanged off the sword blade.

Annja frowned. Did the creature have metallic claws? Were they implants or some sort of supernatural wickedness?

She came back up and immediately stabbed straight in at Khosadam's chest, intent on piercing the tunic and the heart she assumed lay beating beneath it.

But Khosadam jerked itself out of the path of the blade and, as Annja came in, flicked its claw across Annja's cheek.

Annja cried out as the razor-sharp blades sliced through her skin. She felt the rush of blood down her face and the sting of the cuts.

I'll need a rabies shot for sure, she thought as she jumped back and away. Those things are definitely not natural.

Khosadam came closer, as if seeing the blood had energized it. Annja could almost feel the glee in the creature as it sniffed the air and let out another roar.

This time, when it cut in, Annja swept the sword blade up at an angle. She felt the blade make contact and then cleave into Khosadam's left arm. There was a spurt of blood as the sword met flesh and bone.

Khosadam screeched and Annja almost dropped her sword to cover her ears, the sound was so wrenching. But she kept herself from doing so and steeled herself for the counterattack.

Instead, Khosadam reared back and held its wounded arm. Blood continued to jet from the wound. The creature's breathing seemed harsher now. And the look in its eyes was death.

With its free hand, the creature tore off the muzzle and Annja saw the gaping maw lined with pointed teeth. But they weren't white. They gleamed in the dim light. Their metallic points clicked as Khosadam brought the upper and lower rows together in a tight chomp.

What is this thing? Annja wondered. For sure, it's not supernatural if I was able to hurt it like that. But the metal claws and teeth—it's like a machine.

Annja drew the sword up and into a different stance. Khosadam roared and leaped right at Annja. Its feet landed first, shoving the flat of the blade into Annja's chest. Annja fell back, crashing into the table and knocking over the chairs she'd stacked on top of it.

Khosadam came closer. Annja tried to roll but as she did, the creature stomped down on the sword, trapping it underneath Annja's hand. Annja let go of the blade and completed her roll.

Khosadam leaped on top of her again.

Annja stared up into the metal jaws of the beast. The wounded arm leaked blood all over her, and Annja felt a rush of bile in her throat as she struggled to keep from retching from the horrible stench of Khosadam's breath.

The weight of the creature seemed impossible to hold at bay. Annja had its arms pushed back at the shoulders, but she could feel the thing leaning in with even more weight. Worst of all, the head and those metal teeth clicked and clacked ever closer to Annja's face.

Annja brought her legs up and in, trying to get her knees to her chest. She finally did so and then kicked back, launching Khosadam back and off her. It stumbled back, crashing into the wall of the cellar.

Annja made a move, but Khosadam blocked her path. Annja dodged right and Khosadam moved with her, always keeping the good claw out in front.

Khosadam slashed at Annja. She jumped back and away and then came in as Khosadam retracted its claw. Annja was on the outside of Khosadam's right arm, trying desperately to gain leverage by what she hoped was an elbow joint.

Khosadam's head spun and took a bite at her head.

"No!" Annja shouted. She jerked her head back and as she did, she lost the leverage she had gained. Khosadam slashed at her and the claws tore into Annja's jacket, shredding the material, but missing Annja's flesh by a mere inch or so.

Annja punched at Khosadam's head and caught the side of its jaw. Instantly her hand exploded in pain. It was like punching an I-beam. Khosadam's entire jaw seemed forged out of steel.

Annja let her hand go limp by her side. She wouldn't be able to use it again for much.

Khosadam swung toward her, seeing that Annja now had a useless limb, as well. It raised its wounded arm and then let out what Annja could best describe as a chuckle. But she saw no humor in the situation. She had to resolve it and fast.

As Khosadam came at her, Annja whipped her right leg up and out in a high arc that caught the creature on the side of its neck. Annja's foot made impact and Khosadam roared in pain again.

As she retracted her leg, the creature moved in

and head butted Annja in the forehead. Annja's eyes immediately filled with tears and her vision vanished.

Khosadam roared and jumped on top of her again. Annja crashed back to the floor with the creature on top of her. She heard a crack as the full weight of the creature came down on top of her. Every breath felt like a hot lance was being plunged into her body and Annja knew she had broken a rib.

There goes sleeping for a few weeks, she thought.

Khosadam leaned in, its teeth searching for Annja's head. Annja's good hand scrambled for anything she could use. She came up with a fistful of dirt and threw it in Khosadam's eyes. The creature reared back and as it did, Annja bucked her hips and dislodged it. She rolled and came to her feet. Khosadam wiped the dirt from its eyes and hissed at Annja.

I guess it's through playing with me now. This time it will try to kill me once and for all, she thought frantically.

Khosadam leaped through the air again, aiming its good claw at Annja's midsection. Annja pivoted and as Khosadam's claw shot through the space, Annja shot her fist into the creature's throat.

It fell to the ground retching.

Annja summoned her sword.

The beast got to its feet and spun around, looking for Annja. Annja spun, as well. She could hear the gagging noises slowly diminish in Khosadam's throat. She might have injured it, but it was nothing the creature didn't seem able to handle.

Annja brought the sword up in front of her, aware that she was only able to wield it with one hand. It would be tougher to use, but it was still her best means of defense.

Khosadam coughed once and hacked a bloody bit of phlegm on the floor. Then it looked back at Annja and roared again. Annja steeled herself and as the beast launched its attack, she dropped to her knees and shot out her foot.

The rear kick caught Khosadam square in the lower abdomen, doubling it over and dropping it to the floor. Annja rose and heard the labored breathing of the creature as it struggled to get its wind back.

Annja brought the sword high overhead and cut straight down at Khosadam's head. One cut would finish it. But as she did, the creature rushed in under the blade and tackled Annja around her waist. They tumbled to the floor, Annja losing her blade as they crashed to the ground.

Khosadam was on top of her again, and despite the incredible pain in her hand, Annja used her injured limb to hold it at bay.

She could see the sword lying on the ground out of the corner of her eye.

Khosadam's teeth came closer. Annja's fingers clawed at the dirt. Khosadam's teeth were inches away from her face.

The room swam as her vision clouded. And then she saw something move nearby.

Gregor!

He kicked the blade toward her, and Annja felt her hand close over the hilt of the sword.

She turned the point and plunged it straight into the

side of the creature, running it in deep until the point emerged from the other side of its body.

Khosadam stiffened, shrieked and then fell away from Annja. It toppled onto the floor of the cellar and everything went silent.

Annja got to her feet and then drew the sword out from Khosadam's body.

Gregor's voice was a barely audible whisper. "Is it—"

"Dead," Annja said.

She closed her eyes. When she opened them again, the sword was gone.

But Khosadam's body remained along with a lot of unanswered questions.

21

"Took you long enough."

Gregor nodded. "When you crashed into the table, one of the chairs caught me on the way down. I had to extricate myself."

"Well, better late than never, I suppose." Annja cradled her left hand and examined it. It was very tender.

"You're injured?" Gregor asked.

Annja frowned. "I was a few minutes ago. But now, it doesn't seem to hurt that much."

Gregor took her hand and ran his fingers over it, gently probing the skin. "Does this hurt?"

"No."

He nodded. "Nothing is broken. Perhaps you only strained it when you punched the beast in its head."

Annja glanced at the unmoving body. "Parts of it are made out of metal."

"Not exactly a recipe for the supernatural, I suppose," Gregor said.

"No. But it does raise some other questions. Like who the hell made this thing?"

Gregor knelt next to the corpse. "You think it was made?"

Annja pointed. "Look at the claws. They've been discolored to look blackened but they're metal, as well. It could have sliced me open if I hadn't been careful." Annja took a breath and winced. Her ribs still hurt like hell.

Gregor lifted Khosadam's claw. "Looks like folded steel. Extremely tough and very sharp."

Annja fingered her jacket. "Sliced right through my parka here. An inch more and it would have been my intestines draped all over the place."

"You were extremely skilled in the fight," Gregor said. "I was very impressed with your fighting ability."

"I'll bet," Annja said, waiting for the inevitable.

Gregor stood. "And that sword. Where did that come from?"

Annja shrugged. "I don't know." She was suddenly exhausted and didn't have the energy to try to explain the unexplainable.

"You don't know?" Gregor said.

"It's something that started showing up a while back. I don't know where it is or how it gets here. It does seem to pop out at moments when I need it most." Annja watched Gregor's face for signs he thought she might be insane. But she didn't see any.

"Well, it certainly happened to be here at the right time. Lucky for both of us, eh?"

"Yes." Annja took another breath and winced.

"Your ribs." Gregor nodded. "I thought I heard something crack."

"You've got good ears."

He shrugged. "I saw the beast land on top of you a number of times. It was a lot of weight to support."

Annja kept one hand over her side and smiled. "Souvenir for me, I guess. A reminder over the next few weeks when I'm unable to sleep that I left my ribs in Siberia."

Gregor pointed at Khosadam. "What do we do with this now? Take it with us to show the villagers?"

Annja shook her head. "I don't know how you're feeling, but I'm beat. Plus that thing weighs a lot, as you said, and the thought of carrying it miles through the deep snow doesn't exactly send warm fuzzies down my spine."

"So we leave it here, then."

"I guess so."

"And how do we get out of here?"

Annja pointed at the secret door. "Through there. May as well see where the steps at the far end of the tunnel lead. Who knows, if we're really lucky, maybe we'll find another Khosadam to play with."

Gregor frowned. "Sometimes I do not understand the American sense of humor."

"That makes two of us," Annja said. "Shall we go?"

Gregor limped toward the shelves. "You're sure it's dead, right?"

Annja stopped and knelt by the creature. She felt along its neck and then down by its wrist. After a few moments of searching, she looked back up at Gregor. "No pulse that I can find."

"And we're done with the whole supernatural story, aren't we?" he asked.

"Definitely," Annja stated.

"Then let's get out of here."

Annja rose and walked through the secret doorway into the tunnel. Ahead of them, they could still see the open side door that must have connected the tunnel leading from the cavern.

"Never hurts to have a couple of egress points," Gregor said.

"It almost caught us unawares, though," Annja said. "I could have done without being surprised like that."

Gregor pointed to the far end of the tunnel. "Stairs."

"Shall we see where they go?"

Gregor nodded and they moved slowly to where the wooden stairs jutted out of the hard earth and led upward. Gregor paused at their base and looked at Annja. "We don't know where these go."

"That's what we're here to find out."

"What I mean is, we shouldn't just go rushing right up them. They could be booby-trapped."

Annja cocked an eyebrow. She wasn't keen on wasting time looking for traps. But on the other hand, Gregor did have a point. And surprise had plagued them on this trip already. No sense repeating the same mistakes.

"All right. But you'll have to take point. I have no idea what I'm looking for when it comes to that stuff."

Gregor held out his hand. "I'll need my flashlight again."

"Be careful, I think the batteries are starting to run down."

"You wasted all the power?" Gregor asked.

"Someone had to find you in the dark, buddy. You're lucky I even bothered at all," Annja replied.

Gregor took the flashlight and switched it on. Then he knelt down by the lowest tread and peered up under it. "This one looks clear."

"You have to do this for every one of them?"

"Yes."

Annja sighed. Staying down in the dark with the body of Khosadam didn't make her feel comfortable at all. She had no idea exactly what it was they were dealing with. She'd seen enough bad horror flicks to know that creatures usually came back to life, even when they were supposed to be very dead.

"Clear," Gregor said as he moved higher up the staircase.

Annja watched him work. He dragged his right leg on to each stair as the other braced most of his weight. The beast had hurt him fairly badly.

She glanced back down the tunnel. The dim light seemed to have waned since the battle with the creature. Darkness bled into the tunnel they were in, blotting out features and anything Annja could use as a reference point.

"It's getting darker," she said without even thinking.

"What?"

She turned. Gregor had paused in his work and was now looking at her intently. "What did you say?"

"It seems like it's getting darker."

Gregor looked away from the stairs, paused, and then frowned. "Looks the same to me." He turned back to the stairs and flashed the light under another tread.

Annja stared down the tunnel. She could almost picture the body of Khosadam starting to twitch back in the root cellar. She could imagine it stirring as the evil that had lived in it came back to life, making the beast shudder and sit upright. Then it would give a gasp, get to its feet and start for the door.

Annja closed her eyes. The sword hovered in front of her.

She took a deep breath. "I'll be right back."

"Where are you going?" Gregor asked, alarmed.

"I need to see something."

"Annja—"

But she was already moving back down the tunnel toward the root cellar. As she did, the darkness around her grew deeper. Annja's heartbeat hammered again. I won't be able to use the sword until I get back into the cellar, she thought. I'll have to be quick about it.

Her footsteps sounded quiet on the dirt floor, but Annja was sure anyone would be able to hear her heart thundering.

Is this thing really supernatural, after all? she wondered. Is it truly some dethroned goddess out to feast on the living? And if it is, how will I ever kill it once and for all?

Ahead of her, she could make out the dim outline of the secret door. As soon as I'm through the door, I'll close my eyes, draw the sword and start swinging.

She knew she would have to clear the shelves first and make sure she had a good bead on Khosadam's head. Decapitating it just might be the most effective way to destroy it once and for all.

Unless it was already alive and waiting for her to return.

Annja stopped. Around her, the darkness felt almost palpable. She half expected to be able to reach out and grab a handful of it.

What the hell is the matter with me? Why do I keep getting sidetracked? she wondered. She looked at Gregor hard at work, halfway up the stairs now.

Was there something else at work here? Or was it just her own imagination conjuring up this stuff?

I'm my own worst enemy, she decided. The stress of losing Bob combined with the superstitious folklore of this area has really got me twisted up inside. She shook her head and looked at the doorway ahead of her. All she had to do was push through it, draw the sword and finish Khosadam once and for all.

Ten feet from the door, Annja slowed her breathing, willing herself to move as quietly as possible. She took deep breaths, flushing her system with oxygen, knowing that in combat her muscles would eat through the fresh air faster than when they were resting.

She was six feet from the door. Was that a noise on the other side? Was it Khosadam rising up again? Annja closed her eyes. The sword was there, ready to draw. She felt her hand reaching out to push the door open so she could fit through the portal.

She heard another noise on the other side of the door. It's true, she thought. Khosadam is still alive. I failed to kill it the first time. I won't make that mistake again.

Her hand made contact with the wooden door. She took a deep breath and shoved the door open.

With a cry, Annja leaped through the opening, closing her eyes in midair. The sword hovered in front of her and she wrapped her hands around its hilt. As she came down and touched the floor of the cellar, Annja opened her eyes.

The sword was nowhere to be seen.

Annja looked around.

Khosadam's body still lay on the floor.

Annja slumped over. Hot tears flowed from her eyes, staining her face as they rolled down only to fall and be swallowed by the dry dirt on the floor of the cellar.

Annja looked up at the corpse. There's been too much death here, she decided. Too much heartache.

I need to go home.

22

"Are you all right?"

Annja looked up. Gregor stood in the doorway, his flashlight in one hand and concern clearly evident on his face.

"I heard you cry out. I thought there might be some trouble."

She got to her feet. "I'm okay now."

"Why did you come back here?"

Annja shook her head. "I thought this thing might still be alive. I didn't want it sneaking up on us."

"You thought there might be some truth to those folktales after all, huh?"

"I guess so."

Gregor nodded. "Considering where we are, it's pretty easy to imagine it, isn't it? Surrounded by all this superstition, I suppose it's difficult not to fall under its spell."

Annja shrugged. "I'm done with it now. This isn't

some kind of undead goddess. It's flesh and blood. And I killed it."

"You're ready to go, then?"

Annja nodded and then stopped. "Wait a minute." She looked around on the floor and scooped up something in her hand. "All set."

"You're bringing that with you?"

Annja glanced down at Khosadam's brank and nodded. "I think it's an important reminder of what happened here."

"Maybe you can convince the villagers that there's no danger any longer from it. Then they'll get back to their lives. It could be a good thing," Gregor said.

"I've got more questions I'd like to see answered before I hold this overhead as a trophy."

Gregor regarded her and then gestured over his shoulder. "Stairs are clear. I didn't find any traps. We can leave now, Annja."

She smiled and looked around one final time. The corpse remained exactly where it had fallen after the battle. There was no danger here any longer.

She followed him out of the secret doorway and into the tunnel. Gregor's limp was less pronounced now. "Your leg is better?"

"Seems to be."

Annja nodded. "What do you think it was?"

"Khosadam?" Gregor shrugged. "I don't really know. Some sort of village idiot gone horribly awry? An escapee from a mental prison? Hell, it could have been a descendant of someone who worked in the mines. Perhaps they escaped and came out here to live in the forest."

"And the metal jaws and claws?"

"I have no idea." He stopped and looked at Annja. "The truth is, there are plenty of things it could be. Before the end of communism, there were plenty of bizarre experiments going on with the government's tacit approval. That was before my time, obviously, but you still hear rumors of the stuff."

"I suppose."

They reached the stairs and Gregor nodded at them. "You want me to go first or you?"

"I'll take it," Annja said. "You sure they're clear?"

Gregor smiled. "I'll be right behind you. If there's some type of trap, we'll both be killed."

"That's comforting," Annja said.

"What I mean is, yes, they're clear. I'm staking my life on it, obviously."

Annja started up the stairs. The aged wooden steps creaked noticeably as she shifted her weight on them one after another. In the dim light, Annja could see that they ended at what appeared to be another door. Shafts of light outlined the door.

She looked back at Gregor. "You saw the door?"

"Yes."

"Where do you think we are?"

He shrugged. "No idea. Maybe a cabin in the woods. The tunnels are long, though. Perhaps there's a hunting lodge built into the side of the mountain."

"You think we should go through the door hard?"

Gregor paused. "I hadn't thought of that."

Annja smiled. "You're much different now than you were when we met a few days back."

"Well, that was a role," he said.

"And this is the real you?"

"Maybe." He smiled.

Annja smirked. "All right. Let's be cautious in our approach, then."

"Sounds good."

Annja turned back to the staircase and crept up the final steps. The door grew in size until she felt certain it was a regular size.

She heard noises coming from beyond it. She held up her hand to warn Gregor. He patted the back of her leg signaling he understood.

Annja crept closer to the door. The lit outline of the door was interrupted by shadows passing in front of it. There was someone on the other side of the door; that was certain. But who?

Annja eased her weight over to the outside edges of the stairs, knowing they would support her body weight better and be less likely to creak out a warning. She moved up two more steps and then paused.

Sweat had broken out along her hairline. She was nervous again.

The air felt warmer here, as well. In stark contrast to how cold she'd been back down in the cave, Annja now wanted to shed her jacket.

She moved up another step.

She heard the sound of a chair scraping the floor. And then she heard a deep sigh.

She could feel Gregor's body heat behind her. His attention seemed focused on the door, as well.

She looked back at him and raised her eyebrows. He nodded.

It was time.

Annja let her hand go to where she imagined a doorknob would be. She was rewarded when she felt the cool rusted metal in her hand. She rested her hand lightly on it and then placed the other about six inches higher.

She was ready.

She turned the knob and shoved her way into the bright light, rapidly blinking her eyes to acclimate them as she did so. Behind her, she felt Gregor rushing into the room.

A series of images registered as she took stock of the room. A table. A wood-burning stove churning out plenty of heat. And in a rickety old wooden chair, someone sat with their back to the door.

"Don't move!" she shouted.

Gregor looked at her with a funny expression. Annja shrugged. It was the best she could think of.

The figure seated at the table lifted his hands from the tabletop. "I mean you no harm," he said.

There was something familiar about his voice. Annja closed the door behind her and then moved forward. As his face came into view, Annja felt a wave of surprise wash over her. "Father Jakob?"

He looked at her. A sad smile spread across his face. "Yes."

"What in the world are you doing here?"

He looked at the door and then back at Annja. "Is she dead?"

Annja looked at Gregor and then back at the priest. "Yes."

He nodded and then took a sip of the black coffee in front of him. "I suppose it was inevitable."

"You knew?"

He nodded. "Yes."

"And after all the trouble she caused, you still—"

"Refused to tell anyone. Yes. I am guilty of these things. I know this." He gestured to the empty chairs around the table. "Please sit down."

"I'll stand, thank you. You've got a lot of blood on your hands, Father. And I think you'd better start by telling us exactly what the hell is going on here," Annja said.

"I will." He got up from his seat. Gregor backed up and looked at Annja, but she only shrugged. Father Jakob looked old and frail and she had a hard time imagining him being much of a threat to anyone.

He took a kettle off the stovetop and got two mugs from his cupboard. "You'll be wanting some of this, I expect. You were down there for a long time. It can't have been easy for you."

Annja looked around. She had a sense of déjà vu. "Where are we?"

"In the back of my church," Father Jakob said. "You're back in the village."

"We traveled underground back to the village?" Annja asked.

"Yes."

"So, that's how the creature was able to get here without anyone seeing it."

Father Jakob sat back down. "She had a name, you know. At one time, anyway."

Gregor sat down next to him. "I don't know that we are all that interested in hearing it. I'd rather know exactly *what* she was."

Annja helped herself to some coffee. It went down hot but tasted good. She suddenly realized she was ravenous, as well, but didn't think it was the right time to ask Father Jakob to cook them a meal.

She took the brank out of her pocket and slid it across the table in front of the priest. "You'll want this back."

He took it in one of his blue-veined hands. "I found this in the basement of this church, you know. It's very old. I have no idea who it might belong to or what its purpose might have been."

"I think you figured its purpose out well enough. It's a brank. Meant to be a type of muzzle," Annja said.

"So my instinct was correct." Father Jakob sighed. "I found her about twenty years ago."

"That long?" Gregor was incredulous. "You've had her here with you all that time?"

"Yes."

"And no one ever knew about it?"

Father Jakob took a sip of his coffee. "Regrettably, a few did find out about her. But they never lived to tell anyone."

"You killed them?" Annja couldn't believe it.

"Not me. She did," the priest said.

"Where did you find her?" Gregor asked.

"In the mountains. She was naked and freezing and I took pity on her. When she was still able to speak, she told me she'd escaped from a medical laboratory on the outskirts of Kolyma. At first I didn't believe her, but then she showed me some of what they did to her. And then I believed her."

"She showed you the claws?" Annja asked.

Father Jakob nodded. "Indeed. She'd been surgically altered. That along with her teeth. It was horrifying for me and yet at the same time I felt compelled to help her. I don't know if it was compassion or simply pity on the poor creature that she'd been reduced to. I used to imagine her as a happy young girl who'd been plucked out of her innocence by the cruel demands of the Motherland."

Gregor nodded. "I've heard rumors of what they used to do to gifted children."

Father Jakob looked up. "And they're true, my boy."

Annja leaned forward. "But what was she supposed to become? There must have been some purpose for altering her the way they did."

"She did have a purpose," Father Jakob said. "And when she told me what it was, I nearly died from fright."

"What was it?"

He looked at Annja. "The Soviet Union wanted to create a soldier that could be self-sustaining."

"What does that mean?"

"That creature that you killed was meant to be the prototype for a special kind of soldier."

"Special? In what way?" Annja asked.

Father Jakob put his head in his hands. "She was meant to be a cannibal."

23

"A cannibal," Annja repeated, horrified.

Father Jakob nodded. "The goal, at least according to what she told me, was to reduce the need for rations by soldiers. If they could live off the remains of the battlefield dead, then they could go farther faster than conventional troops."

Annja shook her head. "What sick bastard came up with that idea?"

Father Jakob shrugged. "Who knows? The idea isn't necessarily out of the realm of consideration. After all, toward the end of the Cold War, the Soviet Union was beginning to go bankrupt. Perhaps the powers that be decided that rations were a concept they could do without."

"An army's got to eat," Gregor said.

"Indeed, but if they could remove the cost of rations from the war budget, then the country would have that much more money to spend elsewhere."

Father Jakob finished his coffee and poured himself a fresh cup. "I don't claim to understand it, but from what she told me, that's what they thought would be good."

"Insane," Annja said. "The world is completely insane."

Gregor shook his head. "Well, we can be comforted by the thought that those people who did that to the creature no longer exist. I think we'd all agree we're much safer without them around."

"Absolutely," Father Jakob said. He nodded at Gregor's leg. "You are injured, young man?"

Gregor shifted. "Just a bit of a twinge. Nothing too serious."

Annja took a sip of her coffee. "Why did you hide her for so long?"

"I'd hoped to wean her off human flesh. When I found her, she tried to bite my arm off."

"You're joking," Annja said.

Father Jakob rolled up his sleeve. Annja and Gregor peered closer and could see the half circle of tooth mark scars on his skin. "That was twenty years ago."

Annja frowned. "She should have been able to bite right through your arm considering she had metallic teeth."

Father Jakob laughed. "I was wearing about eight layers of clothes at the time I found her. She did her best, but my jacket stopped her. Instead, I got the pressure wounds from her teeth. I was very lucky."

"So you brought her here?" Annja asked.

The priest nodded. "I kept her down there in the cellar."

"But she could come and go as she pleased," Annja said.

Father Jakob sighed. "I had no idea there was another door out of the cellar. Imagine my horror the night I brought down her supper only to find she was gone. I was out of my mind with fear."

"But she came back," Gregor said.

"She had to. There was no other place for her to go. And there was no one she would trust to keep her safe and hidden."

"When did she start to kill?" Annja asked.

"I used the brank there for a little bit. I was trying to keep her from wanting to eat. And I fed her as well as I was able to given my lowly means. Sometimes I took to digging through the trash of the café for their bits of food."

"It didn't work?" Annja asked.

"Oh, I thought it did. She showed signs of being able to keep herself under control. But then she would strike out in a rage." He shook his head. "I have no idea what they must have done to that poor young girl. Possibly they gave her drugs that altered her basic metabolism or drove her to do what she had to do."

"She would have eaten me," Gregor said. "Wouldn't she?"

"Most likely." Father Jakob looked him over. "You're in good shape, strong and still young. She would derive the most energy from you, I believe."

Father Jakob frowned. "Where is the third member of your party, the one you called Bob?"

"He's dead," Annja said.

"Did she—"

"No," Gregor said quickly. "We were ambushed by two men who worked for the *mafiya*. Bob died trying to fight them off."

"I'm truly sorry," Father Jakob said. "Where is his body?"

"Back in the mountains. In a cave," Annja said. "We need to make plans to get it out."

"Then we should be grateful this day is at last finished."

"It was a nightmare," Annja said.

"One that is now over," Father Jakob assured her. "Although, truth be told, I'm not sure if I'm relieved or heartbroken. I strongly suspect I came to view the creature almost like my own child. And now that she's gone—"

Annja glanced at Gregor, who seemed ready to depart. "There are plenty of people who will want to know all about this," she said.

Father Jakob looked up. "Would you give me two days? I'd very much like to bury her. At least give her something dignified in terms of a burial. After that, I know I'll have some questions to answer."

Gregor stood. "Two days, Father. That's it."

The priest smiled through his tears. "Thank you."

Annja turned to go, but Father Jakob stopped her. "Here." He handed her the brank.

"What's this for?"

"You're an archaeologist, right?"

"Yes."

"Take this. As I told you, it's very old. Possibly older than I know. It might help make up for your loss if you are able to find out something of its history."

Annja tried to smile. "I think Bob would like that."

"He shared your passion for items of antiquity?"

"Very much so."

"Then it is good that you should have it." Father Jakob rose slowly, and Annja heard several of his bones creak in protest. "I will see you out. If you don't mind leaving through the front door."

"Better than trekking back down the tunnels," Gregor said. "I'm not sure my leg would hold up."

"It bothers you that much?" the priest asked.

Gregor shrugged. "Just enough to be a nuisance and slow me down some. I'll be fine once I get a hot bath and a good night's sleep."

At the door, Annja turned. "I am sorry that I had no choice but to kill her."

Father Jakob nodded. "I know you would not have done so unless you had absolutely no choice."

"You're right."

"Most likely, I was a damned fool to try and keep her alive or think I could make her normal again. I don't know that anything was possible considering what they did to her."

"You had to try," Gregor said. "You're a man of the cloth. If you don't try to help people, then who will?"

"Who indeed?" the priest said. He opened the door and a strong gust of night wind blew in. "Good night."

Annja and Gregor hurried down the steps as snow pelted them again. "Another storm?" Annja asked.

Gregor shrugged. "We're in snow country. Stuff like this is unavoidable."

"I'm going to a tropical island when I get home,"

Annja said. "I'm already sick to death of all this white stuff."

Gregor smiled. "You think there might be room for a friend to tag along with you?"

Annja looked at him. "After all of this, do you really want to spend more time with me?"

"I've been known to do crazier things," Gregor said.

Annja looked at him closely. "So now *I* count among the crazy things in your life?"

"A woman with a sword that vanishes into thin air." Gregor nodded. "I think you definitely count."

Annja turned back into the wind. She knew he had a point.

Down the street from the church, few lights shone in the houses. Gregor and Annja made their way back to the hotel and banged on the door.

From the other side, Annja could hear movement and a quiet voice asking something in Russian. Gregor moved her aside. His voice called out in Russian, as well, but the deep boom of it made Annja jump.

Apparently it had the same effect on the innkeeper because there was an instant rattle at the door. In seconds, the door opened and bright light spilled out onto them.

The innkeeper's face looked ashen. "Come in, quickly!"

Annja and Gregor hurried inside and stood just inside the door stamping their feet and shaking out of their jackets. The innkeeper looked at them. "Why on earth are you out after dark?"

"We didn't have much of a choice," Annja said.

"Yes, but that thing is out there."

"Khosadam?" Annja asked.

The innkeeper's face paled. "Yes."

Gregor put a hand on his shoulder. "Here is what you are going to do. You will set a hot bath for me and one for my companion. You will then tell your wife to cook us up a hearty meal. And make sure you have tea and juice, as well."

The innkeeper eyed them both. "You've seen it. You've seen the creature."

Gregor nodded. "We have."

"And you lived to be here?"

Annja sighed. "We're here. Obviously we weren't killed."

"What is it like?" the man asked.

"It's dead," Gregor said.

"You killed it!" The innkeeper's face lit up. "You brave, brave man. You did it. You have rid us all of the beast."

"Not me," Gregor said. "Her."

The innkeeper's eyes widened as he looked at Annja. "The girl?"

"The woman," Annja corrected. "And yes, I did."

"Amazing."

Annja frowned and looked at Gregor. "I take it you guys don't have a lot of strong female role models?"

"I think Khosadam was our first." Gregor laughed.

The innkeeper took Annja's hand. "Forgive me for my ignorance. I will do my best to make sure you eat like never before. And you will have your baths. Both of you."

"You know," Gregor said, "we could save time and water if we shared a bath."

Annja glanced at him. "Nice try, Casanova. But don't count on it."

"It was just a thought."

"A bad one," Annja said. But she smiled anyway.

"There's something else," Gregor said to the innkeeper.

"Anything, dear sir."

"There are some bodies up in the caves on the mountains. They will need to be recovered."

The innkeeper looked concerned. "Did they fall victim to the beast?"

"No—to organized crime."

The innkeeper shook his head. "I do not understand."

Annja cleared her throat. "The two men who were here last night, Yuri and Oleg? They worked for the *mafiya*. They followed us out today and hunted us down. They were trying to get this village to sell itself to their gang, which would then exploit the natural resources in this area."

"I had no idea," the innkeeper said.

"Neither did we," Gregor replied.

"And the third member of your party?"

Annja shook her head. "He's dead. And I want him brought back here for a proper funeral."

"I will see to it that some of the men from the village recover the bodies," the innkeeper said. "You have my word."

Annja looked at Gregor. "Perhaps we can impose on Father Jakob to do a service for Bob?"

"I would think so."

"In that case," Annja said. "I'm going upstairs to have that hot bath."

"I thought I was going first," Gregor said.

"Creature killers get first dibs," Annja replied. "See you down here for dinner."

24

By the time Annja got back down to the dining room, she felt much better. The hot bath and change of clothes made her feel almost human again. And while the loss of Bob still weighed on her mind, she felt somewhat better knowing that his body would be cared for at first light.

Gregor came down a few minutes later. Annja watched him from the big chair nearest the fireplace and nursed the glass of red wine she was drinking.

"Pull up a chair," she said.

Gregor sat opposite her, and the innkeeper brought him a glass of iced vodka. Gregor touched his glass to Annja's. "Here's to life."

"Sometimes overrated," Annja said.

"You think?"

"Considering what we do to each other, yes. But I suppose there's enough room left on this planet for a bit of hope, as well."

Gregor drank his vodka and then rested the glass on the small table between them. "I've seen plenty of examples of evil in my time. And there have been times when others might have considered me an emissary of those same forces."

"But?"

"But I think it's possible to turn over a new leaf if you're so inclined."

Annja took a sip of her wine. "Is that what you're planning to do? Turn over a new leaf?"

"I'm thinking about it."

Annja smiled. "I've known men like you before."

"Men like me? What's that supposed to mean?"

"Strong, rugged." She smirked. "Handsome. But as much as they claimed they wanted desperately to leave behind what they were, they couldn't."

"No?"

"No. Because what they wanted to leave behind was what made them who they were in the first place. And that's not being true to yourself, now, is it?"

"Perhaps."

"No perhaps about it. You can't put down what it is that makes you tick. You might want to—you might enjoy telling people you are. But at the end of the day when you're all alone in your bed and the minutes tick by on your clock, you'll always come back to your base nature."

"You say it like it's unavoidable," Gregor said.

Annja sighed. "Maybe it is."

"You don't strike me as the kind of woman who believes much in predestination."

Annja finished her wine. "I never did before."

"But?"

"But things change. And lately, I think I've been wondering if maybe we are really locked into our paths from the moment we're born."

Gregor gestured to the innkeeper for more drink. "That doesn't do a lot to support the notion of free choice."

"No. It doesn't," Annja admitted.

"It's also not a very attractive way to lead your life."

"Probably not."

Gregor smiled. "And you're comfortable with that?"

"No."

"You're a complicated woman, Annja Creed," he said.

Annja accepted the new glass of wine from the innkeeper and lifted it in Gregor's direction. "So I've been told before."

"Here's to being complicated, then," he said.

"We're toasting that?"

"Why not?" Gregor took a sip. "And I should also thank you."

Annja looked at him. "What on earth for?"

"The compliment."

"You've had too much to drink." Annja considered her own glass and then took another sip.

"You said I was handsome. Thank you for that."

Annja shrugged. "You're welcome." She looked past him. "Looks like dinner is on at last."

She rose and walked to the table. The innkeeper had laid out a enormous feast. Meat and potatoes along with what looked like meat pies, roast quail, soup and a green salad of all things.

Annja sat down. "This is quite a spread."

Gregor smiled. "I believe we're considered heroes."

Annja sniffed. "Spectacular."

Gregor spooned out some potatoes on his plate and then passed the dish to Annja. "You're not very comfortable with that label, are you?"

"Are you?"

Gregor shrugged. "It's been applied to me before. Sometimes it's justified and sometimes not. I guess I've made peace with it."

"I'm a little new to the whole thing. Guess it still doesn't feel like it fits me all that well," she said.

"It will."

Annja bit into some of the quail and chewed. "I don't know if I intend on making it a regular occurrence. The hero thing, I mean."

"Well, now, that's the thing about being a hero— no one ever sets out to do it deliberately. And those who do often end up dead as a result of their efforts. True heroism is something else entirely."

"I guess," Annja said.

"We don't have to talk about it if you don't want to. I was only making conversation."

Annja put her fork down and took some more wine. "I know. Sorry. I'm still upset about Bob."

"You weren't lovers," Gregor said.

Annja looked at him. "No. We weren't. I think Bob had a crush on me, but it wasn't something we ever explored. We were better as friends, anyway. Anything romantic would have clouded our professional aspirations."

"He respected you, though. That much was very evident."

"And I respected him. But there you go. We were close friends and now he's gone."

Gregor nodded. "Sometimes there is comfort in knowing that you have vanquished the killer of a friend."

Annja frowned. "I'm not into revenge."

"This isn't revenge. It's closing the circle. There's a difference."

"If you say so."

Gregor leaned back in his chair. "I know you look at me and see someone who has lied and been deceitful for the majority of his grown life." He shrugged. "And you'd be right to see me in that light. Because it's true."

"I'm not arguing with you," Annja said.

Gregor smiled. "It might interest you to know that I entered the intelligence services with only the noblest ideals in mind."

"Doesn't every kid who plays war enter the military with the same sentiments?"

"Very possibly."

"So what makes you different?"

"I'm not claiming difference. I was merely hoping to illuminate some aspects of my character to you."

Annja stopped eating and looked at him. "Why do you care?"

"What do you mean?"

"Why do you care what I think about you? You could be the cruelest man on the planet. Or you could be the greatest guy around. But what's the big deal? Why do you care what I happen to think of you?"

Gregor sighed. "Because I don't want you to hate me for what I did to Bob."

Annja shook her head. "I don't hate you."

"You don't?"

"I hate Yuri and Oleg for being in that cave with us. I hate them for being with the *mafiya*. I hate them for what they represented and for being the cause of Bob's death."

"But not me," Gregor whispered.

Annja shrugged. "Weird, huh? But I guess I can understand. I don't agree with it—don't get me wrong. But I understand that you were doing your job. And doing what you do didn't kill Bob."

Gregor took a breath and let it out slowly. "Thank you for understanding."

Annja finished her glass of wine. "Forget it."

"I don't know that I will."

Annja smiled. "You're extremely stubborn, aren't you?"

"I prefer 'tenacious,' but if 'stubborn' works for you, then that's fine, too."

Annja took another bite of her dinner and then stopped. "You are a clever one, too, aren't you?"

Gregor nodded. "I think that's a bit of a prerequisite for intelligence officers. Not much use for the slow-witted in my service."

"So you entered the intelligence service because you were sly?" Annja asked.

"I entered because my entire family was killed and I had nowhere else to go."

Annja shook her head. "I'm so sorry."

"Forget it—it's ancient history."

"How did they die?"

"Chechen rebels ambushed my family as they drove south for vacation. I was at school at the time. But my mother, father and little brother were all gunned down in cold blood."

"That must have destroyed you," Annja said

Gregor finished his vodka and nodded at the innkeeper for a refill. "They say that true character is forged in the fire of tragedy. I think that's what happened to me. Instead of releasing my emotions, I bottled them up. The anger welled up within me and caused me to develop myself as much as I possibly could. I entered the military first and then the intelligence services. I volunteered for the most suicidal missions they had. I carried out all sorts of covert operations that no one would ever take responsibility for."

"What happened?"

"I hunted the men who had killed my family. I hunted them down and killed every last one of them. And without any degree of mercy."

Annja's throat felt dry. "I don't think anyone would ever hold that against you. You did what anyone else might have done."

"I'm not proud of what I did. But I can't turn back time and undo it. I'll have to live with the consequences of my actions for the rest of my life. I've made peace with that, though."

"And with the death of your family?" Annja asked.

Gregor smiled. "I'd tracked the last one down to a demolished old warehouse on the outskirts of some dump of a city. He was hiding up on the second floor.

He knew who I was and why I was there. Word had spread that I was coming for him."

"The other deaths would have alerted him, I suppose."

Gregor nodded. "I felt like Death. I strode into the warehouse like I was invincible. He shot at me, but the bullets never seemed to touch me. I walked straight at him as he shot every bullet he had. And while he dropped his magazine and fumbled for a new one, I grabbed him around the throat and lifted him onto a meat hook."

Annja watched Gregor's eyes as they looked up to the left. "He didn't die right away—I made sure of that. I did horrible things to him that night. Things I won't speak of ever again."

He looked at Annja. "Do you think I'm a monster?"

Annja shook her head. "I think you were hurting."

"Indeed. When it was finally over and I sat there drenched in sweat and the blood of my last victim, I slumped into a puddle of filth and cried. I cried for hours. And I felt every last vestige of who I'd become fade slowly away into the night of my past."

"What happened?"

Gregor sniffed. "I returned and was promoted. But I'd changed. I'd rid myself of the demons that drove me to do those awful things. I became a better agent because of it."

"And now?"

Gregor smiled. "Now, I see that dinner is over. And I sincerely hope our innkeeper has a delicious dessert and more drink for us."

Annja stared at him. "You're an interesting man, Gregor."

He bowed from his seat. "I am indeed. Perhaps you will get to know me a little better…sometime."

Annja smiled. "Perhaps."

25

The innkeeper had indeed prepared a lavish dessert of fresh fruit and a chocolate torte. Annja felt herself growing more and more exhausted. Gregor himself looked as tired, if not more.

Annja yawned after her second helping of dessert. "That's it for me."

Gregor pointed. "You'll be able to sleep after two cups of coffee? What about all the caffeine you just ingested?"

"Doesn't affect me at all," Annja said. "What about you? All that vodka has to be doing something to you."

Gregor nodded. "I'm fine as long as I don't stand up."

"How are you going to get upstairs?"

He shrugged. "I was hoping I could impose upon a beautiful woman to assist me."

Annja grinned. "Good luck finding one around this dump."

Gregor leaned forward. "Do you always play this game with men you find attractive?"

"What game?"

"This game of tease. This cat and mouse." Gregor leaned back. "It grows wearisome after a while. At first it is fun, but then later—"

"There's no game here, Gregor. It's just how I am."

"You're as stubborn as I am, aren't you?" he asked.

"Probably."

Gregor put both of his hands on the table and then hefted himself to his feet. "In that case, I may as well say good-night to you now."

Annja stood. "I'll help you upstairs."

"Ah, my charm has won you over at last."

Annja shook her head. "I don't want your death on my conscience when you take a header down the stairs."

Gregor shrugged. "Whatever."

Annja came around the table as the innkeeper started cleaning up. She got her arm around Gregor's back. In the next instant, she felt him put most of his weight onto her.

"Are you quite sure you can't manage to carry yourself a little bit more?" she asked.

Gregor chuckled and Annja could smell the alcohol on his breath. "I thought I was carrying most of my weight." He shifted himself and Annja felt a little weight come off.

They made it to the stairs and Annja had to direct him. "Step up now."

"You see? You are sent from God to make sure I do not die tonight."

"I'm just a designated stair climber," she said.

"There's that heroism again."

Annja sighed and got Gregor up another step. And then another. At last they crested the staircase and Gregor pointed down the hall. "My room is that way."

"Thanks."

Annja walked him down the hall and then Gregor pointed. "That one."

Annja stopped. "That's my room."

Gregor shrugged. "What a coincidence. Who would have thought we would end up being bunkmates?"

"Not me. Now, come on, which one of the rooms is yours?"

"You'd turn down an opportunity to spend the night with a famed member of the Russian intelligence service?"

"Yes."

Gregor looked shocked. "That line usually works quite well."

"I'll bet."

He leaned closer to Annja. "You sure I can't convince you of the error of your ways?"

"Positive. Besides, what good would you be to me? You're drunk as an ox."

Gregor nodded. "This is very true. But in the morning, I shall rise like the Phoenix from its ashes and be a brand-new lover."

"Delightful," Annja said.

Gregor snorted and then pointed farther down the corridor. "That room. That is mine."

Annja walked him down to his room. She turned the doorknob and opened the door. Then she walked

Gregor to his bed. He fell, pulling Annja down with him. She landed on top of his chest.

Gregor looked up with joy in his eyes. "Ah, at last you have come to your senses."

"You dragged me down here," Annja said, trying to extricate herself from his clutches. "Watch my ribs," she said.

"Sorry." Gregor gently pulled her close. "How about a good-night kiss?"

Annja frowned. "Will you leave me alone after that?"

Gregor held up his hand. "I swear it on my honor as a completely drunk Russian."

Annja laughed and then leaned forward. She found Gregor's lips warm as they touched hers. She could smell the vodka on his breath, but it wasn't offensive. And when Gregor put his hand behind her head and pulled in tighter, even she had to admit that the big guy could kiss.

She pulled away and took a breath.

Gregor's eyes danced. "Wow."

Annja sat up. "Happy now?"

"I may never walk again."

Annja smiled. "That's all, lover boy. Now good night."

She walked to the door and took a final glance at Gregor, propped up on his bed looking at her with sad puppy-dog eyes. She took another deep breath and pulled the door shut behind her.

Outside in the corridor, she paused. It was tempting to go back in there and let Gregor ravage her. Or would she ravage him? She grinned.

But in the morning, how would it play out? She

didn't have enough of a read on him to know if he was looking for a quickie or a commitment. And there was no way Annja was interested in a commitment. Not yet.

She walked down the hallway and listened to her footsteps creak along the wooden floor. She could hear the wind howling outside. Snow blew against the inn's walls.

Siberia. She shivered. It would be a long time before she'd want to come back to this remote part of the world.

If ever.

She reached her room and got changed for bed. She could still hear the dishes clanking as the innkeeper cleaned up from their dinner. It was certainly nice of him to go to such lengths in preparing that feast. Annja's stomach rumbled in appreciation. Everything had been utterly delicious. She wasn't sure if the innkeeper was a world-class cook or if it was simply that Annja had been so starving when they returned from the caves.

Probably the latter, she surmised.

She leaned back in her bed. The fluffy pillows encased her head as she stared at the ceiling. She thought about Bob and how much he lived for crazy adventures like this.

At least he went out on one of them, she thought. Better this than to go out in some hospital bed languishing away from a terminal illness.

She'd mourn for him, but his memory also made her happy.

And to think she'd almost passed up this trip.

Outside her room, it sounded as if someone was in the hallway. A creak of the floorboards broke the silence.

Annja frowned. She hoped Gregor wasn't coming to proposition her again.

Part of her wanted nothing but the release a sexual dalliance would grant her. It could be a great way to work off all the excess adrenaline from the day's adventures. And she had to admit that Gregor wasn't a bad prospect. He certainly had the body for it. And he had a quick mind, as well.

I wonder how much of what he told me tonight was the truth?

Another creak outside her door made her stop.

There was no way that Gregor could move that quietly in the drunken state he was in.

Unless he was playing drunk.

Annja frowned again. Why would he pretend to be drunk? That didn't make any sense. Khosadam was dead and gone and they were going to leave as soon as possible. They'd had a celebratory dinner, almost a send-off for them.

No, Gregor hadn't been lying about overdrinking—of that she felt sure.

But who was in the hallway?

The wind rattled a shutter against the side of her bedroom window, and Annja almost jumped out of her bed. She took a breath and leaned back, straining her ears to listen.

This is just like last night, she decided.

Maybe the inn is haunted.

No, she thought. *Too many superstitions were*

floating around for her pragmatic mind to endure. She was falling for any little tale that came up, and it was starting to annoy her.

She turned over in the bed and closed her eyes. I'll see Gregor in the morning and ask him then, she decided.

Then she heard another creak in the hallway. And then a thump.

Annja sat up in bed. "Hello?"

Her voice sounded higher from the anxiety she felt. She realized it sounded ridiculous to even break the silence like that. She rolled out of bed and crept toward her door. She heard nothing outside in the corridor.

The doorknob felt cold to the touch, but she gently turned it. I'll just go check on Gregor and make sure he's okay, she thought. Then it will be back into bed and off to dreamland.

Her door opened and Annja stepped out into the corridor. No more sounds reached her ears from downstairs. The innkeeper must have finished cleaning and gone to bed, as well.

Everything seemed silent.

Annja padded down the hallway, her feet making little noise as she moved. Once she stepped on a loose floorboard, but after adjusting her weight, she traveled the rest of the way in silence.

A line of sweat broke out along her hairline as she reached the end of the hallway and stood in front of Gregor's door.

Am I sweating out of fear or excitement? she wondered. She grinned. This will be like Gregor's best wish come true when I walk in there to check on him.

I wonder if he's wearing anything? Annja shook her head. Enough. Open the door, check on Gregor and then get back to bed. There's a lot to do tomorrow.

Annja reached out for Gregor's doorknob. It felt warm.

A thought crossed her mind as Annja turned the doorknob. The door slid open and she stepped inside Gregor's room.

Ahead of her, she could see the bed. Gregor had drawn the covers up, over his body.

She smiled.

The wind banged another shutter against the side of the inn, and Annja moved to the window to close the drapes. No sense waking him when the sun comes up first thing, she thought.

She looked at him sleeping and realized she couldn't hear any breathing.

"Gregor?"

She moved to his side and shook him.

A pillow fell out from under the covers.

Annja tore back the blankets and saw the rest of the pillows bunched up to make a line in the bed.

Gregor was gone.

26

Annja ran downstairs. After shouting for the inn-keeper a number of times, the sleepy-eyed man came out of his room.

"What is it?"

Annja pointed upstairs. "Gregor is gone. Have you seen him?"

"Not since you and he left me with a pile of dishes to clean. Now I am going back to bed." He turned to leave.

Annja grabbed him by the arm. "You don't understand. Gregor was drunk when I took him up to bed. There's no way he could have made it down the stairs without making a ruckus."

The innkeeper sighed. "So, what are you saying?"

"Someone must have taken him."

The innkeeper grinned. "Are you joking with me, miss?"

"No, I'm not."

The innkeeper pointed at the front door. "Do you see that plank? It is five inches thick and ten feet long. Nothing is getting through that door. And nothing has gotten through that door since you and Gregor came back this evening."

"Don't you have a back door?" Annja asked.

The innkeeper shook his head. "When Khosadam started hunting people in the village, we boarded it up and moved a shelf in front of it. It is as impenetrable as the front door."

"What about windows, then? Surely the windows down here open."

"They are all bolted when winter comes around."

"Could someone have unbolted them?"

"Who would do such a thing?"

Annja looked at him. "What about you?"

The innkeeper shook his head. "You had also a lot to drink tonight, yes? Perhaps you should go back to bed. I am willing to bet that in the morning, your friend Gregor will be right back where you left him."

Annja leaned back. "You don't believe me."

The innkeeper sighed. "I am very tired."

Annja ran back upstairs and threw on her clothes and parka. Then she stomped back downstairs to find the innkeeper huddled over a cup of coffee. Annja cleared her throat and pointed to the front door. "Open it."

The innkeeper's eyes widened. "What?"

"You heard me. Open the door. I don't care if you don't believe me. I'm going to look for my friend with or without your help."

"It is freezing outside. If you wish to go out, you will do so alone."

"Fine," Annja growled.

The innkeeper grumbled but got to his feet. He shuffled over to the wooden plank and grunted as he lifted it. He set it down next to the door and then looked at Annja. "Once I let you out, I am putting this back in place. You will not be able to get back in here until after sunup. Do you understand?"

Annja pulled her hat and gloves on. "Just open the door."

The innkeeper shook his head but slid back the bolt on the door. As soon as he cracked it, a gust of wind blew it all the way open, sending a barrage of snow inside that pelted Annja and the innkeeper in the face.

Annja stalked past the innkeeper out into the night.

The man had been right. The temperature felt as if it was at least ten below. Annja pulled up the collar on her parka and turned into the wind, taking a face full of snow as she did so.

She stared at the ground.

There were no footprints of any kind marking their way through the drifts. And while it was snowing heavily enough, it hadn't been long enough to cover any prints.

There had to be another way out of the inn. But how could she find it?

Annja turned and looked around the village. Every light was off. Every window was dark. She turned and looked down the main street. A glint of dull yellow burned through one of the windows in the church.

Father Jakob?

Annja started walking toward the church. Perhaps he was still up. Maybe he was even still grieving about the creature.

If nothing else, maybe he would be able to shed some light on what might have happened to Gregor. He seemed to have good insight into people, and he had known Gregor for a number of years. Plus, she couldn't go back to the hotel.

As Annja waded through the snowdrifts, her boots left twin lines in her wake. She kept her head down to ward off the wind. Why would Gregor have gone out on a night like this? Annja shook her head. No, that was stupid. He was too drunk to do so. Someone must have taken him.

Annja reached the church. She slipped on the first step, falling back into the snow. She brushed herself off as another gale of wind blasted her in the face. She could feel the snow melting on her skin as her breath made steam clouds in front of her.

She mounted the steps again and made her way to the porch. She could still see faint light coming from somewhere inside.

Annja knocked on the door.

She knocked again, this time louder until she could hear her pounding over the snowy wind.

No one seemed to stir from within the church.

Annja turned away from the door. Maybe she could walk around the church to see if she could look into any of the windows. If Father Jakob was still awake, he might hear her if she banged on a window.

At the bottom of the steps, she turned right and walked along next to the church. She could see the light better now, and it seemed to be coming from the kitchen at the back of the church.

Annja continued until she reached the back window. It was too high to see in through. She needed something to stand on.

Across the yard, she spotted some overturned wooden barrels. She rolled one over and placed it in front of the window. She tapped it down into the snow, hoping that the buttressing would help support her weight.

Here goes nothing, she thought. And she jumped onto the barrel and stood up on it. She could see a single candle flickering on the kitchen table. But no Father Jakob.

Where is he? Annja tapped on the window. Nothing moved within the church.

I've got to get in there, she thought. But there were bars on the kitchen window. So much for that.

Annja hopped down from the barrel and walked around to the front of the church again. By the front door, there was a window to the side that she presumed was the office for the church.

It's not like I'm breaking stained glass, she thought as she elbowed her way through the window. Pieces of glass shattered on the floor inside the church.

Annja felt for the window catch, found it and then eased the window up so she could squeeze through.

The wind howled inside the church, as well, now that she'd broken the pane. But Annja managed to get through and found herself on a threadbare carpet in the office.

She stood and looked around. A small battered desk and chair stood in the corner. The outside wind scattered the papers that were on top of it. Aside from the desk, bookshelves lined the wall. But the writing was all Cyrillic and Annja couldn't read any of it.

She found the door to the main part of the church and turned the knob. She closed the office door behind her. At least she could keep the wind contained.

Annja passed the pews and looked around. Churches at night always made her nervous. With nothing going on inside them, they seemed so dark and inhospitable. The statues, the candles and the faces all peering down at her made her distinctly uncomfortable.

She walked down the aisle, running her hands over the rough-hewn wood of the pews. She could see hymn books stacked neatly just inside on the benches themselves.

All around her, the church lay dormant. Annja wondered when mass was. She'd forgotten to ask Father Jakob about that. Not that she was exactly a churchgoing kind of woman, but she did like to cover her bases.

Annja shook her head. Forget about that for now, she told herself. We're supposed to be looking for Father Jakob so he can help us find Gregor.

She heard a noise in the back of the church. "Father Jakob?" she called out.

Annja waited, but nothing sounded in reply.

"Father Jakob?"

Outside, the wind battered the church with more snow and ice. Annja shivered in spite of herself. The church was cold and her breath still made steam in front of her face.

Another noise sounded in the kitchen. Maybe he's hard of hearing, she thought. Maybe he takes a hearing aid off each night and doesn't know I'm here. He could be back there enjoying some coffee.

Coffee sounded good to her.

She walked farther down the aisle.

She heard another noise in the kitchen. This time it sounded like a door opening.

The door to the root cellar?

Annja licked her lips. Her throat felt dry. "Hello?"

She stood still, but heard nothing. She kept walking toward the altar. Beyond it, the door to the kitchen beckoned. She passed the altar and headed for the door. She grabbed the doorknob and turned it.

Inside the kitchen, she saw the candle she'd seen from outside.

It had been extinguished.

Annja felt the wax. It was still warm and pliable. Whoever had blown out the candle had done so only recently. Was it Father Jakob? Had he heard her and hidden? Maybe he didn't know it was her.

A sound from the main church made her jump.

Annja turned and walked back through the door into the church. From where she stood, the darkness and the faint light from the snow outside twisted together, forming intricate shadows that seemed to grow and shrink with every breath.

Annja's eyes searched the depths of the church, but she could see nothing.

She turned.

A thunderous explosion slammed into her head and Annja dropped as more blackness raced for her.

27

A steady drumming in her head woke her. Annja groaned as she tried to open her eyes. Fortunately, bright lights that might have made her wince didn't greet her. Instead, she woke in total darkness.

She couldn't move.

I'm on my back. Tied down? She flexed her wrists and found them bound somehow, as were her legs.

Her parka had vanished, but she still had her sweater and pants on. She shivered, aware that she was cold.

But where was she?

Annja closed her eyes again, straining her ears for any sound that might help her figure out her location. But she heard very little.

No wind. No sounds of shutters banging into the sides of windows.

Am I underground?

A thought came at her. Maybe Khosadam had

knocked her out and dragged her back into the root cellar. Maybe Annja was going to be the next meal.

No, I killed that thing, she recalled.

Whoever had knocked her out, it wasn't Khosadam.

But who did that leave? Father Jakob? Annja sighed. The old priest didn't seem a likely candidate. He could barely move earlier when she and Gregor had come up from the root cellar. His body was old and looked racked with arthritis.

Gregor?

It wouldn't be the first time a guy had double-crossed her.

In the darkness, Annja couldn't see what bound her hands and feet. She worked her fingers, trying to get at the knots, but it was impossible. Someone who knew how to restrain humans had bound her wrists. Another sign that it was probably Gregor.

Bastard!

Annja shook her head. And to think, I almost slept with him. God knows what would have happened if I had.

She listened again. Now that her ears had adjusted a little bit more to her environment, she could pick up small sounds. And from what she heard, it definitely seemed likely that she was somewhere underground.

But where?

She and Gregor had explored the cave in the mountains that led to the tunnel to the root cellar and up into the back of the church. Was it possible that an entire network existed? And that it ran under the town?

Annja thought about it. It made sense. Considering the history of the area, perhaps there'd been some sort of underground railroad set up for refugees from the Kolyma mines. Maybe workers who fled hid out under the town.

And if there was an underground network, then that might explain how Gregor had disappeared. Maybe there was a secret entrance into the tunnels from the inn itself.

Annja nodded. It could happen.

But how did Gregor know about it? And how did he know where to look? He was with Bob and Annja for most of the time except at night. And Annja didn't know if that would be enough time to discover the secret entrance.

More to the point, why would Gregor be doing this? What did he hope to gain from it all? Was he working on another agenda entirely?

I've got to get out of here, she thought. There's got to be something I can do to loosen these bonds and slip out. If Gregor is behind this, then I don't trust him to keep me alive much longer.

Especially since he knows about the sword.

Annja slumped back. He knows about it. Why the hell did I take it out when he was around? Gregor knowing she had the sword meant he would make damned sure that she couldn't bring her hands together and grab it from wherever it waited.

She heard a sound in the darkness. Annja stiffened. Was someone in the room with her? Was it Gregor? Was he here already to kill her?

Annja waited, straining her eyes to see. But the room was absolutely dark and she couldn't see anything at all.

Another noise, which sounded like someone shifting. Annja's throat felt dry again, although the steady drumming in her head seemed to be waning.

"Hello?" she called out.

It came out as a croak, but Annja felt better at least making a noise. She wasn't going to be surprised again on this trip. Better to let them know she knew they were there.

"Hello?" she called out.

"Ughhh."

"Who's that?" she asked.

"Annja?"

Annja stopped. It couldn't be. There was no way.

"Bob?"

He chuckled but it came out sounding weird. "Yeah, it's me."

Annja's eyes felt burning hot and sticky. "It can't be…. I saw you…. You died in my arms!"

"I thought so, too. I guess we were wrong," he said.

Annja shook her head. "How can this be? Where are we?"

"I don't know. I woke up a few hours ago, felt like hell and then someone came in and gave me something. I passed out again."

"Are you in a bed?"

"I think so, but I've got some straps around me. I can't move."

"I'm tied down, too," she said.

"Damn."

Annja looked over in the darkness. "I was devastated when you died. I thought…"

"I know," Bob said. "I can't believe this isn't heaven or hell. I thought for sure I was a goner."

"You were. That's what I don't understand. I checked your body. It seems impossible that I'm speaking to you right now."

"Maybe we're both dead," Bob offered.

Annja smiled. "Thanks for cheering me up."

"Just a thought."

"What's the last thing you remember before waking up here?" she asked.

Bob paused. "I was in your arms. I remember it being very cold. And then I think I just saw blackness coming for me. That was it."

"Any pain?"

"Surprisingly no. And the next thing I knew, I was here."

Annja sighed. "Well, we can't stay like this. We've got to get out of here before whoever did this comes back and decides to kill us for good."

"Maybe they don't want us dead," Bob said.

"Huh?"

"I don't know—I'm just thinking out loud here. But if I was already dead and gone, why would someone save me like this? You'd think they'd just want me out of the way, right?"

"Maybe."

"No, it makes sense, think about it. I could be dead right now, but I'm not. And clearly whoever took me also took you, right?"

"Yeah."

"And you're not dead yet, either."

Annja frowned. He made a good point. When

they'd knocked her out, they could have easily killed her right then and there.

But they hadn't.

"What do you think they want?" Annja asked.

"I don't know, but clearly us being alive is a vital part of it."

Annja licked her lips. If they were being kept alive for a reason, that meant there might be a chance for escape. Good. As soon as their captors made a mistake, Annja would be right there to capitalize on it.

"I guess things will get interesting from here on out, huh?" Annja said.

"Sure looks that way," Bob replied. "Although part of me wishes it ended back there in the cave."

"Why do you say that?"

Bob chuckled in the darkness. "I kind of liked going out like that. A dig on a remote site. Surrounded by legends and strange creatures. A mighty gun battle. You gotta admit, that's a pretty kick-ass way to go out."

Annja smiled. "I think you just wanted the glory."

"Just imagine the play I'd get with that up in heaven."

"You could have gone to hell," Annja pointed out.

"I suppose, but I guess it wasn't my time to find out," he said.

Annja took a deep breath. Bob, alive! She never would have thought it possible. But here it was. "I think Gregor might be behind this," she said seriously.

"What makes you think that?"

Annja pursed her lips. "It's just a feeling, I guess. Like how he wasn't honest with us about being an intelligence operative and all that."

Bob laughed. "Poor Gregor. He really is a nice guy and all. He's not as smart as he thinks he is, though."

"What do you mean?"

"I knew he was a spy."

"You did?"

"Of course."

Annja shook her head. "Thanks for letting me in on the secret."

"Don't be upset, Annja. I couldn't tell you. I needed you thinking him weird from the start. It would make the ruse all the better."

"What ruse?"

"I've been feeding him false information. While Gregor has been thinking he's wormed classified data out of me, he's actually been getting bogus material supplied to me by the government."

"You just keep unloading surprise after surprise on me," Annja said.

"They knew about Gregor a while back. My brother contacted me about it and we set up a plan. Gregor's a nice guy and I'm genuinely fond of him, but the whole thing has been a setup."

"Wow."

"We decided the best way to really seal the deal was to bring you in on this dig. You're naturally suspicious of everyone, anyway."

"I am?"

"Sure. So, Gregor wouldn't suspect a thing. And it worked perfectly."

"Up until you died," Annja said.

"Nah, that just helped things even more."

Annja smirked. "You're an amazing man, Bob."

A noise in front of them made them both stop talking. It sounded like a bolt being drawn back on a door. Someone was coming.

28

As the door opened, brilliant light blinded Annja. She heard Bob groan. She blinked furiously, trying to adjust her eyes so she could see who had come in.

"I see you're both awake."

Gradually, Annja's eyes cleared, although the person remained silhouetted in front of the bright lights. "Who are you?" she asked.

"You don't recognize me?"

"No. I can't see."

The shadow turned and said something to someone behind him. Immediately, the lights dimmed enough for Annja to make him out.

It wasn't Gregor.

"Father Jakob?"

He bowed low. "You may also refer to me as Dr. Dzerchenko. It is my real name, after all, not some silly concoction dreamed up by my superiors when I came to this wretched outpost."

"What is this all about?" she asked.

Dzerchenko shook his head. "I'll tell you, but not yet. I don't want to ruin the surprise. And I have so few things left in life that grant me some measure of happiness that I will keep the truth from you a little longer. I believe you'll indulge me this final time, won't you?"

"What choice do we have?" Annja asked.

"You ought to be showing more gratitude than that," Dzerchenko said. "After all, I saved your friend's life."

"You did this?" Bob asked.

"Of course. And you were in need of help, my dear man. If I'd gotten to you much later, you wouldn't have had a chance. As it is, you're still in rough shape."

"I feel great," he said weakly.

Annja looked and saw the multiple tubes and wires connected to Bob's bed. As he'd noted, wide leather straps held him in place.

Dzerchenko pointed. "The straps are for your own protection, I assure you. I couldn't risk you waking up and trying to move. Any action like that might tear the sutures I used to repair all the damage the bullet caused."

He turned his attention to Annja. "In your case, however, the bonds are more for our protection than yours."

"I don't know what you're talking about," Annja said.

Dzerchenko laughed. "I'm sure you do, my dear girl. I can't take a chance that you'd ruin my laboratory here."

"Laboratory?" Annja asked.

Dzerchenko held up his hand. "I'm sorry, I failed

to mention where you are. You are in an underground network that lies beneath the village. I'm sure you already surmised such a thing. You do strike me as much more observant than the majority of people I've encountered in life."

"Gee, thanks," Annja said.

"Be that as it may, you must still appreciate my position in this. I apologize for the physical restrictions I've placed upon you, but I will clarify my work here in just a few more minutes."

"Let me guess—you're doing the mad-scientist routine." Annja leaned back against the board she was strapped to. "Another crazy genius hell-bent on creating something, right?"

"The mad-scientist label has never applied to me, I assure you. What I'm after here is nothing less than revolutionary."

Annja looked at him. The guise of Father Jakob no longer seemed relevant. Dzerchenko seemed healthy and strong, even if he was older. That would make him more dangerous than before, Annja thought. I'll have to remember that.

"Does this have anything to do with what you told me and Gregor earlier about the cannibal soldier?" she asked.

"So you were listening," Dzerchenko said. "Excellent."

"It's a crock, though," Annja said. "It's impossible, right?"

"Is it? Didn't you yourself see the results and battle it in the root cellar? The thing you called Khosadam. She was one of my earliest experiments."

"You did that to her?" Annja asked, horrified.

He smiled. "She tried to escape from the mines. She was found by the KGB and told she would die by firing squad unless she volunteered to be used in my experiments."

"She volunteered?" Annja couldn't imagine such a thing.

"Oh, indeed she did. Although I must admit the poor thing probably would have opted for death had she known what awaited her. Regardless, she came to my lab and the rest, as they say, is history."

"You destroyed her."

"I gave her a new life," Dzerchenko said. "Don't be so presumptuous as to think I robbed that girl of anything. I gave her power and strength beyond her wildest imagination."

"You turned her into a beast," Annja said. "And one I would not have killed unless I absolutely had to. You left me no choice."

"Yes, well, it was a shame, but she was getting a bit out of hand. Her nocturnal forays were becoming troublesome."

"So, why not just kill her yourself?"

Dzerchenko frowned. "Believe it or not, I found I was unable to do so. I had become fond of her over the years. She was like my own child. And I could never do that to her."

"So, you went out and found a fool to do your errand for you," Annja said. "Glad I could oblige."

"You put her out of her misery," Dzerchenko said. "Isn't that what you claim she was enduring?"

"Metal teeth, metal claws and wearing the brank? I'm sure she was miserable," Annja said.

"So you did her a favor." Dzerchenko smiled. "And me, as well. Thank you for that."

"If you're looking for a creative way to thank me, I'd suggest letting me and Bob go."

Dzerchenko shook his head. "And ruin the surprise? Not at all. I wouldn't hear of it."

"Is it about Gregor? We already figured out he was a bad guy."

Dzerchenko laughed. "You really think you know it all, don't you? You've got it all figured out. Well, your theories are full of nothing but hot air."

"So, what is it, then? You saying Gregor's not involved?" Annja asked.

"Gregor was a nuisance. Just as you were. When you three came poking around the village and got caught up in the silliness of the Khosadam legend, I was forced to take steps that I would not have otherwise taken."

Bob shifted in his bed. "So what now?"

Annja glanced at him. "Hang on a second." She turned back to Dzerchenko. "Where is Gregor? What did you do with him?"

"Not so much *with*," Dzerchenko said. "The better question is what did I do *to* him?"

Annja's stomach cramped up. This can't be good, she thought.

Dzerchenko stepped back and Annja could see into the next room. Bright lights illuminated the entire scene. She could see a gurney and on top of that, she saw Gregor's body. Limp. Lifeless.

"You killed him." Her voice was quiet.

Dzerchenko shook his head. "Why must everything be about death with you, Miss Creed? Isn't it possible that I could be redefining life?"

"What have you done to him?"

"Gregor will be the next generation of my experiment. And I will finally see it as a total success. The lessons I learned from my prototypes were invaluable to me. Gregor is giving me a chance to put those lessons into action."

"You're turning him into one of those…things?" Annja cried.

Bob groaned next to her. Dzerchenko held up a finger. "I wouldn't do that if I were you. If you rip the sutures, I will not be able to save you again and you will most definitely die."

Bob stopped struggling. "How long until I'm able to move?"

"A matter of days, I'd think. You took the repairs quite well. Better than I would have expected, actually. But I imagine that's due to your heightened athletic state. Still, don't go abusing the repairs just yet."

"When I'm able to move again, you'd better be dead already, because I'm going to wrap my hands around that scrawny neck of yours and squeeze until brains leak out of your ears," Bob said.

"Unfortunately, it'll be too late," Dzerchenko said. "By that time, I will have completed my work on Gregor and he will be ready to unleash upon the world."

"You're going to set him free?" Annja asked.

Dzerchenko smiled. "Why not? It's the reason I've been in this horrid village for over thirty years, masquerading as a priest, so I can continue my work unabated."

"But the people who originally set you up…surely they're not still in power?" Bob said.

Dzerchenko grinned. "Why is it Americans think they know everything? Just because the Cold War is over, don't think for a moment that there is no animosity between our two countries. And don't ever make the mistake of believing that the people who grew up hating your country have fallen out of grace."

"You're saying they're still around?" Bob asked.

"Certainly."

"Great," Annja said. "So much for world peace."

"World peace is a fallacy perpetrated by dreamers who know nothing of how the world truly works."

"I must be an idealist," Annja replied.

"Most people are. But they fail to realize that everything in this world boils down to one thing— money. And even in war, the ultimate goal is to secure the land, resources or riches of the other country. They want to become more powerful and wealthy than the other."

"Isn't that a shortsighted view?" Bob asked.

"It's pragmatic," Dzerchenko said. "And the world could use a bit more pragmatism." He pointed at Gregor's limp body. "That in there is an example of ultimate pragmatism. A soldier who can subsist on the dead around him. He can keep going for days without needing rest, able to eat on the go, scavenging from corpses. It's brilliant and cost-effective."

"So this is all about economics?" Annja said.

Dzerchenko shook his head. "My dear, that is what the Cold War was about. And it's why the Soviet Union lost. But with a new breed of soldier, we can turn the tables once and for all. Then our government, which has been cheerfully masquerading as a fledgling democracy, can finally revert to its true nature and conquer the West."

"My god, you really are insane," Annja said.

Dzerchenko smiled. "The greatest minds have always had to endure ridicule from the mediocre."

"You're paraphrasing," Bob grunted. "Completely unoriginal."

Dzerchenko frowned. "Very well, you'll see how it all plays out. Because within the next hour, Gregor there will be reborn as a new man. A fantastic soldier capable of extraordinary feats."

"Sounds like a pipe dream," Bob said.

Dzerchenko chuckled. "Yes, well, I suppose you'll change your mind once you get a look at him."

Dzerchenko came farther into the room and Annja could see the smile on his face. "You see, when Gregor awakens, he will be quite hungry."

Annja's stomach hurt even more.

"And naturally, he'll want to eat." Dzerchenko leveled a finger at Bob. "You will be his first meal."

Annja took a breath. "No!"

Dzerchenko looked at her. "Don't worry, Annja. I haven't forgotten about you. Once Gregor is finished eating Bob, we will put him to his first field test. You will face him in combat, Annja Creed. And one of you—most likely you—will die."

29

"I'll leave you two alone to mull over what I just told you," Dzerchenko said. He flipped a switch near the door, and a dull yellow bulb overhead offered out some light. Dzerchenko slammed the door.

For a moment, neither Bob nor Annja spoke. Then Bob cleared his throat and said, "Well, that certainly wasn't what I was hoping to hear."

Annja nodded. "Nothing like being saved from death only to learn that you're going to die again, huh?"

"I never saw this coming, I'll grant you that."

"And I'm supposed to fight Gregor?" Annja said. "This is insane."

"At least you're not getting eaten," Bob said. "That's always been a fear of mine."

"Cannibalism?"

"Just the eating part. I always thought it would be by a shark, though. You know, a nice vacation somewhere, an early-morning swim and then chomp."

"You've seen *Jaws* one too many times."

"Probably. But at this point, I'd take the shark over Gregor. Something about that just seems so utterly awful."

Annja flexed her wrists again, but there was no give. "I need to get out of these bonds if we have any hope of escaping," she said.

"Uh, we have a problem there."

"What?"

Bob nodded. "Look at me. I'm not exactly in mint condition here. You might be able to escape somehow, but I'm stuck where I am unless, like the quack says, I want to rip out all the sewing he did."

Bob was right. Annja looked at him again. In order to get him out safely, she'd need a team of trained medical professionals. If she tried it alone, Bob would die as soon as she started to move him.

"Then we won't escape," Annja said.

"We won't?"

Annja shook her head. "No. We will stay here and kill Dzerchenko. It's the only way to ensure our own survival."

"And Gregor? What about him?"

Annja sighed. "I'm hoping it won't come to it, but if I have to, I'll deal with him, as well."

"You like him, don't you?" Bob asked.

Annja took a breath. "I don't know. Part of me thinks he's okay. Part of me isn't sure what side he's been on throughout this entire trip. He's been handy, yeah, but he's also left me with a lot of questions."

Bob chuckled. "I always get a kick out of hearing you dismantle potential lovers."

"I'm not dismantling anyone."

"Okay."

She looked at him. "You want the truth? I was starting to like him, okay? But now I don't know what to think."

"Doesn't seem like there's much to think about. If Dzerchenko is right about what he plans to do, then Gregor is pretty much finished, anyway. That, I believe, removes all the pressure from you," Bob said.

"Yeah, but I've still got to face the idea that I might have to kill him."

"First and foremost, it would appear that we need to figure out how to get you free," Bob said.

Annja flexed her wrists again. "I'm tied down too tight." She knew she couldn't draw the sword with her hands bound. Even if she could, her wrists were braced so stiffly that the sword wouldn't be able to cut the restraints.

"That's a problem," Bob said.

"A big one." Annja leaned back against the board and chewed her lip for a moment. There had to be something she could do to draw the sword and somehow use it to free herself.

"What about your feet?"

"What about them?" she asked.

"Are they tied as tightly as your hands?"

Annja tried moving her feet. There was a bit more give to the bonds, but she didn't think it was enough to free herself.

"I don't think there's anything I can do there, either."

"Just a thought," Bob said.

Annja nodded. "Keep thinking. It's the only hope

we have of staying alive. And I don't intend to lose you so soon after I got you back."

Bob smiled. "Thanks. I'm glad I asked you to come along on the trip. I'd say I chose wisely."

"Save it," Annja said. "We're not free yet. And I hate premature praise. Once we get out of here, you can uncork the bubbly."

"Fair enough."

Annja took a deep breath and closed her eyes. She needed an idea. A solution to the problem they faced. Somehow, somewhere inside of her, there had to be a way to get to the sword and use it even though she was restrained.

Something.

Her mind swam as images flooded her consciousness. She could see the sword cutting her bonds. She could visualize it in the air doing what she needed it to do. She could imagine her being free and able to rescue Bob.

But how?

Her eyes snapped open.

It was a crazy thought.

But what other options did she have?

"You thought of something?"

She looked at Bob. "A long shot."

He smiled. "Long odds are what we're all about right now. I'd say take a stab at anything and hope for the best."

Annja nodded. "That's just what we'll be doing."

"What's the idea?"

Annja smiled. "Ever hear of telekinesis?"

Bob nodded. "Sure, I don't think there's a guy

alive who never wished for the ability to move objects with his mind. If only to blow up skirts on women as they walked by."

Annja smirked. "Well, aside from your pubescent fantasies, there's been some groundbreaking research done on it in the past. The Soviets did a lot of research into it during the Cold War."

Bob sniffed. "Maybe you should ask Dr. Nutjob in there if he was on the committee. He might be able to give you some pointers."

Annja sighed. "Just close your eyes and focus all your energy on escape. I'm going to try and loosen my bonds."

I want to draw the sword out with my mind and see if I can wield it that way. For a limited time only, just long enough to cut me loose. Then I'll use it with my hands again like I always do, Annja thought.

Bob's eyebrows jumped. "Wow, that would be amazing."

"Wouldn't it, though?"

"You think you can do it?"

"I don't know. I guess it depends on how well we visualize it."

Bob nodded. "Well, good luck."

"Thanks." Annja closed her eyes.

"Annja?"

She opened her eyes. "Yes?"

"I don't mean to put any more pressure on you than you already have, but, uh, we're under a deadline here," Bob said.

Annja grinned. "Thanks for the reminder."

"Just doing my part."

"Now shut up, Bob."

"Okay."

Annja closed her eyes again. Her thoughts seemed jumbled and fuzzy, as if she were fighting to clear them. Annja frowned. What was wrong? She could usually picture the sword immediately and then draw it out. It had always worked like that in the past. Ready at a moment's notice.

But now it was a jumbled mess in her mind. She couldn't see clearly at all.

Annja opened her eyes. "I can't make out anything in my mind. It's like there's all this interference or something. My thoughts are a mess. They're jumbled and confused."

"That's not good."

"That's not good at all," Annja said. "If I can't think clearly, we're both dead."

Bob sighed. "Any chance you can force yourself to think clearly?"

"I wouldn't know how."

The door opened again and Dzerchenko came into the room. He smiled at Annja. "How are you doing, my dear?"

Annja didn't respond.

Dzerchenko held up a vial of liquid. "You see this? It's a mild pharmacological drug that I sometimes use on my patients."

"What's it do?" Annja asked, alarmed.

Dzerchenko shrugged. "Oh, nothing much. But in your case probably plenty. You see, I gave you some earlier after I knocked you out." He leaned in close and whispered in her ear. "It interrupts your thought patterns. In other words, it makes it very hard to concentrate on anything. That, I'd be willing to guess, includes your ability to summon the sword Gregor told me about."

Annja glared at him in shock. "You'd be surprised what I'm capable of doing."

"I would be surprised," Dzerchenko said, "if you had the ability to suppress the effects of my special concoction." He glanced at his watch. "You've got about thirty minutes left, anyway. And then, I believe all bets are off."

He turned and left the room.

Annja let out her breath and closed her eyes.

Thirty minutes wasn't a lot of time at all.

30

"Was he right?"

Annja nodded. "I think so. My mind's a mess right now. I can't seem to make heads or tails out of anything."

"How strong do you think the drug was that he gave you?"

"I don't know. I guess plenty." Annja frowned. "There's got to be a way to fight it, though. I just don't know how."

"What about if you concentrate really hard?"

Annja looked at Bob. "Don't give up hope," she said. "I'll try to think of something." But it was easier said than done, and Annja knew it. She closed her eyes and watched the mishmash of images and thoughts and emotions come flying at her randomly. She tried to direct her thoughts, but found she was completely unable to focus for long on even the smallest thing.

She exhaled a long breath and tried to relax her muscles. Even though she had pins and needles firing off in her arms and legs, Annja kept breathing.

"I'm going to try something," she said to Bob. "So please be quiet and don't interrupt. Okay?"

"You got it. I'll just sit here all quiet like."

"Thanks."

Annja kept her eyes closed and started breathing deeply. She inhaled long and slow and exhaled in the same manner. After a minute of this, she started counting her breaths. She reached ten and would start all over again at one. Each time she completed a series of breaths, she felt more relaxed.

I could fall asleep here, she thought.

But she redirected herself back to counting breaths. She was surprised at how difficult it could be. Every time she started counting, her mind wanted to wander away and think of crazy things. She had to bring it back into line and force herself to count the breaths. She could feel her muscles relaxing even more. She kept breathing.

And she kept counting.

Annja could see the fog in her mind and it looked like gray, bloated rain clouds hanging in the sky. She kept breathing and counting, hoping that the clouds would part and the blue sky of her clear mind would shine through.

Annja's chest rose and fell as she breathed in and out. The pins and needles in her arms and legs started to fade away as she continued her metronomic respirations. All she had to do was think about breathing and counting.

That was all.

Annja reached a ten-count again and redirected herself back to one. Long inhale and long exhale. All the stress and tension would melt away.

On the next series, Annja felt her heartbeat kick up a notch.

What's going on? she wondered.

She kept breathing and counting. Her heartbeat continued to increase. She kept breathing and counting. She reached ten quicker and quicker, always going back to one.

Over and over again.

Sweat broke out and ran down her face. Her entire body felt awakened instead of relaxed, as if she'd unlocked some powerful reservoir of hidden energy. Annja kept breathing and counting.

She could feel her wet skin brushing against her clothes. And still her heart kept beating faster and faster and she kept breathing and counting.

Annja's eyes popped open with a sudden gasp.

"You okay?"

She could hear the concern in Bob's voice. She looked over at him. "I don't know."

"You look like hell."

"I do?"

"You're pale as a ghost. And you're soaked through with sweat. I was watching you. Your chest heaved like a bellows, for crying out loud. I thought your heart was going to jump out of your chest."

"Makes two of us," Annja said. "I knew I was sweating, but I couldn't do anything about it."

"How does your head feel now?" Bob asked.

"Hang on," Annja said. She closed her eyes and prepared herself to see nothing but more fog.

Instead, everything seemed still. "It worked."

"What did?"

Annja opened her eyes. "I tried a breathing technique to purge my system of Dzerchenko's drugs. It must have worked. I can think clearly again."

Bob nodded. "Good news."

"Well, that's one task down. Now let's see if we can make the other thing work."

"Better make it snappy," Bob said. "You've got about five minutes left."

"How long was I breathing?"

Bob shook his head. "Seemed like forever. But must have been at least twenty minutes."

"I had no idea I was out that long," Annja said. "It only felt like I was gone a moment or so."

"I suppose that's why it worked," Bob said. "Now, really, if you wouldn't mind helping out a pal here so he doesn't have to get eaten by a former employee, that'd just be swell."

Annja smiled and closed her eyes again. She visualized the sword. At first, it seemed like it might not work, but then she really focused and suddenly she could see the sword hanging in front of her in brilliant light.

I have no hands, Annja thought. But I can still summon my sword if I want it badly enough. All I have to do is concentrate.

In her mind's eye, Annja saw her hands reaching out for the sword. They closed around the hilt of the sword. Annja opened her eyes.

The sword was not there.

"Dammit!"

Bob's voice was quiet. "Easy, Annja. You can do this. I know you can. Just take it easy and try it again. Okay?"

"Okay."

Annja closed her eyes. The sword was there, right where she had left it. She tried again to draw it out with her hands.

Again it did not come out.

"I don't know if this is going to work, Bob."

"Keep trying, okay? We really need this to work. Otherwise, we're both dead."

"I'm trying."

"Try harder."

"Easy for you to say."

Bob grunted. "Sure, with all these tubes and all. Please, just do what you can."

"All right." Annja closed her eyes again. She saw the sword hovering in front of her. What is it that I'm missing? she wondered. The sword is right there. I can see it. I can wrap my hands around it. But I can't get it out. Why?

She studied the sword, marveling at the length of the blade and how it seemed to have an aura all its own. She looked at the hilt. She knew how it felt when it rested in her hands. How secure she felt when she wielded it. And how much a part of her it was.

She heard something.

A sound in another room. Bob was right. They didn't have much time. She had to do this now.

Dzerchenko sounded as if he was unlocking the door.

"Annja…" Bob's voice was low and hurried, but Annja could sense the fear welling up within him.

She could see the sword. *I need you,* she thought.

She concentrated. She saw the sword. She saw her mind's energy wrapping itself around the hilt. She saw her mind drawing it out into this world.

Annja opened her eyes. The sword was lying on her stomach. She looked at Bob. He had his eyes closed and was muttering in prayer or concentration. Annja worked her hands over the edge of her blade and ran the restraints over it until they released. "Hurry, Annja. He's coming," Bob said. His eyes were still shut tight.

Dzerchenko muttered something on the other side of the door. Maybe he forgot the key, Annja thought.

She leaned forward and undid her feet restraints. Then she clutched the sword in both hands.

Annja hopped off the table and stood to one side of the door. Here goes nothing, she thought.

The door suddenly flew open.

Dzerchenko came in with his head down, shaking it as he thumbed his way through several keys on a ring. "Sorry to keep you waiting, but I forgot which key it was for the lock."

He looked up.

Annja watched as surprise exploded all over his face.

"What—?" Bob said.

Annja grinned. "Howdy, Doc."

Dzerchenko turned.

Annja leaned over and placed one edge of the sword blade under his chin.

"I think it's time you and me had ourselves a little talk."

31

"Where did you get that?" Bob asked.

Annja ignored the question.

Dzerchenko's eyes narrowed. "I am surprised you were able to overcome the effects of my drug. It was a recipe I made myself. Now, I think I will have to go back and reexamine it."

"Or maybe you'll be dead before you get the chance," Annja said.

Dzerchenko shrugged. "It is always a possibility."

"You're not fazed by that?"

He laughed. "You've seen what I have created here. Do you think I was so naive that I wasn't aware of the potential for danger? That my creations could go out of control at any moment and turn on me?"

"She did go out of control. Or did you already forget?" Annja said.

Dzerchenko laughed again. "I lied. She never went

berserk. I released her. I allowed her to explore what she was. It was all part of the research."

"You deliberately killed those villagers?" Annja asked.

"Indirectly."

Annja shook her head. "You're guilty of so many crimes, I don't even know where to start."

"I'm guilty of no crimes," Dzerchenko said. "As I mentioned already, my work is protected."

"Doesn't matter," Annja said. "Once we're done here, we'll make sure your work is brought to the attention of the rest of the world. You'll be held accountable."

Annja felt her anger welling up. She could slice his head off right now and make sure that Dzerchenko's work never saw the light of day. One cut and it would be over.

She snapped the blade away from his neck.

He sneered. "Don't tell me you're beholden to some sort of honor system."

Bob cleared his throat. "Annja? Maybe you just ought to kill him."

Annja shook her head. "Not yet." She gestured to Dzerchenko. "Get back into the laboratory."

"Why?"

Annja pressed the blade against Dzerchenko's cheek. A razor-thin line of blood appeared, and Dzerchenko winced. "I can cut you a million times and never kill you. It will hurt like hell, though, so I suggest you do what I say."

"Fine."

Annja glanced at Bob. "I'll be next door for a moment. You okay?"

"Yeah, just don't take too long," he said.

Annja nudged Dzerchenko into the laboratory. She could see the gurneys and all kinds of medical equipment. It looked as if they were in a large underground cavern that had been hollowed out many years ago. "How long have you been down here?"

"I told you. Almost thirty years."

"And before you?"

Dzerchenko nodded. "There were others. This place used to be a bunker. It was convenient to set me up here."

Across the room, Annja could see Gregor's body. Tubes and wires ran to various machines. She recognized some of them, but others looked completely alien to her.

"Is he dead?"

Dzerchenko sighed. "I told you I had no intention of killing him."

"He looks dead."

"He's resting. The transformation tends to be quite exhausting."

"Transformation like what you did to the girl," Annja said quietly.

"Better," Dzerchenko replied. "I had to make adjustments that would enable him to defeat skilled opponents. I thought I'd done so with the girl, but you proved otherwise when you killed her."

"I want him put back the way he was," Annja said.

Dzerchenko turned. "What? You're kidding."

"I'm not."

Dzerchenko shook his head. "It would kill him. I

cannot make him the way he was. He has implants now that would be impossible to remove."

"Why?"

"I had to make it that way. What if others like him found out they could be transformed back? They would attempt to do it themselves and the entire project would fail. No, they must realize that there is no going back. Only then will they learn to accept the new reality of their situation."

"You really are sick," Annja said.

Dzerchenko sighed. "My genius will be recognized at a later date. I have no problem with posthumous glory."

"How did you get him out of the hotel so quietly?"

"It wasn't hard. He was drunk."

Annja nodded. "Yeah, but you're not exactly a physical specimen. And Gregor weighs a fair amount. I should know—I hefted him upstairs."

"Did you, now?"

"Yes."

"Well, he proved pretty easy to move when I got to him."

"Was that you I heard moving about in the corridor?"

"You heard me? Why didn't you come to investigate?"

"I did. Eventually."

Dzerchenko grinned. "Waited too long, did you? And now your friend is here. All because you failed to act quickly. Just think, if you'd interrupted me, you could have stopped me from doing this. You might have been able to save Gregor."

Annja gritted her teeth. "You're evil."

"Of course," Dzerchenko continued, "there'd be no homecoming for you and Bob. You had no idea I had him. And then I would have simply transformed Bob into one of my new soldiers."

"Why didn't you?" Annja asked.

"Gregor is more physically gifted than your friend Bob. He is bigger and will probably endure punishment more."

"He won't get the chance," Annja said.

"Oh? And how will you stop it? You're going to kill him. Put him out of his misery. Is that it?"

"I was thinking about it," Annja admitted, terrified at the thought.

Dzerchenko leaned against the gurney by Gregor's feet. "No. I doubt you will. You don't have it in you to strike down an unarmed person. And you especially won't kill someone you were friends with."

"You don't know that," Annja said.

"You kept me alive, didn't you?"

"Because you're going to transform him back into a normal human being."

"I told you that is impossible."

Annja sliced open his other cheek. "Do it. I won't ask again. And if you tell me it can't be done, then I *will* kill you. Bet on it."

Dzerchenko sighed. "You really mean to go through with this?"

"Yes."

"All right. But don't say I didn't warn you." He pointed at a closet. "I need a gown and mask. Is it okay?"

"Fine."

She moved with Dzerchenko to the closet and watched as he pulled on a set of scrubs. He placed a face mask over his mouth and then walked to the sink.

"Would you mind turning on the water? I need to scrub up before I crack him open again."

Annja leaned in and turned on the tap. Dzerchenko scrubbed his hands, lathering them up and rinsing several times before he nodded that Annja could shut off the water. As he toweled off, he kept staring at her.

"He could die, you know."

"Make sure he doesn't," she said.

"It's not up to me, Annja. It's up to him. It's how his body reacts to getting cut into for the second time in several hours. The sheer shock of the procedure could send him over the edge."

"You saved Bob from a gunshot wound that would have killed anyone else. You can make sure Gregor doesn't die."

"Those are two different things. Bob's gunshot wound was bad, yes, but the repair was easy. For me, it was a piece of cake, as you might say. But this procedure is long and involved. And there's no guarantee that he will survive it."

"You're stalling because you want him to wake up and attack me," Annja said. "Now get to work."

"I'm not hoping he wakes up," Dzerchenko said. "In fact, it would be better for all of us if he stayed asleep."

"Just get working. Tell me what you have to do."

Dzerchenko sighed. "You wouldn't understand."

"Try me."

"I've injected liquid metal into his hands, feet and jaw. It has already cooled and hardened. To undo it,

I must superheat the metal to make it pliable again. Only then would I be able to remove it."

"That sounds difficult and dangerous."

Dzerchenko nodded. "I told you that it would be. It's incredibly dangerous."

"How hot do you have to get the metal?"

"Much too hot for humans to endure. There's a chance his system could go into shock from that alone."

Annja looked at Gregor's naked body. He was a mess of stitch marks from where Dzerchenko had cracked him open. Blood had splattered the edges of the gurney. The procedure didn't look as if it had gone easily.

Was Dzerchenko telling the truth? Would she be killing him if she ordered Dzerchenko to proceed? And could she live with herself if he did die?

"Annja?"

She looked at Dzerchenko. "What?"

"I'm going to start now. Are you sure this is what you want me to do? Are you absolutely sure you want me to do this?"

Annja bit her lip. Gregor. Poor Gregor. Look at him. A shell of the man he used to be only hours before. And now he's some freak of nature waiting to wake up.

And eat.

"Do it," she said firmly.

Dzerchenko nodded. "Very well. Just so you know— you have officially signed his death certificate."

"Make sure he doesn't die. Or you will."

Dzerchenko pointed at a tray of surgical instruments. "I need a scalpel to cut into him. Is that okay?"

Annja backed up. "Go ahead. But don't try anything funny or I'll cut you in half before you get two steps closer to me."

Dzerchenko nodded. "I wouldn't dream of it."

Annja frowned. Why is he so cooperative?

Dzerchenko lifted a scalpel from the tray and held it up to the light. "Isn't this a marvel? The way it can be so brittle and yet so lethal? Amazing tools, these scalpels."

Annja looked at Gregor again. This is it, she thought. Was this the right thing to do?

Dzerchenko brought the scalpel down. "Here we go."

"Do it," Annja said.

Dzerchenko looked up. "Yes. Do it."

Annja felt something pierce her skin from behind. She dropped the sword and slumped to the floor.

She heard Dzerchenko's laughter echo in the shadows of her mind.

32

Annja heard voices rattle through her head as she came around. Unlike any of the other times she'd been knocked out lately, there was no throbbing in her skull as she opened her eyes.

"Welcome back."

Bright light made her wince, but then she adjusted. Dzerchenko leaned over her. "How are you feeling?"

"Why do you care?"

"Just checking for any aftereffects of the drug."

"I'm fine."

He nodded. "Probably better than all those knocks you've been taking on your head, eh?"

"How did you know about them?"

Dzerchenko waved her off. "I took an X-ray of your skull when I knocked you out to make sure there was no serious damage. I could see the contusions you'd gotten before. You've been taking some good knocks recently. You want to tell me about them?"

"I nearly got run off the road biking into this dump of a village. Then I fell in the cave and banged my head against the rocks."

"Ouch. You ought to be more careful."

Annja frowned. "Tell you what—from now on I'll make sure to ask that all my head injuries be done with a pillow."

"Or a drug like my good friend gave you," the doctor said.

Annja turned. Beyond Dzerchenko, a face she recognized smiled back at her. He didn't look as demure and submissive as he had back at the hotel, though.

"So, it's you," she said.

The innkeeper smiled and took a bow. He seemed distinctly pleased with himself. Annja found it nauseating.

"This," Dzerchenko said, "is my good friend and assistant Tupolov. I believe you've met him before, under very different circumstances."

"We've met," Annja said. "And now that I know who he really is, I'll be sure to kill him after I kill you."

Dzerchenko and Tupolov laughed. Dzerchenko shook his head. "I told him you were a funny one. He didn't believe me."

Annja sat up on the gurney. "Why didn't you restrain me?"

Dzerchenko shrugged. "Why bother? Since you proved so capable of ruining one set of restraints, I saw no need in sacrificing any more. Besides, take it as a measure of my good faith."

"Good faith? Are you insane?"

Dzerchenko shrugged. "Hardly. I'd like to offer a truce."

"Why?"

"I can use someone like you," he said.

"For this? Forget it."

Dzerchenko leaned closer. "But you've got skills and abilities I would love to study. Together, we could really do some pioneering work in the field of psychic-spiritual research."

"There's no way I would ever work with you. Not after what you've done to my friends and to innocent people alike," Annja said.

"But don't you understand the importance of this research? It can help people. Isn't that what you want? You could help people, Annja."

"I can barely help myself most of the time," Annja said. "And the people I help are the ones I choose to help."

Dzerchenko frowned. "Tupolov didn't think you'd go for it, but I insisted on trying."

"Maybe he's the smarter of the two of you."

"He suggested I just kill you and get it over with."

Annja shrugged. "Whatever."

"The concept of your own death doesn't seem to faze you much," the doctor said.

"I'm comfortable with the thought of dying."

"Really?"

"Sure."

Dzerchenko laughed. "More bravado, I'm afraid. You might claim such, but I don't buy it. You've got too much loneliness in your eyes to be so nonchalant about death. You still long to find someone you can share your heart with. You want love, like everyone else in this world. And until you have that, you'll always wonder."

"What about you? Are you ready to die?" she asked angrily.

"I've been ready to die for years," Dzerchenko said. "Both of us have. But we're not allowed to die until our work is successful."

"What in the world does that mean?"

Dzerchenko sat down in a plastic chair. "How old do you think I am?"

"Sixty?"

"Thank you. I'll take that as a compliment."

"Is this where you tell me you're actually five hundred years old?" Annja asked.

Dzerchenko shrugged. "No, don't be ridiculous. But Tupolov and I are both ninety-five years old."

"I don't believe you."

"I kid you not. We were hired by Stalin to work on this project. And we've been working on it ever since. Oh sure, they move us from time to time—thirty years ago to this place. And they'll probably do it again, but we've always kept going. The last thing he said to us—Stalin, that is—was that we could not die until we successfully completed the project."

"And how did you manage that?"

Tupolov held up a vial of serum. Dzerchenko gestured at it. "Our fountain of youth. It's a genetic mixture of stem cells combined with supernutrients. We inject ourselves with it once a week, and that keeps us going."

"And you won't ever die?" Annja asked.

"Well, not from old age. At least not yet as far as we can tell. We only developed the serum about twenty years ago. When we started faltering because of old age, we knew we had to take steps to ensure our survival. We had to keep our promise to Stalin."

Annja shook her head. "It's not possible."

Dzerchenko laughed again. "You're one to talk about impossibilities, Annja. After all, you seem to have the ability to summon some kind of sword at will. Now really, is it fair to say we're an impossibility?"

He had a point, but Annja kept glancing around. The gurney that held Gregor had vanished.

"Where is he?"

"Who?"

"Gregor."

Tupolov grinned. "I would have thought she'd ask about Bob first. I guess we were wrong about who she cares about more."

Annja looked toward the door she'd come through originally. It was closed. Was Bob still in there? "Where's Bob?" she said.

Dzerchenko shook his head. "No fair. You asked about Gregor first."

"Just tell me where they are."

"Gregor is fine. He's awake."

"You fixed him?"

"Of course not. I left him just the way he was. He'd be dead otherwise—I told you that."

Annja frowned. "And what about Bob?"

"Ah well, Bob is also awake. Although I suspect at the moment he is quite anxious."

"Why?"

"I told you what would be happening, Annja." Dzerchenko shrugged. "It's not like it was a surprise or anything."

Annja hopped off the table. Tupolov leveled a gun on her. Dzerchenko held up his hand. "Now, now, is this really necessary? Tupolov there has a trigger finger that is unrivaled for a ninety-five-year-old man, I assure you. If you make a move that looks even vaguely suspicious, you'll be dead in short order."

"Tell me where they are," Annja demanded.

Dzerchenko pointed at a window at the end of the room. "You'll find them over there."

Annja walked to the window. It looked down upon a wide area roughly thirty feet in diameter. In the center of the room Bob lay in his hospital bed.

Across from him, Gregor stood.

But he didn't look like Gregor anymore.

His hands hung by his sides. Annja could see the sharpened metal claws. She could see his pointed toes. And she could hear the clacking of his metallic teeth.

Gregor was gone. A monster had replaced him.

"I'll bet he's hungry," the doctor said.

She turned and saw Dzerchenko and Tupolov coming toward her. She turned back. Bob's face was a mask of terror.

"It's all in the name of research, my dear. All we have to do is switch off the force field and Gregor there will be all over Bob."

"So why haven't you done it already?" Annja asked.

"We wanted to give you a choice."

"What choice? You've created a monster and

you've placed one of my oldest friends in harm's way. What choice is there in that?"

"Plenty," Dzerchenko said. "You can still save Bob."

Annja looked at him. "How?"

"Fight Gregor. We need field data to surmise how well he will adapt to a skilled foe. You fit the bill quite well. Much better than any of the locals we could hope to kidnap thanks to Tupolov's inn."

"And if I fight him?"

Dzerchenko shrugged. "No guarantees. He should kill you. But you might also kill Gregor. And if that happens, then obviously, Bob doesn't get eaten."

"And we go free?"

Dzerchenko smiled. "Well, now, I suppose that would be something we'd need to discuss when the time came. Let's not get too ahead of ourselves, after all."

"I'm not giving you what you ask unless I've got some sort of guarantee," Annja said.

"Then you'll stand here and watch Bob die."

"Horribly," Tupolov added. "It truly is a grisly sight watching them devour another human. Cannibalism is a terrible thing."

Annja looked down on the horrible scene. Bob's face had paled. She could see him trying to flex against his restraints. But he was held fast. He might tear out his sutures if he keeps doing that, she thought.

"What's it going to be, my dear?"

Annja looked at the two old men. She'd never known such hatred before. They looked evil and wicked, and the thought of what they'd done to so many people sickened her. But she was trapped.

She noticed that Tupolov held a remote control in his other hand. "Is that for the force field?" she asked.

He nodded. "Just in case you had any bad ideas about drawing your sword and cutting us down. My last act would be to release Gregor. And I'm willing to bet he can eat Bob before you can break the window."

Dzerchenko's voice was quiet in her ear. "It's decision time, Annja. We can't wait any longer."

"Too much to do," Tupolov said.

Annja looked back into the improvised arena. Gregor was already straining at the edge of the force field. Twice he tried to punch through it, but he was forced back as the electricity jolted him.

Bob was yelling. But Annja could hear nothing through the window.

"What's it going to be?" Dzerchenko said.

Annja looked at him. "You're asking me to kill one of my friends to save the other."

Dzerchenko nodded. "The power over life and death is never easy, is it?"

Annja looked back at the arena. "You'll bring Bob out of there if I go in?"

"Immediately."

"And you'll take care of him?"

"Of course."

Annja looked at Dzerchenko. "If I die inside there, Bob goes free."

Dzerchenko smiled. "Whatever you say."

Annja knew he'd never keep his word. But she had no choice.

"Show me how to get inside."

33

Dzerchenko led her down a set of metal stairs that Annja hadn't noticed in the corner of the room. In front of her, she could see a metal door that looked as if they'd stolen it from a submarine.

"It's a security procedure for us," Dzerchenko said. "We find that the new creatures are somewhat likely to have temper tantrums. They stay down here until they get acclimated."

"How many of them have you made?" Annja asked.

"About half a dozen, but the one you killed was the only one that survived for any length of time. That's why we were understandably upset to find out she'd been killed. Anyway, we've got very high hopes for Gregor. His physical stature alone should be enough to ensure his survivability."

"It's not all about the body," Annja said.

"True enough. That is why we hope he does well. Gregor has a very interesting background. He has a sharp mind, and we think his cunning might just make him an exceptional talent."

"But first you have to make sure he'll kill—is that it?" Annja said.

"Something like that."

Annja nodded. "Well, let's get this over with."

"You'll use your sword, right?"

"Yes. I will."

"Fascinating," Dzerchenko said. "I wish you'd indulge me a little bit and tell me how it is that you came by it."

Annja looked at him. "It's a long story. And you wouldn't believe me if I told you anyway."

"How many people would believe this? It's one of the things that keep us safe here. No one in their wildest imagination would think that a couple of old fogeys are trying to develop a cannibalistic soldier. It's stuff out of cheap movies and science fiction. But the truth is real enough."

"I'm not interested in revealing myself to you, Dzerchenko."

"Very well. But I fear we might not have this chance ever again."

"Because I'm going to kill you?"

Dzerchenko smiled. "No. Because Gregor is most likely going to kill you."

"And that saddens you, huh? You big softie."

"I'm inquisitive and curious by nature," Dzerchenko said. "That's how I came to be involved in this experiment. I'd very much like to know as much as possible before I shuffle off this mortal coil."

Annja looked at him. "As soon as I go in, you

wheel Bob out. You make sure he's okay. That his sutures haven't come out."

"I will check. It did look like he was getting a bit frantic in there, didn't it?"

"Of course he was."

"I hope you enjoy yourself, Annja."

Dzerchenko spun the wheel lock on the door. Annja heard the hydraulic hiss as it opened. She heard Bob's screams instantly.

"Bob!"

He turned, his head and face all sweaty. "Annja! Thank God!"

Annja ran to him. Being down here with Gregor so close, it was no wonder that Bob was terrified. She was starting to get scared, as well.

"It's going to be okay."

"How the hell is it going to be all right? They're going to let him eat me!"

Annja shook her head. "You're safe. Dzerchenko is going to look after you." Annja spotted some blood on the sheets. "And he'll make sure you didn't do anything to injure yourself. Okay?"

"What about you?"

Annja smiled. "I've got some business to attend to."

"What kind of business?"

"Don't worry about it."

"Annja."

"Bob." Annja shook her head. "I've got to fight Gregor. They want to see how well he does against someone like me."

"You mean someone who knows how to fight?"

Dzerchenko put his hands under the back of Bob's gurney. "It's time for us to go, Bob."

Annja gave him a hug. "Take care of yourself. They said they'd let you go if things don't work out for me."

Bob sniffed. "Like they'd keep their word."

Dzerchenko cleared his throat. "Now, now, you don't know that."

Bob glanced up at him and then back at Annja. "I know this won't be easy for you. But trust me, I don't think there's anything of Gregor left in that thing. I've stared into his eyes for the last twenty minutes. And it terrified me."

Annja nodded. "I'll be okay."

Dzerchenko pushed the gurney out.

Bob raised his hand. "See you soon."

"See you soon," she said.

At the door, Dzerchenko looked at Annja and smiled. "Best of luck. I think you'll need it."

Annja glared at him. "When I'm done with Gregor, I'm coming for you and Tupolov. If you've got any last-minute things to do, I suggest you take care of them now. I won't grant you any quarter."

Dzerchenko slammed the door shut. Annja heard the wheel lock engage.

She turned.

Gregor grunted across the arena. His feet scraped the dirt floor, sending up whorls of dust. Annja stared at him, but saw no recognition in his eyes.

So this is it, she thought. It comes down to this.

She knelt in the center of the arena. And closed her eyes. The sword hung there in front of her. Annja wrapped her hands around it, felt the warmth of it seep into her body.

I don't want to do this, she thought.

Annja opened her eyes. The sword was in her hands. Ahead of her Gregor roared when he saw the brilliant blade. He pawed at the ground like some kind of human bull. Annja could see sweat and spittle shooting out of his mouth.

Annja stood.

Above her, Annja saw Dzerchenko and Tupolov at the window. Tupolov had a video camera. Dzerchenko held a notebook and the remote control for Gregor's force field.

He looked at Annja and smiled. Annja stared back at him. Just wait, she thought. Your turn is coming soon.

She heard a fizzle and saw the lights go out on the poles that marked the containment area Gregor stood in. The force field was off. Gregor emerged.

Annja circled as he stalked her. She could see the long claws that his hands had become. His toes had similar claws.

I'll need to stay clear of those if I have any hope of ending this fast, she thought. Otherwise, if he gets a clean shot at me, I'll be sliced open. And this time, it'll be worse than Khosadam. She didn't have toe claws.

Gregor's mouth parted and Annja could see the long teeth that Dzerchenko had given him. They looked sharp.

I'll bet he'd like to sink those things into me, she thought.

Gregor continued to circle her. He's being wary

because I have the sword, Annja thought. Well, good. At least he'll keep his distance for a bit.

But even as she thought that, Gregor lashed out with a high roundhouse kick aimed right at her head. She barely had time to duck as the limb sailed over her. She heard the swish as the toe claws cleaved through the air.

That was too close, Annja thought as her heart pounded in her chest. He's already using the limbs that give him the most distance. Gregor wasn't wasting time trying to punch at her because he knew the sword would give Annja added reach.

Smart. Just as Dzerchenko predicted.

Annja wanted to look up at the window to see what they were doing, but she knew Gregor would never forgive her. The moment he sensed an opening, he'd be all over her.

I've got to end this fast, she told herself.

Annja dipped low and cut up at a diagonal angle as Gregor shifted to his left. He lifted his left hand and deflected the blade. Annja heard the sharp clang of metal on metal and knew that Gregor had used his claws to thwart the attack.

Gregor launched another kick at her right side, coming up and in with a lifting front kick. Annja backed away as his toes cut through the bottom part of her pants.

She shook her head. Gregor continued to circle. She could see mucus running from his nose. He really did not look anything like the man she'd almost gone to bed with. He'd been replaced by something else—something that seemed culled from the pages of science fiction.

But this was real. And Annja was in real danger.

Gregor launched another attack, coming at her with a front kick and then driving down with a straight slash with his right hand. Annja pivoted and then ducked under the slash. She came up and cut left to right, swinging down at Gregor's leg. Her blade cut into the top of his thigh muscle, drawing blood.

Gregor didn't roar in pain. Instead he started laughing.

Annja winced. It sounded like a raspy cough. Drool flowed from Gregor's mouth and he put one of his hands on the wound. It came away bright red. He licked his hand clean and then smiled at Annja.

With one hand, he reached out. His fingers curled into a fist except one. Pointing at her, he whispered, "I'll taste you next."

He talks? Annja's mind swam. Gregor was definitely an improvement on the Khosadam that she'd fought before.

Gregor came flying at her in the next instant, raining his claws down on her. Annja brought the sword up again and again, deflecting each strike. She backed up, and Gregor kept driving her back.

Annja knew she was running out of room.

And then Gregor jumped into the air and lashed out with both of his legs. They caught her square in the chest, and Annja braced herself, expecting to feel his toe claws bite into her at any moment.

But instead, the jolt of the kick sent her flying backward right into the wall. Annja crashed to the ground and the wind was knocked out of her.

Her sword lay nearby. Annja grabbed it and tried to get back to her feet.

Across the arena, Gregor laughed again.

He's having fun with this, Annja thought. I mean nothing to him. I'm just a toy.

Gregor prowled around the arena. He would start to come for her and then he'd back away. His face bore a wide grin, and drool dripped from his jaws.

The next time he comes in, he'll try to kill me, Annja thought. This is just the foreplay.

Gregor pawed the ground and put his head down as if he were a bull. Whorls of dust jumped into the air. Annja could hear the breaths coming out of Gregor's nose. More snot and drool dripped to the ground.

He's getting ready, she thought.

She held her sword up in front of her and took a deep breath. I've got to end this thing.

Here and now.

34

The beast that had once been Gregor roared long and loud at Annja. She winced at the noise but kept her sword up in front of her for protection.

There's nothing left of Gregor in there, she thought. Dzerchenko and Tupolov have killed every last bit of him. She eyed him as he circled, drawing down the distance between them.

Gregor's eyes flashed from side to side as if trying to figure out a weakness in Annja's defense. His toes dug up dirt and dust and his hands snapped together like pincers.

In the next instant, he was airborne again, driving down at Annja's head with his hands and feet fully splayed. Four sets of wicked claws streaked toward Annja with terrifying speed.

She brought up the sword. She dropped and stabbed upward.

She heard a shriek in the next instant as her blade

punctured Gregor's sternum and drove all the way through. Gregor's momentum finished the job, and he landed on top of Annja with a sickening crash.

She could feel his final breaths coming out hot and sticky. She felt the sudden rush of blood drenching her.

Gregor's voice sounded far away. "Thank…you…"

Annja's eyes felt hot and wet. "I'm so sorry," she cried.

She pushed him off her, and Gregor's body slumped to the side. His eyes rolled back.

Gregor was dead.

Annja looked at his claws and found they looked almost like toys rather than lethal killing tools. But she'd come close to feeling them and wouldn't trade places for anything.

She drew her sword into the air. The blade had a thick, slick coating of crimson. Annja wiped it on the ground, watching as the dirt absorbed much of the blood.

Annja wiped her brow and turned to look up at the window. She was sure that Dzerchenko and Tupolov would be watching in horror.

But there was no one there.

Annja frowned. She wanted to put the sword away, but she didn't know what might be waiting for her. Dzerchenko and Tupolov might be planning to double-cross her.

She couldn't take the chance. Not with Bob in desperate need of medical evacuation.

Annja walked to the door and waited. Nothing happened. She placed the sword against the wall close by and tried turning the wheel lock. It was stuck. She looked back at the window.

Dzerchenko and Tupolov were back.

Uh-oh, Annja thought. This can't be good.

Dzerchenko waved to Annja and then pointed to a grille near the door. Annja looked and then heard a buzz of static. "Congratulations."

Annja frowned. "I did what you asked. Now let me get Bob out of here."

"Ah yes, well, I'm afraid that's not going to be possible. We can't trust you not to tell anyone about our experiments here."

"I'm not interested in blowing the whistle on you guys. I just want to get Bob out of here and to a hospital in one piece," Annja said.

"You did quite well with Gregor. We were very impressed."

Annja looked over at Gregor's corpse. She felt horror at what she'd done. And a measure of relief that it was finally over. "I'm thrilled you enjoyed the show. Now let me out of here," Annja said angrily.

"What would you say if we told you that we were so impressed that we'd like you to stay here with us for a while."

Annja frowned. "That wasn't part of the deal."

Dzerchenko grinned. "Deals are made to be broken, my dear Annja."

"Not this one. Now let me out."

"I'm afraid not."

Annja gritted her teeth. "Dzerchenko, you are really doing your best to make me mad, aren't you?"

"Not at all. I'm simply asking you to understand our position."

"Which is what, exactly?"

Dzerchenko held up a clipboard. "We have several instruments located throughout the arena that measure all sorts of things, including reaction speed, power, endurance, that sort of thing."

"So?"

"So, you were off the chart on all of them. It was quite amazing. We wonder if it has something to do with your special sword there."

Annja shook her head. It always amazed her that people said she moved fast. To her, it felt as if she were moving through quicksand most of the time. "I don't know what the sword can and cannot do," she said honestly.

"Exactly," Dzerchenko said. "That's why we'd like you to stay around for a little bit. Humor us by showing us how it all works. And once we're done, we'll let you go."

"Why should I believe you? You were supposed to let me go when this was all over."

Tupolov laughed. "Well, honestly, Annja, we didn't think you would be able to survive a fight with Gregor. That's why we made that promise. Your odds simply were not good."

"Thanks a lot."

"We had a lot of faith in our creation."

"So you lied."

"See it from our perspective, Annja. We're scientists. We want to study things that are incredible to us. And you were certainly incredible. You defeated something that should have been undefeatable."

Annja smiled. "I guess you guys weren't as good as you thought you were, huh?"

Tupolov frowned. "We think the problem was with Gregor and not with our research."

"Always the way," Annja said. "It's never about the people in charge. It's always the little guys that get the blame." She pointed at Gregor. "For what it's worth, I think he was pretty damned impressive."

"It's worth nothing," said Dzerchenko. "You killed him and made our experiment worthless. Now we've got to come up with something new."

"Something new?" Annja asked, frightened by the thought.

He smiled. "You, my dear."

I'm really getting tired of him calling me "my dear," Annja thought. She shook her head. "I'm not going to be your guinea pig."

Dzerchenko shrugged. "Then Bob will die."

"Bob's got nothing to do with this!" Annja grabbed her sword. "I did what you asked and you're supposed to let us go!"

"Bob has everything to do with this," Dzerchenko said. "After all, he seems to motivate you in some way. Are you in love with him?"

"No. He's a dear friend."

"And naturally you'd like to see him live out his life with many more happy years. Wouldn't you?"

"Of course," Annja said.

"Then the choice is, once again, yours."

Annja leaned on her sword. Somewhere up there

Bob lay on a gurney, probably completely unaware of what was going on. Maybe they'd stashed him in the other room again so he couldn't hear. If he could hear, he would have shouted something about Annja refusing to do it and to not worry about him.

But she couldn't do that. She'd lost Bob once on this trip, and the thought of losing him again made her heart ache. Worse, knowing those two crazy loons, they'd probably make some big spectacle out of it.

And that might be the worst thing of all.

Annja bit her lip and felt the tang of blood as she tore off some skin. "What do you want from me?"

"Just a chance to ask you some questions."

"That's it?"

"Of course."

Annja frowned. "You'll forgive me if I'm not exactly a trusting soul when it comes to your declarations. After all, you just admitted that you lied to me in order to get me to fight Gregor."

"True enough, but we have nothing to gain from lying to you this time."

Annja looked at Dzerchenko and Tupolov. Both of them wore such sweet smiles it made her stomach churn in disgust.

I don't trust either of those two idiots any farther than I can throw them. But what choice do I have?

"All right," she said.

"You agree?"

She looked up. "I said yes."

Dzerchenko clapped his hands. "Excellent. That is really good news, Annja. And we'll make sure Bob is taken care of straightaway."

"What do you mean?"

"We were about to remove him from life support when it looked like you weren't going to play ball with us."

"Well, get him back on it!" Annja shouted.

Tupolov disappeared and returned a moment later. Dzerchenko pointed at his clipboard. "This will be so enthralling, I assure you. Once we get our questions answered, that will be all there is."

Annja nodded. "Fine, fine. Whatever." She rested her hand on the wheel lock of the door leading out of the arena. "Just let me get the hell out of here already, would you? Gregor's body is starting to smell for some reason."

"That's due to some of the chemicals we pumped into him to accelerate his reaction time and thought processes. They're probably just leaking from his orifices and his wounds."

"Wherever they're leaking from, it's really beginning to stink down here," Annja said.

Dzerchenko and Tupolov smiled.

Annja heard a hiss and turned around.

At the far end of the arena, she could see grill-work high up on the wall. A faint yellow gas was seeping out of it.

She spun around. "What the hell is that?"

Dzerchenko's smile widened. "Just a little security for Tupolov and me."

Annja shook her head. This was getting ridiculous. "I told you that I would agree to answer your questions. There's no need for any gas."

"What if you try something on us? After all, you've still got your sword."

Annja hefted her blade. How she wanted to cut them both open. Instead, she frowned again. "I thought you wanted to ask me questions about it. Isn't it better if I have it available for you?"

"We'd prefer you put it away."

Annja smiled. "Turn the gas off."

Tupolov shook his head. "Not yet."

Annja glanced back at the grates. More of the yellow gas floated into the arena. Already she was starting to feel faint and somewhat woozy. Why would Tupolov and Dzerchenko want to gas her when they needed her to answer questions?

It didn't make sense.

Annja clenched her jaw. Those bastards weren't going to ask her questions at all. It had been a stall tactic in order to get the gas ready to pump in. They don't care one little bit about what I can do, Annja thought.

They want to turn me into another Gregor. Only better. One equipped with a sword.

Annja looked up at the window. She held up her sword and pointed at them. "This isn't going to work. I know what you're up to. I won't let you do it to me like you did to Gregor."

Dzerchenko and Tupolov just laughed and pointed at the yellow gas rapidly filling up the arena area.

Annja turned and looked back at the grates.

I have got to get out of here before it's too late.

Otherwise both Bob and I will die.

35

The gas continued to seep into the arena. Annja wasn't sure what kind of gas it was, but she knew for sure it was beginning to affect her. She tried to keep herself higher than the gas, which seemed to hover at about waist level.

Once it knocks me out, they'll drain the room and then come in and get me, Annja thought. After that, I'm the guinea pig I never wanted to be.

She glared up at Dzerchenko and Tupolov. They were engaged in conversation and not looking at her. How many times have they done something like this? she wondered. It's already old hat to them.

The thought of all the other people they'd probably killed made Annja sick. If not for me and Bob, I have to find some way to avenge their deaths at least.

Was she just being silly? Since when did she feel the need to avenge people she'd never even met before? It was a weird feeling that came over her.

What, am I channeling Joan of Arc now, too?

Annja frowned. The gas. It had to be the gas. The yellow mist was floating higher now, roughly on the same level as her stomach.

She hefted the sword. I wonder if this blade can shatter glass?

Annja moved farther back into the arena. Dzerchenko and Tupolov still paid her no mind.

She grinned. That's right. You boys just keep on about your business and don't mind me. As far as you know or care, I'll be unconscious soon enough.

Annja judged the distance and the angle. It just might work.

But what about me? How am I going to get up there to escape?

The viewing platform stood about ten feet above the arena area. And there was no way Annja could leap that high on her own.

Her head swam.

I have to try, she thought. I have to try to jump it. And if I fail, then at least I might take one of those sick bastards with me.

She backed up some more and turned the sword so it sat in her hand like a spear. I hope my aim is decent.

Annja aimed the tip of the sword right at the space between Dzerchenko and Tupolov. With any luck, she might rip them both apart. And if the sword penetrated the glass, then there might be a chance the gas would dissipate through the break.

Annja shook her head. It's the only option I've got.

She took one more step back, then jogged forward and hurled her sword.

As the sword rocketed toward the window, Dzerchenko and Tupolov suddenly saw the movement out of the corners of their eyes. As if in slow motion, they both turned. Annja saw the looks of surprise dash across their faces and she smiled.

Dzerchenko and Tupolov might have been ingesting stem-cell shakes, but their reaction to the sword looked incredibly slow to Annja. Dzerchenko started to move forward and bumped into Tupolov, who had turned to run in the opposite direction.

The tip of the sword impacted the glass.

Annja heard the crash as it shattered through, piercing and sending zigzag fault lines scoring through the rest of the viewing-window panel.

But the sword didn't stop there. It kept moving through the glass and in the next instant, it ripped into Tupolov's body from behind, shish-kabobing him as the tip jutted out of his chest.

He screamed once and then fell silent.

Annja wasn't through. She took a running start at the wall, trying to generate momentum as she did so. As she moved, the yellow gas churned in her wake.

Annja hit the base of the wall and drove herself up, taking another step off the wall as if she was running up it vertically.

She reached up and grabbed the ledge.

She grabbed with her other hand and then pulled herself up and into the laboratory.

Dzerchenko had been knocked off his feet when Tupolov took the sword in his chest. Bob was nowhere to be seen.

Tupolov was definitely dead. Annja grabbed her

sword and ripped it out of his body. Then she went over and hauled Dzerchenko up by his lapels and thrust the sword blade under his chin.

"Turn off the gas!" she screamed.

He nodded, already coughing as some of the gas leaked into the laboratory. Annja watched as he punched some buttons on a control panel and then leaned back against it, coughing some more.

"Where is he?" she said.

"Who?"

"Bob."

Dzerchenko pointed at Tupolov. "You killed him in cold blood."

Annja nodded. "And you should remember that. I'll do the same thing to you unless you do exactly what I tell you to do."

"Why did you kill him?"

"You would have killed me," Annja said.

Dzerchenko shook his head. "It wasn't about killing you. It was about using your talents to enhance our experiments. You would have truly been the unstoppable soldier we've always dreamed of creating."

Annja shook her head. "I'm no one's soldier."

Dzerchenko spit a stream of blood out of his mouth. "Bah, another idealist who thinks she doesn't have to stand for anything."

"The only thing I'm interested in standing for right now is my life and the life of my friend Bob."

Dzerchenko nodded. "Yes, yes, you've made that abundantly clear." He eyed her. "But tell me something. Do you really think you'll get away with this?"

Annja frowned. "Get away with what? I just want to leave."

"Yes, but it's really not that easy, now, is it?"

"Why wouldn't it be?"

"Well, obviously, Bob is in need of medical care. And there's really not a doctor around these parts for miles. The closest hospital is back in Magadan." He grinned. "You're a long way from rescuing Bob, my dear."

"Stop calling me that," Annja said.

Dzerchenko shrugged. "As you wish."

"Where is he?"

"He's back in the holding room. He's fine right now, but as I've already warned you, moving him would be a grave mistake."

"So what would you have me do—leave him here?"

Dzerchenko coughed once and spit a bit more blood. "I doubt very much you'd entrust him to me. Unless I'm mistaken."

Annja shook her head. "You're not."

"So, your option is to either move him and watch him die, or leave him here while you go get help. Quite the choice."

Annja looked at him. "What is it you want, Dzerchenko?"

"I want amnesty, of course. I don't want to be tied to this fiasco. Tupolov is dead—let him take the fall for it."

"Wow, I'm in awe of your loyalty."

Dzerchenko waved her off. "Please. We always knew it might come to this. And we were prepared to do what was necessary to ensure our own survival.

We had to make sure we weren't prosecuted for what we've done here."

"But I thought you said you had help from higher-ups. Surely they wouldn't allow you to get into trouble," Annja said mockingly.

Dzerchenko pushed himself off the control console and took a step around Tupolov's body. He bent and patted Tupolov on the head before looking back up at Annja. "Our backers aren't the people who are overtly in power. Nor would they be willing to expose themselves for the sake of two doctors. They're interested in results, not in controversy."

"I see."

Dzerchenko sighed and then stood back up. "We are something of a deniability, if you get my meaning."

"I do. But that doesn't make your life any easier."

"No. It does not."

Annja looked around. There was a lot that could implicate both of the scientists. "So, what now?"

"I propose something of a truce," Dzerchenko said.

Annja smiled. "You're kidding me."

"I assure you, my dear—" Dzerchenko caught himself. "Sorry. I assure you there is nothing humorous about my proposal. At the end of the day, I must be a pragmatist, as I've said before."

"And ensure your own survival," Annja said.

"Exactly."

"So how does this work? I leave you here with Bob? I go get help? Then what? You disappear or something?"

Dzerchenko took a breath and let it out slowly. "Actually, I think I'd probably be fine right where I am. I think I can go right back to playing the role of Father Jakob, the poor, unaware soul who had a network under his feet and never knew it."

"Oh, come on. You really think anyone will fall for that?"

Dzerchenko smiled. "Never overestimate the intelligence of the average person, Annja. They are more gullible than most people would admit."

"So, Tupolov takes the fall?"

"Yes. He will be seen as the main instigator of this mess."

Annja pointed at the computers. "They'll shut all this down. Confiscate the entire setup."

"Perhaps. But I will get more equipment."

"And you'll continue to do what you've been doing."

Dzerchenko smiled. "Would you believe me if I told you I'd be a good boy now?"

"Definitely not."

He laughed. "Then I won't insult your intelligence."

Annja hefted her sword. "What guarantee do I have that you won't kill Bob as soon as I leave?"

"Why would I?"

"Spite?"

Dzerchenko shook his head. "I have no reason to kill Bob. And I'm more than content with fading away for the time being. You go. I'll look after Bob while you're gone. When you get help and are on your way back, simply call me on my cell phone and let me know so I can extricate myself from this."

"And resume your role as the village priest."

Dzerchenko spread his arms. "These poor people, they need all the spiritual guidance I can offer."

Annja frowned. "The Bible. You ever read that book, Dzerchenko?"

"Of course. My role demands I am well versed in it."

"Any of it ever stick with you?"

He laughed. "Not one silly word of it."

"You're a real man of God."

Dzerchenko leaned closer. "I'm a real man of myself, Annja."

Annja didn't like it. She hated making a deal with Dzerchenko, but she needed his expert help to take care of Bob. A serious gunshot wound wasn't something she could afford to take lightly, even if he'd already been patched up. One small misstep could reopen the wound and Bob could bleed to death. Annja was determined not to see him die twice. Especially after losing Gregor.

"I need a minute with Bob before I go," she said.

Dzerchenko lit up like a bad aluminum Christmas tree. "I take it we have ourselves a deal?"

"Yes."

Dzerchenko held out his hand. "Care to make it official?"

Annja seriously thought about cutting his hand off, but resisted the urge. Instead, she simply looked at him. "If you double-cross me, I will slice all the skin from your body and roll you in salt."

Dzerchenko merely grinned. "That actually sounds like it might be fun."

36

"You're leaving me here?" The look in Bob's eyes made Annja's heart ache. She could tell it was taking all his strength to maintain his sanity.

"Your wound is too critical to try and get you out of here myself. It could tear open the sutures, and you'd bleed out before we got out of the village. I can't have that." She took his hand. "I saw you die once already. I'm not going through that ordeal again."

He sighed. "And the psycho doctor?"

"He says he'll take care of you."

Bob smirked. "You believe him?"

"I don't have much choice. I'm kind of stuck here."

"What's he get out of the deal?"

"Amnesty. His partner, the one I killed, takes the fall for all of this stuff, and he plays up the role of the victim in it."

Bob frowned and cleared his throat. "The poor village priest caught up in the middle of some horrible experiment. Tidy. He'll come out looking none the worse. Meanwhile, all sorts of people are dead."

Annja slid her parka on. "It's the best solution to the problem we're facing here."

"It's not a solution at all. That guy will get off and be free to keep doing what he's been doing. More people will die." Bob sighed. "I'd almost rather you killed him now and not worry about me."

"I can't do that," Annja said.

"Kill him or leave me?"

Annja smiled. "Leave you, pal. I'm getting you out of this situation intact. I swear it."

Bob nodded. "Where is he now?"

"Cleaning up the place so there's no evidence tying him to this. I don't know. Hell, he could be getting back into his priest robes for all I know."

"Don't be long," Bob whispered.

Annja squeezed his hand. "I won't. I promise. I'll be back as soon as I can get some real medical help to transport you back to Magadan."

Bob's eyes shone in the dim light. Annja gave him one last squeeze and turned away.

Back in the laboratory, Dzerchenko had indeed changed back into his robes. Annja shook her head. As a priest, he looked utterly disarming and kindly. But she knew what he really was—a monster of the worst magnitude.

"I'm leaving."

"So I see."

Annja thumbed over her back. "You keep an eye on him. Both eyes. And you'd better make sure he's good to go. As soon as I get back, I'm getting him the hell out of here."

Dzerchenko smiled. "I still know how to take care of people, Annja."

"Yeah, I know. You did a good job patching him up. Just make sure he stays that way. You're his guardian angel now. And if you screw that up, you won't like what I do to you."

Annja turned and left the laboratory. She quickly traversed a dimly lit tunnel to the set of stairs that led to the kitchen of the church. Annja stood in the doorway looking at the dim gray light of dawn just starting to peek into the church. The old lingering scent of incense hung in the air, and Annja took a deep breath.

Please keep him safe.

She ducked down the center aisle and then opened the front door. A breeze blew into her, but the air felt warmer than it had overnight. For the first time in a couple of days, Annja could see clear sky overhead. A break from all of the snow would be a welcome change. She headed down the main street of the village. She needed a truck or a car, something she could use to drive back to Magadan and get help.

She looked around. Most of the village looked to be one giant snowdrift. And even though there was no more snow falling, the wind blew the light, fluffy flakes up like a desert dust, clouding her vision. Annja could see piles of snow, but couldn't figure out if any vehicles lay beneath them.

She needed help.

A thin plume of smoke wafted out of a stovepipe

by the café. The windows were fogged up. Annja smiled. The cook might help her if she asked.

She knocked on the door and waited. Another brisk breeze sent a puff of snow into her face. She felt it melt and the ice-cold water run down her face.

On the other side of the door, she could hear the clicks of a bolt being thrown back. There was a grunt and then the door swung open.

A blast of hot air belted Annja like a right cross. She leaned back and then smiled. "Good morning."

The cook recognized her and smiled. She stepped back and invited Annja inside.

Annja stepped in and looked around. No one else was in the café. The tables were all set. The cook rested her hands on her hips and smiled broadly. *"Da?"*

Annja frowned. Communicating was going to be a challenge. "I need a car. Or a truck."

The cook looked at her and frowned.

Annja sighed. "Automobile? I need to get to Magadan. My friend is injured badly and he needs a doctor."

At the mention of Magadan, the cook's face lit up. "Magadan."

Annja nodded. "Yes."

The cook made a shape with her hands and then the appropriate car sounds. Annja smiled. *"Da."*

The cook nodded and then pointed to a seat at the table. "You. Sit."

Annja sat at the table and took a breath. Something smelled delicious. She hadn't realized how famished she was.

The cook returned from the kitchen with a plate of what looked like scrambled eggs and some type of meat. She brought a cup of steaming coffee and set it in front of Annja.

"You."

Annja smiled. "Thank you. But I have to get back to Magadan. My friend is hurt."

The cook frowned, shook her head and pointed at the plate. "Eat."

Annja picked up a fork. Perhaps it wouldn't make a difference if she bolted a bit of breakfast first. At least this way, she'd be in good shape for traveling.

The cook watched her eat. Occasionally, she'd nod and say something indecipherable in Russian.

Annja shoveled forkfuls of food into her mouth. She couldn't stop eating the breakfast. "It's really good," she said around mouthfuls.

The cook sipped a cup of coffee. "Magadan?"

Annja nodded. "Yes. *Da.* My friend is hurt." She made a show of impersonating someone who had been injured.

The cook laughed.

Annja sighed and pushed the plate away. "That was fantastic. Thank you so much. But I really need to get going now."

The cook shook her head and pointed at the clock high up on the yellowed wall. "Magadan. No."

Annja frowned. "What? You mean it's too early? No one's up yet? Something like that?"

The cook just looked at her. Annja sighed and stood. "I need to get going. I'll find someone else to help me with the car."

The cook stood up and tried to push Annja back into the seat. *"Nyet!"*

Annja dodged her and set her feet. "Cut it out. Don't try to stop me. I need to get back to Magadan."

The cook's face fell. *"Nyet, nyet, nyet."*

Annja slid her gloves on and walked to the door. "Thanks again for breakfast. Really. I appreciate it."

She pulled the door open and walked outside.

Weird town, she decided. I need to get out of this place. With Bob.

She looked up and down the street. Where to find a car?

She headed back to the hotel. Maybe Tupolov's wife would have the keys to a vehicle she could take. She smirked. It'd be the least she could do, considering her husband was a dead nut.

I'll have to tell her, Annja thought.

But not right now. Her priority was getting the vehicle and driving back to Magadan. When she got back, she could break the news.

As she approached the inn, she could make out several muddled sets of footprints in the deep snow. By the look of it, people were at least awake now.

She stepped into the inn.

Small puddles of water lay about the floor just inside the door. She could see coats hanging off the line of pegs stuck into the knobby wall by the fireplace. There were several pairs of boots underneath them.

"Hello?" Annja's voice rang out, but she could hear nothing. There seemed to be no activity within the inn.

She walked over to the kitchen and pushed through the swinging door. The kitchen was rustic but functional. Big iron pots hung from a rack suspended overhead. A block of wood housed several large knives. In the back, she could see a bunch of garlic garlands dangling from another rack. And the air smelled of last night's big meal.

Annja walked through the kitchen and toward the back pantry. She thought she could hear something.

Static?

As she approached the back of the pantry, Annja could see a small radio transmitter. A base microphone sat nearby.

Maybe she didn't have to drive to Magadan after all. Maybe she could radio for help.

She sat down on a nearby chair and flipped a few of the switches and dials. Sharp bursts of static echoed throughout the pantry. Annja keyed the mike.

"Mayday, mayday, mayday. Trying to reach anyone in Magadan. Over."

Nothing but static replied.

Annja frowned and tried to remember anything she knew about radios. With the clear skies overhead, she shouldn't have any trouble getting reception or transmitting a signal.

Unless the antenna was down.

If the storm wrecked the antenna, Annja thought, I could be wasting my time here.

She changed the frequency and was rewarded with a break in the static as a voice came from the speaker.

"Hello?"

The static burst cleared again. *"Amerikanski?"*

Annja grinned. "Hello? Can someone help me? I need help from Magadan."

Static reclaimed the airwaves and Annja swore under her breath. She'd heard someone and they'd heard her. She had to keep trying.

The static cleared then. "Magadan?"

Annja keyed the mike. "Yes, Magadan! I have a friend here who is injured. I need medical help sent immediately."

She released the send key and waited. Through the static, she heard the voice again. "Magadan. Magadan. *Da*. Okay. I hear you. You are okay?"

Annja keyed the mike again. "Yes. I'm okay. My friend is not okay. He needs help."

The voice came back immediately this time. "Where are you? I will send doctor."

Annja exhaled a rush of breath. "Thank God." She keyed the microphone again and cleared her throat. "Thank you, thank you. We're in—"

"Stop." The voice came from behind her.

Annja turned.

The innkeeper's wife—Tupolov's mate—stood there holding a very ugly pistol in one hand. The barrel was aimed at Annja's heart.

Annja held up her hands. "Don't."

Behind her, the voice at the other end of the radio kept talking. "Hello? Where are you? Hello?"

But Annja couldn't respond.

37

Annja eyed Tupolov's wife. The gun she held didn't waver at all. And her eyes looked as cold as steel left out in the Siberian winter. Annja moved very slowly, turning around so she could fully face her. "Don't shoot."

Tupolov's wife responded by thumbing the hammer back on the pistol. "You killed him."

Annja took a breath. There didn't seem to be much point lying about it. "Yes." But how had she found out?

"Why? Why did you kill him?"

"He meant to kill me. I did it in self-defense."

"That's not what I was told."

Annja licked her lips. She had to play this carefully if she had any hope of avoiding the bullet. The situation was worsened by the fact that Annja was sitting in a chair. Her movement would be restricted.

"Who told you?" she asked.

Tupolov's wife smirked. "Who do you think?"

Dzerchenko. It had to be. Annja frowned. If Dzerchenko had been in touch with Tupolov's wife, that meant Bob might be in grave danger. Annja had to take care of Tupolov's wife and get back to Bob.

She eased the chair around some more. The gun barrel was now aimed at her head. Tupolov's wife shook her head.

"Do not move any more or I will shoot you."

Annja kept her hands up. "I understand. Did you know what your husband was doing?"

She shook her head. "Whatever he did, it was the right thing for us. I loved him dearly."

Her English was too good, too polished, Annja thought. "You've been schooled abroad."

Tupolov's wife smiled. "You have keen ears. But you don't speak Russian?"

"Not much. It's a language I've never been able to get to grips with."

Tupolov's wife shrugged. "No matter. It doesn't matter if you speak the language or not. Either way it translates to you dying."

"Tupolov was bad. He did horrible things to people. He killed people. You understand this?" Annja said.

"The people he killed deserved what they got."

Annja looked around. There was nothing within reach she could use as a weapon. "You ran this hotel and lured travelers here so he could experiment on them with Dzerchenko," Annja said with a sudden realization of the woman's role.

"No one missed them. No one ever came looking for them."

Annja shook her head. "That doesn't make it right."

"Does it make it right that you killed him, then?"

"Self-defense," Annja said. "I had no choice."

Tupolov's wife nodded. "Just as I have no choice. Now stand up."

Annja stood. "Where are we going?"

"You saw the boots and coats in the other room?"

"Yes."

"We have company. Some people here are eager to meet with you."

Annja frowned. What the hell did that mean? No one even knew she was here. How could there be anyone here to meet with her? It didn't make sense.

The woman gestured with the pistol. "We're going upstairs now. Go through this door and go upstairs. I will be right behind you the entire time. If you try anything, I will shoot you."

"I won't," Annja said. If nothing else, she wanted to see who these people were.

She pushed through the kitchen door and then turned right to the steps. She could sense Tupolov's wife behind her, but at a measured distance. She was far enough away that Annja wouldn't be able to attack her without taking a bullet.

Not a good position to be in, she decided.

The stairs creaked as they walked up them. Annja kept her hands held up so Tupolov's wife wouldn't get jumpy on the trigger. "You could give me the gun now, and we could settle this in a better way," she tried.

Tupolov's wife jammed the barrel into her back. "Stop talking and keep moving. I don't want to present you to our guests as a corpse."

Annja crested the steps. "Now where?"

"Down the hall. The last room on the left."

Annja started down the hall. Her boots sounded loud on the wooden floor and threadbare carpet. She passed her old room and then Gregor's. She winced at the thought of what he'd become. And what she had been forced to do to him.

The door at the end on the left beckoned. From behind her, Annja heard Tupolov's wife clear her throat. "That's far enough."

Annja stopped and turned slightly so she could see. Tupolov's wife gestured at the door. "Open it."

Annja rested her hand on the doorknob and turned it. The door opened easily. Inside, Annja counted four men. All of them looked stocky. Their faces were a bright red. Annja spotted several open bottles of vodka on the table in the room.

The largest of the men smiled broadly as Annja entered. "Ah, so here she is!"

Tupolov's wife came in behind Annja and stood off to the side. Her gun stayed on Annja the entire time.

Annja looked at the portly man in front of her. "Sorry, do I know you?"

He laughed. "No, I would be surprised if you did."

"You know me, though."

He nodded. "Oh yes, I most certainly do. Annja Creed, world-famous archaeologist, television host and all-around interesting woman."

Annja cocked an eyebrow. "Thanks. I think."

He stood back and gestured to a seat. "Please, please, sit down. We'd like to talk to you."

Annja sat. The portly man held out his hand. "My name is Mischa. I have other names but you can call me Mischa. It makes everything that much easier than long Russian names, don't you think?"

Annja glanced at the other men in the room. They all seemed to have paused, as if waiting for something. Annja could see the look of death in their eyes. Whoever they were, she didn't feel any safer now than she had with Tupolov's wife.

"Nice to meet you, Mischa."

He grinned and then spoke rapid-fire Russian over his shoulder. One of the men chuckled and Mischa glanced back at Annja. "Vladimir thought you would be…difficult. That you would make trouble for us. I told him otherwise and we bet on it. Needless to say, he now owes me."

Annja smiled. "Very nice."

Tupolov's wife stood nearby still shooting daggers at Annja. Mischa glanced at her. "You can go now."

Tupolov's wife shook her head. "No. I must kill her to avenge my husband. You said I could. I was only to bring her here and you would let me have her when you were through with her."

Mischa sighed and Annja saw him nod. There was a brief puff-puff sound and Annja heard two shell casings clink to the ground. She turned and saw Tupolov's wife crumple to the ground, twin black holes punched through her forehead.

Her gun slid to the floor.

Mischa shook his head. "People are always so temperamental. And really, there's no need for it. Business is business. It gets complicated when people allow their emotions to interfere." He eyed Annja. "Don't you agree?"

"I suppose," she said cautiously.

Mischa smiled. "You're wary. I was told you are a careful one." He shrugged. "I don't blame you. If I were in your position, I would feel exactly as you do now. I would make sure I said as little as possible while trying to fathom the people across from me."

"That's about it," Annja said.

"Aren't you curious?"

"About what?"

Mischa leaned back. "About who we are?"

"I'm more curious about Tupolov's wife."

Mischa sniffed. "She became problematical. We no longer need her."

Annja nodded. "All right. Now I'm curious as to who you are."

Mischa took a drink of vodka and then put his glass back on the table next to him. "I think you met some associates of ours."

Annja swallowed.

Mischa caught it, though, and laughed. "Yes, Yuri and Oleg were my men. Scouts, so to speak. We sent them ahead to handle things here and it looks like they got themselves handled instead, eh?"

Annja shook her head. "They were going to kill us."

Mischa laughed. "You're going to use the same excuse on me that you used on Tupolov's wife there? That you killed them in self-defense?"

Annja shook her head. "I don't go around purposefully killing people, Mischa. If I kill, it's always in self-defense."

"I see."

Annja waited while Mischa finished his drink.

Then he rubbed his hands together. "Fortunately for you, I'm not upset."

"You're not?"

He shrugged. "Yes, they were dear to me. All of my men are. But they knew the risks associated with our line of work. And they embraced those risks. They should be commended for falling in battle."

"They fought hard," Annja said.

Mischa nodded. "I know they did." He eyed her. "And you should be commended for killing them."

"I wasn't alone," Annja said.

"Regardless," Mischa said. "Your skill prevailed. And that is worth a nod of respect."

Annja said nothing while Mischa got himself a refill of vodka. He took a sip and then belched into his hand. "Pardon me."

Annja smiled. "I don't mean to be rude, but what are we doing here?"

Mischa pointed at her. "What I am doing is trying to figure out whether I should kill you or not."

"Ah," Annja said.

"You see, while I am not one to hold a grudge, my men here were very close to the men you killed. And as such, they want revenge for their fallen brothers. I am trying to decide if I should honor their request for your death or not."

Annja leaned back. "Well, don't let me interrupt your thought process."

Mischa smiled. "Why don't you tell me what happened here?"

"In town?"

"I sent Yuri and Oleg here to scare the villagers into

moving and giving up their land rights. The area is filled with natural resources my companies can exploit."

Annja nodded. "I think they were trying to do just that when they followed us into the mountains."

"Why did you go into the mountains?" Mischa asked.

Annja took a breath and related the entire story of Khosadam and how things had unraveled to the point that Annja was looking for medical help for Bob.

When she finished, Mischa looked at her curiously. "And no part of what you just told me was fabricated for my pleasure?"

Annja shook her head. "I couldn't make this stuff up if I tried."

Mischa nodded. "Interesting. And you say this Dzerchenko character is creating supersoldiers?"

"He's trying to. Supposedly, he's backed by someone very powerful."

Mischa pursed his lips. "Fascinating. I never thought I would ever hear a story like this, but then it just goes to prove you can't assume anything in life, eh?"

"That's what I've been learning," Annja said.

"And so here we are," Mischa said.

"Here we are," Annja agreed. She was unsure how much more she could take.

Mischa looked at Annja for another full minute before finally clapping his hands and standing up. "All right, then."

Annja started. "You're going to kill me?"

"I don't know yet. But for right now, I want to see this man Dzerchenko. His work intrigues me."

Annja shook her head. "He'll pretend he's just a priest."

Mischa laughed. "He can pretend he's an earthworm for all I care. But when I ask him questions, he had better be honest with me. Otherwise, he may just die in his fantasy world."

Annja followed Mischa out of the room, wondering just how much longer Bob could hold on.

38

Mischa's men led the way back down the street to the church. As they walked, Mischa stayed close to Annja. "You've been enjoying your stay in my country?"

Annja shrugged. "I haven't really seen all that much, to be honest. I flew into Moscow and then took the train straight to Magadan."

"Shame," Mischa said. "That's no way to experience Russia. You should take your time. There is a great deal to see."

Annja spread her arms. "Supposedly there's a tunnel that runs from the hotel to the underground laboratory at the church. But I had no idea where to look. Sorry."

"The fresh air does us all good," Mischa said. "After all, we never can tell when it might be our last, eh?"

Annja glanced at him. Was he implying she might be killed and she should relish this moment? She closed her eyes for a split second and saw the sword ready to draw out. Seeing it gave her a bit of comfort.

What did Mischa want with Dzerchenko, anyway? Why not just storm the laboratory and kill him? That way, Mischa and his men could take over the village and plunder its natural resources. While Annja might normally frown on that activity, she wanted nothing more than to get Bob to safety and see Dzerchenko's operation stopped.

They reached the church. Mischa looked at Annja. "Now, let me ask you something very important."

"Yes?"

"You haven't led us into a trap, have you? This man Dzerchenko isn't waiting up there ready to ambush us, is he?"

Annja shook her head. "The last thing he knew, I was on my way out of this village. I was supposed to get a car or truck and drive back to Magadan. Once there, I'd get help and alert the police about what happened here."

Mischa's eyes never left her. "Anything else?"

"When we were headed back, I was supposed to call his cell phone and let him know. That way, he'd be able to get ready."

"Ready?"

Annja sighed. "The deal was I'd blame everything on Tupolov. Dzerchenko would play the unwitting dupe, the humble country priest."

"I see."

Annja looked at him. "That's the truth. I've been nothing but honest with you. All I want is to get my friend out of here," she said.

"What happened to him?"

"During the fight in the cave with your men, he

took a bullet. I watched him die, but this guy Dzerchenko apparently brought him back to life."

Mischa's eyes widened. "Is that so?"

"Yeah."

"All right." He nodded at his men, and they fanned out on either side of the church. Two of them crested the steps and waited on either side of the front doors. Annja watched them move in perfect choreography as they swung low and entered the church, each man taking a side.

After a few seconds, they reemerged and waved Mischa and the others in.

"Impressive," Annja said.

Mischa nodded. "I never settle for mediocre talent. I want my men to be the very best. I've had them all trained to a fine edge and I believe it shows."

"It certainly seems to."

They walked into the church. Mischa leaned closer to Annja. "You lead the way. My men will back you up. If any shooting starts, I advise you to hug the ground and let us handle things. Okay?"

"Okay," Annja said.

Annja walked down the center aisle. Somewhere beneath her, Dzerchenko waited with Bob. The key, she thought, would be getting Bob away from Dzerchenko as fast as possible. Once Dzerchenko heard them coming down, he would suspect a trap and might kill Bob out of spite.

She reached the kitchen door and pushed through it. The air seemed still. Annja couldn't tell if Dzerchenko had even been up top since she'd left.

He's probably waiting for my phone call, she thought.

One of Mischa's men tapped her on the shoulder. Annja turned and he gestured that he should go first at the door leading down. He held a compact Kalashnikov submachine gun in his hands and he looked very able to use it.

Annja leaned out of his way and he approached the door. He set the gun down and ran his fingers all over the lip of the door, peered underneath and generally tried to examine the door structure as much as possible.

Booby traps. Annja hadn't even thought that Dzerchenko might try something like that. She'd made the mistake of assuming he wouldn't do that.

Mischa's man came away from the door with a low whistle. In his hands, Annja spotted a monofilament wire and a palm-size grenade. Not only had Dzerchenko booby-trapped the door, but he'd also done so with enough explosive to kill everyone nearby.

Mischa stepped forward and examined the booby trap without saying a word. He nodded to his man, who pocketed the grenade. Mischa glanced at Annja and waggled his eyebrows. It seemed that Dzerchenko was a bit more careful than Annja had given him credit for being. She cursed her mistake. She should have known better from Gregor's cautions.

Another one of Mischa's men moved to the door. He cracked the door and Annja felt a warm breeze waft into the room. Mischa's man edged his way into the darkness, and Annja strained her ears to catch any sound that he might make.

He was completely silent.

These guys are good, she decided. Mischa certainly wasn't lying about the talent pool he hired from.

The man reemerged about four minutes later and nodded at Mischa. Their hands seemed to carry on a silent conversation, almost like sign language, but a different dialect entirely.

When it was over, Mischa nodded at his other men and they all vanished down the black rabbit hole. Then Mischa nodded to Annja and pointed.

Time to go down.

Annja went first and Mischa floated along behind her. She noticed that his footsteps were as light and quiet as those of his men, despite his bulky size. Annja figured him for military at some point in his life. He seemed far too disciplined to not have had any such experience.

Annja's boots gripped the stairs. From below, she could see the dim outline of Mischa's men as they descended. They were nicely spaced, on alternating sides. Annja could barely make out the barrels of their submachine guns nosing their way through the darkness, ready for any sign of trouble.

Remarkably, Annja felt safer then than at any other point during the trip thus far. There was something strangely comforting about the presence of Mischa and his men. And while Annja knew that they could just as easily shoot her dead as anyone else, she was happy not to be alone for this battle.

Dzerchenko wouldn't be able to spring any nasty surprises on them. The numbers simply weren't in his favor.

Annja reached the bottom of the staircase. Mischa

came up behind her and she could feel his body heat. His voice tickled the hairs on her neck as he whispered into her ear. "Now where do we go?"

Annja could make out the tunnel she'd traveled down on her way out a few hours before. She pointed in the dim light and instantly, Mischa's men headed down the tunnel, still with their guns ready to fire.

"Come along," Mischa said quietly.

Annja glanced down and saw the silhouette of a small pistol in Mischa's hand. Something about that made her smile. Mischa wasn't taking any chances with Dzerchenko.

Or maybe he just doesn't trust me, Annja thought. Smart guy.

But she really didn't have a plan to escape. She merely hoped to get to Bob and get them both out of there. Mischa could talk to Dzerchenko, and they could work out a deal where they ruled the world for all Annja cared. As long as she and Bob got out of there, that was what mattered the most.

Annja kept walking and could see more light coming from somewhere up ahead. We're getting close, she thought. Her heart started beating faster. She closed her eyes for a second and saw the sword still ready for her.

She almost smirked at the thought of the expressions on the faces of Mischa and his men when they saw the sword an instant before it cut them down.

But Annja would only kill them if she absolutely had to. There had been enough horrors already.

If she could get away without killing any more people, Annja would definitely be happier for it.

The light grew stronger as she continued down the

tunnel. Funny how many details of this I missed in my rush to get out of here earlier, she thought. The tunnel had smooth walls, and small, dim lights spaced every fifteen feet. The lights did little more than keep the tunnel from being in absolute darkness. And the majority of the light came from the door ahead of them.

Annja turned a corner and saw the brilliant yellow light flooding the tunnel. Mischa's men had stopped just short of where it got bright, waiting for their boss to show up.

Mischa glanced ahead and then nodded at them. They slunk closer to the door, trying to squeeze into the walls of the tunnel on either side, rather than allow themselves to be framed in the bright light. They stacked on either side of the door.

Mischa held up his hand and they froze.

Annja stopped, as well, although she didn't know why. Maybe Mischa had such dominant spirit that her body simply responded to it.

He whispered in her ear again, "Is that it?"

Annja nodded. "He'll be in there with my friend."

"You will go in first," Mischa said.

Annja turned and looked at him. "Me?"

He smiled. "Better you than us. When he sees you, he'll let his guard down and then we'll rush him so we can have a nice chat."

Annja shook her head. "He'll wonder why I didn't call."

"Tell him your phone is broken—I don't care."

"He'll wonder how I happened to get past his grenade booby trap."

Mischa smiled and his teeth seemed to glow in the

dim light. "Tell him you were an army brat and your dad worked in explosive ordnance disposal." He frowned. "Look, it doesn't matter. Just walk in and let him see you."

Annja sighed. "Fine."

She turned and faced the open doorway. Beyond it, Bob waited for her. She only hoped Dzerchenko wasn't standing over him with a scalpel. Knowing Dzerchenko, I'll be lucky if he hasn't turned Bob into one of those creatures, she thought.

Annja held her breath and walked forward. She could feel the eyes of Mischa's men on her as she moved closer. Their guns looked terribly lethal close up, and Annja felt a shiver run down her spine as she moved past them.

So much death in such a tiny little thing, she thought.

The light hurt her eyes as she got closer. She could feel Mischa somewhere behind her. He'd move in with her, but at a distance. Annja expected that his men would move as soon as she said anything to Dzerchenko.

She took a moment to check that she could still draw her sword. With her eyes closed, she could see it hovering in her mind's eye.

She exhaled. I'm ready.

She opened her eyes and walked forward. Ten more steps and she'd be through the door. She kept blinking her eyes, trying to acclimate them as fast as possible to the sudden illumination.

Two of Mischa's men nodded at her as if she were a part of some special-operations team ready to storm a building. One of them actually winked at her.

She walked through the doorway.

The lighting was intense and Annja brought her hands up to her eyes, shielding them somewhat from the harsh glare.

"Dzerchenko?"

Her voice sounded louder than she'd wanted it to.

"Dzerchenko?"

She felt movement around her and knew that Mischa's men had come rushing in.

She blinked again and her vision finally cleared. Around her, she could see the laboratory. Most of the equipment had vanished. Only a few large units remained, humming away in the corner.

Mischa stepped up beside Annja. "It would appear that we have ourselves a small problem."

Annja nodded.

Dzerchenko was gone.

And so was Bob.

39

"Where are they?"

Annja shook her head. "I don't know. This is where I left them." She turned and looked in the holding room she and Bob had been held in. "He's gone."

"Your friend?"

"Yes."

Mischa pulled at his lip. "I'm not going to insult you by suggesting you lied to me and my men. You seem much too intelligent for such juvenile antics."

"Thank you," Annja said.

"However, the fact remains that we have a problem. If neither Dzerchenko nor your friend are around, then they must be somewhere. We need to find out where they went."

"I'll gladly help you."

Mischa waved over one of his men. Annja recognized him as the one who had disarmed the booby trap. Mischa spoke to him in low mutters for a moment. The man responded and Mischa nodded.

He looked back at Annja. "My man here says that it's possible the booby trap was positioned from the outside rather than down here underground."

"Which means what?" Annja asked.

"Which means that Dzerchenko could have set it as he exited the door. We were supposed to be killed by it. It wasn't a precaution at all."

Annja sighed. Dzerchenko had tricked her and she'd fallen for it. And now Bob was once again in harm's way. "When I find that guy—"

Mischa grinned. "When *we* find him. We're together on this, Annja. I hope you realize that."

"You're not going to kill me after this?" she asked.

Mischa shrugged. "I don't see any need to. You just want to get home. I don't imagine what we do interests you that much, now does it?"

"Get me and my friend on a plane and you can have at it as far as I'm concerned."

"You really are quite smart." Mischa chuckled. "Too bad you won't stay around for some sightseeing. I'd very much love to get to know you better."

"Some other time," Annja said.

Mischa nodded. "So, where would he go?"

Annja looked around the laboratory. Dzerchenko could have made his way back down the other tunnel to the caves and gotten into the mountains. But would he? Annja doubted it. With Bob in critical condition, he had to stay close to civilization if he wanted to keep him from dying. And like it or not, Annja had to admit that Dzerchenko was probably looking to turn Bob into another experiment. He'd keep him alive.

"They've got to be in town somewhere."

Mischa nodded. "That's what I would think, too."

Annja looked at him. "When did you and your men get here?"

"Last night. We arrived at the inn very early this morning."

Annja smirked. "We probably missed each other by a few minutes. I went out looking for Gregor last night after he disappeared."

"Gregor?"

"Another man we were traveling with."

"What became of him?"

Annja paused. "Dzerchenko made him into something awful. I faced him in combat."

"And you killed him?"

"Yes."

Mischa looked impressed. "You really are something else, aren't you, Annja Creed?"

Yes, I am, she thought. But what I am, I have no idea. She shrugged. "I did what was necessary to ensure my survival."

Mischa looked at her. "So, we're going back to the village, then."

"Yes."

Mischa's men cleared out of the laboratory. They returned along the tunnel to the steps and climbed back up into the kitchen. Mischa's bomb man went to the door again, checking to make sure they hadn't been lured into the cellar to kill them. He pronounced it clear, and they got back into the kitchen without event.

Instantly, Mischa put his finger to his lips.

Voices. Annja could hear them clearly. But something about the tone of them seemed odd. She glanced at Mischa. "What is that?"

Mischa listened and then seemed surprised. "Praying?"

He waved two of his men to the kitchen door. Both of them framed it and then slid the door open a tiny crack.

The volume of the voices grew louder with the door open a speck. Mischa's men returned and one of them whispered into his ear. Mischa nodded and looked at Annja.

"The church is full of worshipers."

"Mass?"

"That's right."

Annja shook her head. This was bizarre. "Who is the priest leading the service?"

Mischa shrugged. "They say he's fairly nondescript. Slightly stooped over. Nothing remarkable about him."

Dzerchenko. It had to be him. Who else would be leading a church service in this village? "I think that's our guy."

"The priest?"

"I told you that was his disguise."

Mischa looked a bit uncomfortable. "Yes, but, well, he's a priest."

Annja cocked an eyebrow. "Has that ever stopped you before?"

"Well, I don't know. I've never had to deal with the church in this way before."

"It's not the church," Annja said. "He's an imposter trying to hide among his flock. It's not like he's a real priest."

Mischa didn't look convinced, but he glanced at Annja and nodded. "All right. I need a moment to figure out how we're going to pull this off."

He huddled up with his men and while he did so, Annja crept to the door and peeked out. All of the pews were filled with people. Annja saw villagers she'd never seen before. She saw men and women only, no children.

Their heads were bowed in prayer as Dzerchenko led them with his arms raised toward heaven.

The only place you're going is straight to hell, Annja thought.

She scanned the crowd but couldn't see Bob anywhere. Maybe he's in the office near the front of the church, she thought.

Dzerchenko's flock seemed serious about their worship. Their low monotone voices hummed through the church, making Annja's head buzz a little bit. Dzerchenko's voice was easily distinguishable from all the others since it carried them along.

Mischa's hand rested on Annja's shoulder. "We have a plan."

Annja let the door slide shut again and turned back to Mischa. "Okay, I'm listening."

Mischa thumbed over his shoulder. "Two of my men will exit here by that window. They'll proceed around to the front of the church and at the countdown, they'll come in and post at either of the far corners."

"Got it."

"At the same time, we will exit here and my other two men will post at these nearest corners. You and I will handle Dzerchenko."

"So, you're trying to bottle up the church and keep anyone from leaving."

Mischa nodded. "I think that's the best plan. If we can keep it contained, we don't have to kill anyone. We can grab Dzerchenko, get him to reveal where he's stowed your friend and then he and I can have ourselves a talk about his future."

It was a simple and easily workable plan. It just might work. Annja nodded. "I like it."

Mischa smiled. "So glad you approve."

"Well, it's easy and it has a strong chance of working."

Mischa looked at her. "It *will* work. My men will see to it." He looked away and nodded at his two men by the window.

Annja watched as they pushed hard on the window, forcing it up from the sill. Both men snaked through the opening and vanished.

Mischa checked his watch. "Two minutes."

His other men each held up two fingers. Mischa nudged Annja away from the door. "Let my men take control first and then we will come out."

Annja nodded and stepped back. Mischa's men took up their positions by the door. Annja heard Mischa say something low and inaudible. Both of his men nodded.

Mischa's voice was lower now, and Annja could tell there was some tension in it. "One minute now."

Annja closed her eyes. Her sword still hovered

right where she expected it to be. She felt a wave of calm wash over her. For the first time, she felt as if she wasn't about to bite off more than she could chew.

"You okay?"

She opened her eyes. "Fine."

Mischa nodded. "Thirty seconds."

Mischa's men did a final check on their weapons, each one carefully checking the safety and making sure he had a round in the chamber, ready to fire. They looked at each other and nodded.

"Twenty seconds."

The men looked a bit more tense now. Annja could see it in the way they hunched forward. She could see the barrels of their weapons held obliquely low, just off the horizon. She recognized the position as low-ready. From where they slung their weapons, both men could bring target and fire to them in an instant.

These guys are good, she decided. Trained professionals about to do what they did best. Annja was glad she was on this side of the door.

She smirked. What strange bedfellows the world could make. Here she was about to storm a church with Russian *mafiya* members in the hope they could rescue Bicycle Bob from crazy scientist Dzerchenko.

Annja wondered what Mischa intended to do with Dzerchenko. Then she just as quickly decided she didn't care.

"Ten seconds."

Mischa's men were breathing deeply now. Annja knew they were trying to flush their systems with as much oxygen as possible. As soon as they broke into the main church, their muscles would devour the oxygen supplies as adrenaline kicked into overdrive.

She found it fascinating to watch them prepare for it.

Mischa's voice was quiet but urgent in her ear. "Five seconds."

Annja took a breath.

Mischa counted down the final seconds.

Mischa's men seemed to explode through the kitchen door as one entity. From somewhere down near the front of the church, Annja could hear the main doors burst inward.

Mischa's men shouted commands in strident Russian to the parishioners.

Mischa's hand stayed firm on Annja's shoulder. "They'll call us out when they've got it under control."

Annja nodded. So far, she hadn't heard a single scream ring out. That was weird. If armed men broke into a church service she was attending, she could count on at least some mild hysteria from some of the older folks in the church.

But nothing seemed to surprise the parishioners here.

She glanced at Mischa. "They're not screaming."

His eyes narrowed. "Maybe they're in shock. They might confuse my men for the second coming."

"I don't know," Annja said.

One of Mischa's men shouted something. Mischa released his hold. "Let's go."

They pushed through the kitchen door, and Annja could see Mischa's men at every corner, their guns trained on the crowd.

Annja turned and looked at Dzerchenko.

He smiled at her. "Welcome back, Annja Creed."

Annja shook her head. "Forget it—where did you put Bob?"

Dzerchenko smiled some more. "Aren't you even interested in meeting my flock?"

He spread his arms and Annja heard a sudden rumble of movement from behind her.

She turned.

Every parishioner stood up. But something was wrong. Their hands.

Annja whipped her head back at Dzerchenko. "You didn't."

He grinned. "Meet my life's work, *my dear*. And prepare for the ultimate demonstration of my power."

40

Mischa's men waited just long enough for him to nod once, and then all hell let loose. Their submachine guns opened up and ripped into the parishioners. They howled as the bullets tore into them, shredding clothes and skin. Blood sprayed everywhere as Mischa's men kept up their assault.

Mischa gripped Annja's shoulder. Annja looked at him and he simply shook his head. There would be no mercy given to the parishioners.

One of Mischa's men dropped a magazine and slid another into its place, but as he did so, one of the parishioners reached out a metallic claw and sliced into his gun hand. He screamed and dropped his gun.

Instantly he was pulled to the floor by the claws.

His screams were drowned out by a renewed burst of gunfire from Mischa's other men.

Mischa brought his own gun up and double-tapped a parishioner attempting to crawl out of the nearby pew. His bullets slapped into the parishioner's forehead, exploding his skull all over the floor.

Annja bit back the flood of bile in her mouth.

Stained-glass windows exploded as stray bullets broke them into a million bits of colored glass. Behind her, Dzerchenko looked horrified as his creatures were being cut down.

Another one of Mischa's men took a slash across his belly. Annja watched as the crimson line on his stomach seemed to unfurl the contents of his abdomen onto the floor. He sank down beneath a tide of corpses.

Mischa's two closest men backed up a few steps, trying to get some distance from the parishioners who hadn't been shot and who were clambering over the pews like zombies.

Mischa's own pistol barked three more times, and Annja saw two more creatures go down.

"This is getting dangerous," Mischa said.

Annja nodded. "Get Dzerchenko. Maybe he can stop them."

Mischa nodded and made a run for the altar, where Dzerchenko stood. He put his pistol up to Dzerchenko's temple and eased back the trigger. "Make them stop," he ordered.

Dzerchenko smiled. "I don't want to do that."

Mischa pressed the barrel of the pistol into his temple. "You either tell them to stop right now or I will decorate this place with your brains."

Dzerchenko eyed him and then nodded once. "Very well. I will stop them for the time being. However, they are very hungry. And they haven't eaten in days. I may not be able to control them for long."

"Just do it."

Dzerchenko held up his hands and then shouted, "Stop!"

The effect was instant. The creatures stopped and sank back into the pews as if nothing had even happened. Aside from the corpses of their fallen comrades, and the puddles of blood and empty shell casings, nothing much had changed.

A stiff breeze blew in from the broken windows. Mischa's men changed magazines.

Mischa looked at them and nodded. "Finish it."

Their guns erupted.

Dzerchenko screamed, "No!"

But it was too late to save his creations. Mischa's men systematically cut down every last one of the parishioners. They sat there accepting their fate as the men walked up and down the pews, slaughtering them all.

Annja shook her head. Such barbarism. At one time all of those creatures had been people. But Dzerchenko had gotten his hands on them and turned them into something not of this world.

She glared at him. "Their deaths are on your hands."

Dzerchenko pointed at Mischa. "He ordered them killed."

"You killed them a long time ago. They've only been wishing for death to free themselves. You stole their lives from them. You deserve nothing less than the same," Annja said.

Dzerchenko frowned. "I still have something you want. Very badly, I'd imagine."

Annja leaped onto the altar and grabbed Dzerchenko. "Where is he? If you've hurt him, I swear to God—"

"You'll kill me? Roll me in salt as you promised?" Dzerchenko smiled. "I don't think so. You won't touch me if you ever want to see Bob again."

Mischa's hand was on Annja's shoulder again. "Annja."

She released Dzerchenko, who straightened himself up. Mischa walked over to him. "Where is this Bob?"

Dzerchenko smiled. "Why would I tell you that?"

"Because I'm a smart man. If you tell me where Bob is and I get Annja and him out of here, then you and I can discuss a possible future together."

"What kind of future?"

Mischa shrugged. "Seems to me you might just have a valuable commodity here. I'm sure there are plenty of people in the world who would be interested in…import opportunities."

Annja shook her head. "You're not serious."

Mischa looked at her. "Annja, this is business."

"This was wholesale slaughter! You can't seriously be thinking about going into business with this guy?"

Mischa looked at Annja. "What's more important to you—Bob or what I do with my time and business?"

Annja swallowed. "Bob."

Mischa nodded. "That's what I thought. Now, give me a moment here and I'll see if I can't oblige you, okay?"

Annja frowned. "Fine."

She turned away and walked behind the altar. High above, a wooden crucifix hung on the church wall. Annja looked up at it and felt incredibly sad. So much death in a holy place like this. She shook her head. It shouldn't have happened this way. She never should have fallen for Dzerchenko's trap.

"Annja."

She turned and saw Mischa beckoning her over. She cleared her throat of the lump in it and walked over. "Yes?"

"Bob is in the back office. Go find him."

Annja turned and hurried down the steps of the altar. She had to pick her way through the bodies littering the floor of the church. Twice, she almost fell in the bloody puddles. At the door of the office, she cracked the door. "Bob?"

A lamp hit the door with a crash.

"Bob! It's me, Annja."

"Crap, sorry."

Annja pushed the door open and saw Bob on his gurney. How he'd managed to get a lamp and throw it at the door as she opened it amazed her. "Got some strength back, huh?"

He nodded. "What the hell happened out there?"

"Don't ask."

"I'm asking, I'm asking."

Annja filled him in as best she could. When she was finished, Bob shook his head. "This is unbelievable."

"I know."

"When you left, I had a bad feeling about it. And then he came in and laughed the entire time. Said something about gullible women. It was ridiculous blabbering that just made my head hurt. He got me up here as his… people were filing in. I've never been so scared my whole life. They all just looked at me like I was dinner."

"I think you were," Annja said.

"I think we all were."

"I guess it's a good thing I ran into Mischa and his men, then."

"Depends on how you define luck, I guess." Bob smiled. "Can we get out of here now?"

"I think so. Mischa's talking to Dzerchenko. It seems obvious they're going to work some kind of deal. It sickens me but there's nothing I can do about it right now. My priority is getting you out of here."

Bob frowned. "They'll keep this up, won't they?"

"Very probably."

"Damn."

Annja nodded. "There's nothing we can do. This is a matter for the authorities, not us. I wish there was something more I could do, but right now…"

"Yeah."

The office door opened and one of Mischa's men came in. He pointed toward the altar and Annja nodded. "Okay, I'll be right there."

He left and Annja got behind Bob's gurney. "We have an audience with the pope, apparently."

She pushed him back out into the church. Bob groaned. "My God, look at this place. It's a slaughterhouse." Bob whistled. "I wonder what the penalty is for killing inside a church?"

"I don't want to find out," Annja said.

She pushed Bob as far as she could before the bodies barred her way. Mischa came over. "You are free to go."

Annja nodded at Bob. "I need help getting him out of here."

Mischa agreed. "I'll tell one of my men to help

you. We came in two vehicles. You take one of them and drive him back to Magadan. He can get the care he needs there."

Annja looked over Mischa's shoulder to Dzerchenko. "What about him?"

Mischa smiled. "Oh, I think he's got enough on his mind right now to not worry about what you and Bob are up to."

Annja sighed. "You've been good to me and I appreciate that. But I implore you not to do anything with Dzerchenko. Look at these poor people. Each one of them used to have a life and now they're dead. But before they were killed, they endured horrific suffering. What kind of price can you put on that?"

Mischa looked around and then back at Annja. "Plenty. These things will fetch millions with the right buyers. It's too good a deal to pass up. And if we control the village here, we can use it as a base of operations. We'll be safe and secure. And Dzerchenko can continue his work."

"You're enabling his nightmare to continue," Annja cried.

Mischa eyed her. "You have a better idea?"

"Kill him. And stop this madness."

Mischa smiled. "You can really be cutthroat when you want to be, huh?"

"I think it's necessary in this case."

"Perhaps, but the profit is too immense."

"And what about your men who were killed? They won't be the only ones. And when Dzerchenko thinks he can get the better of you, he will try it. You might even die at the hands of one of these things."

Mischa nodded. "It's a chance I'm willing to take."

"I wish you wouldn't."

"What you wish isn't a factor here."

Annja took a breath. "All right, then."

Dzerchenko appeared at Mischa's shoulder. "Are we all set here?"

Mischa glared at him. "I told you to wait over there."

Dzerchenko smiled. "Forgive an old man his passion for working an open wound." His eyes twinkled and Annja hated him all the more.

"You're scum," she said.

Dzerchenko bowed. "Thank you." He stood and looked at Mischa. "Has she told you about her magical sword yet?"

Mischa's eyes opened. "What?"

"She has a sword she can summon at will."

Mischa looked at Annja. "Is this true?"

Annja shook her head. "I told you you wouldn't be able to trust this guy. He's insane and he's already lying to you."

Mischa eyed Annja and brought his gun up. "This sword…show it to me."

41

Annja looked into Mischa's eyes. "There is no sword. Dzerchenko is making it up in order to gain favor with you."

"How would lying gain him any favor with me?"

"If he is able to convince you that I have a sword and I tell you I don't, he'll just accuse me of lying until you get angry with me. At that point, you'll probably shoot me and he will get exactly what he wants—me dead."

Mischa smiled. "Your mind works very well, doesn't it?"

"I have no idea. Lately, it's been getting me into a lot of trouble."

Mischa looked at Dzerchenko. "I'm inclined to believe her. She hasn't lied to me yet."

"That's because you're allowing yourself to be wiled by a beautiful woman."

Annja frowned. "Thanks for the backhanded compliment."

Dzerchenko ignored her. "Don't let her fool you. She can summon it at will. She used it to kill the man I sent to kill her."

Mischa smiled. "All right, if she's got a sword, where the hell is it?"

Dzerchenko frowned. "I don't know. She can summon it forth at will, though."

"So it just…appears?" Mischa asked

"Yes!" Dzerchenko said.

Mischa chuckled. "You realize how crazy that sounds? Especially coming from a man of science? I wouldn't think that you'd fall for that superstitious mumbo jumbo so easily."

"It's not crazy. I saw it."

Mischa leaned close to him. "Could be time to get your eyes checked out."

Dzerchenko turned away. "Fine."

Mischa looked back at Annja. "Don't worry about him. Are you ready to get going?"

Annja nodded. "We are."

"All right, then—"

As Mischa continued talking, Dzerchenko suddenly let out a bloodcurdling scream and launched himself into the air.

Annja saw it all happen as if in slow motion. She saw the wicked knife Dzerchenko had in his hands. She closed her eyes and summoned the sword.

As Dzerchenko came down, Annja deflected the blade and then pivoted, dropping as she did so. Her blade cut horizontally across Dzerchenko's midsection, cutting deep into his body.

He dropped, cut almost in two by Annja's sword.

Dzerchenko's knife clattered away.

"My, my."

She looked up at Mischa, who had a pistol trained on her. "It would appear as though my former would-be colleague was correct." He looked shocked.

Annja said nothing, but got to her feet. "Yeah, well, you can't blame a girl for trying to keep her stuff safe."

Mischa smiled. "You want to explain this to me?"

"Not really."

"I could offer to kill Bob here and make you talk that way. Or I could give you to my men and they could have some fun with you before you spit out the truth."

"You won't do that," Annja said.

Mischa's eyebrows jumped. "And what makes you think I won't?"

"Because as bad a man as you are, you're not a beast." Annja looked at Dzerchenko's corpse. "Not like him."

Mischa considered that and shrugged. "Perhaps."

"No perhaps about it. You're as good a man as is possible for someone in your line of work."

"Don't flatter me too much, Annja. I might have to kill you just to protect my reputation."

Annja walked around to Bob's gurney. He was staring at her. "We're leaving," she said.

"Are you?"

Annja stopped. "Which one of your men is going to help me?"

Mischa chewed his lip. "None."

Annja took her hands off the gurney. "What are you talking about?"

"I want that sword."

Annja smirked. "Trust me, if I could give you this thing, I would in a heartbeat. But I'm afraid it's not that easy. For some bizarre reason, the sword chose me. Now I'm stuck with it like a bad set of luggage."

"There must be a way," Mischa said.

Annja leaned against the gurney. "Tell you what—you come up with a way to do it, call me. We can talk."

Annja started to push the gurney, but one of Mischa's men blocked her way. Annja stopped again and looked at Mischa. "Are we really going to go through this again?"

Mischa kept the pistol on her. "Let me have it. I want to see it."

"You know," Annja said, "the Japanese samurai used to believe that if you unsheathed a sword, you had to cut something. That if the blade was only brought out for show, it was an insult to the sword itself."

Mischa laughed. "So we'll cut Bob, then."

"I don't like the way this conversation is heading," Bob said.

Annja patted his arm. "The sword stays with me. That's my final offer."

"Not much of an offer," Mischa said. He leveled the pistol on Bob. "Here's my counteroffer."

He fired one round into Bob's leg. Bob screamed in agony as the small-caliber round tore through his thigh. A spurt of blood spread across the sheets.

"I shot him in the quadriceps. He'll be fine…for now. But given the extent of his other injuries, you need to get him to a doctor. Soon. Otherwise, who knows? Shock could settle in. And he could very likely die."

Annja was sweating. This can't be happening.

"The sword, Annja. Now."

Annja glared at him. "Maybe I was wrong."

"Oh?"

"Yeah, you're as big a piece of garbage as Dzer-chenko was."

Mischa laughed. "That's better."

Annja looked at Bob. He'd clamped one of his hands over the wound to stop the bleeding.

Mischa leveled the pistol at Bob's head. "Last chance. The next bullet goes into his head. And then I start on you. And you know, there's only so much pain a human being can tolerate."

Annja started to say something, but her words were drowned out by the sudden report of multiple gunshots.

Mischa turned, but as he did so, his body took four bullets that caused him to twist and buck as if some-one had touched him with a live wire. He pirouetted and crumpled in a heap on the floor.

His other men took rounds and dropped, as well.

Annja ducked down, but saw the church being overrun with men dressed in black coveralls and respi-rators. They shouted for her to stay down. Two of them rushed over and covered her while the other members of the team cleared the remainder of the church.

After twenty seconds, it was over.

One of the commandos helped Annja to her feet. "Are you all right?"

Annja nodded. "My friend needs medical attention."

The commando called over a medic who went to work on fixing Bob.

"Who are you guys?" Annja asked.

The commando removed his respirator. Annja

could see the marks on his face from where the rubber housing met flesh. His eyes looked sharp and they reminded her of someone.

"We're friends of Gregor's."

Annja could see it now. The way he carried himself, the way he spoke and stood. It was as if Gregor had come back from the dead.

"I see," Annja said.

"Where is he?"

Annja sighed. "I don't know. He was underground in a secret laboratory. But I don't know where he might be now."

"All right, we'll find him." The commando turned and gave orders to his men, who then fanned out to search for Gregor's body.

Annja watched him and cleared her throat. "How in the world did you ever find us?"

He grinned. "Gregor had a global-positioning satellite transponder on his body. We all have them. It took us a little while to get here when he failed to report in last night. We knew there was trouble."

The medic was doing good work on Bob, who smiled weakly at Annja. The medic said something to the commando leader, who nodded and then looked back at Annja. "He says your friend should be dead. But that he will live."

Annja winked at Bob. "Defying the odds again, huh?"

"I'm like a bad fungus, apparently."

"Apparently."

"We'll fly him out," the leader said.

"Thank you," Annja replied.

A burst of radio static broke out over the leader's radio unit. He spoke into it for a moment and then listened. When the transmission was done, he looked back at Annja. "They found him."

"Downstairs?"

"Yes."

Annja took a deep breath. "I wish I'd gotten to know him a bit better."

"He was a good man." The leader looked around. "What happened here?"

Annja smiled. "How much time do you have?"

"As much as it takes."

Annja explained all the events that had transpired. She hadn't realized how much detail there was in retelling the story of their adventures. Every once in a while, she would look over at Bob and smile. He looked tired and Annja suddenly realized that she was exhausted. The pressure of the past few days had drained her. She needed a vacation in a bad way.

From the rear of the church, she saw movement. Four commandos bore a stretcher out of the kitchen.

Annja could see Gregor's body lying on it covered in a sheet.

As they filed down the center aisle, Annja whispered goodbye to him. The commandos filed outside and down the steps.

"He'll be buried with full military honors. The country owes him a huge debt of gratitude."

"So do I," Annja said.

"Do you know how he died?"

Annja hesitated. "Yes."

The leader looked at her for a long minute. Then

he simply nodded. "Very well. I guess we'll leave that right where it is."

Annja sighed. "That might be best."

"Let's get you out of here. As far as I can tell, this village is deserted."

"It should be destroyed," Annja said.

Bob grabbed her hand and squeezed it tight. "Thank you."

She grinned. "For what?"

"For coming on this trip. I never would have gotten out of this alive without your help."

"You can buy me a beer when you get out of the hospital."

"You bet."

The leader looked at them both. "We'll be having a service for Gregor back at our headquarters. You're both welcome to attend if you like."

Annja looked at Bob. "It might take us a while to get there."

The leader nodded. "We have to do our investigation first. We'll hold the service in a few weeks. That should give you enough time."

Annja nodded. "I think we'd like that. A lot."

The leader stepped away, and several more men came over to Bob's gurney. They wheeled him to the front door, wrapped him in blankets and then carried him down the steps.

Overhead, Annja could hear the steady sound of helicopters coming in.

She took one final look around the church.

And then walked outside into the bright new day.

Epilogue

Annja sat drinking her cold draft beer in a small bar in Brooklyn. Around her, the voices of other bar patrons mingled with the music of a jukebox in the corner. Several wide-screen televisions showed football games.

Annja took another sip of her drink and then wiped her mouth on a napkin. The booth she sat in had a high back. It afforded her privacy, and lately that was something she was coveting even more than she normally did.

Her stomach lurched and she looked up. Threading his way through the crowd was a familiar face, and Annja smiled in spite of herself. As Bob worked through the crowds, he leaned on a cane and waved to Annja.

She waved back and he made it through the throng. "About time you got here," she said.

He rested the cane against the table and then used his hands to steady himself as he slid into the booth.

His left leg stayed straight outside of the booth, jutting out into the aisle. "You try getting around on one of these things. They're a royal pain in the ass, let me tell you."

"At least you get to maneuver around, huh?"

"Yeah, at least." He looked at her beer. "What are you drinking?"

"Sam Adams Winter Lager. One of the best in the world."

Bob nodded. "I'll have one, as well." He waved a waitress over and placed his order. He also slid his credit card onto her tray. He winked at Annja. "I haven't forgotten about that beer I owe you."

"Thanks."

He leaned back. "How're you doing?"

Annja shrugged. "Okay."

"You sure?"

She smiled. "I'm all right. Honestly."

"I think that trip over yonder took a lot out of you. I know it sure as hell devastated me," he said.

"Almost dying can do that to a person." Annja took another sip of her beer. "God knows I've been there enough."

"What we saw over there…well, it was horrible," Bob said.

"The whole village, all his experiments. Even the nice old cook who made me breakfast the day I left you to get help."

"You stopped for breakfast?"

Annja smirked. "She forced me to eat."

"Yeah. Okay." Bob grinned at her as the waitress returned with his drink. She brought a refill for Annja.

"Thanks."

Bob hoisted his glass. "Here's to surviving."

Annja clinked her glass against his. "Always a good thing."

"And to Gregor."

Annja nodded. Despite the fact they'd already celebrated his death in battle with the other members of his unique fraternity, Annja still felt a lingering depression about how he had died.

Bob watched her and drank his beer. "It wasn't your fault. You've got to get over it."

"I'm trying."

"You're not trying hard enough, Annja. You don't go around dealing death with reckless abandon. You showed amazing courage over there and also incredible restraint. When it came down to it, you did what you absolutely had to in order to get us out of there."

"I suppose. I just can't stop thinking about the fact that he was a good man."

"He was a spy."

"Even so."

"The simple fact is this—you did what you had to do. Hell, it could just as easily have been me. And you might be sitting here with Gregor instead."

Annja smiled. "Any one of us could have died over there."

Bob nodded.

"You been home to see your family yet?" Annja asked.

He smiled. "Saw my mom and sisters. It was great seeing them. The entire time I was on that damned gurney, all I could think about was how much I wanted to spend time with them. Stuff like that, I don't know, it makes you appreciate the people you have."

"Yes. I'd imagine it does."

Bob sighed. "So, I've got an offer to do a documentary on what we experienced over there."

"You do?"

"Yep. I pitched the story and they loved it. The cane helped, too. Walking wounded and all. TV execs love that crap. It's too bad I'm so fuzzy on what actually happened. All the meds took their toll, but I'm sure I can give them a good story anyway."

Annja shook her head. "You're certainly getting right back on the horse again, aren't you?"

"It's all I know how to do." Bob's eyes wandered over to the bar. "Speaking of which…"

Annja saw a gorgeous blonde giving Bob the eye. She smirked. "Must be that cane of yours."

Bob nodded. "May as well get some mileage out of it. You mind if I—?"

Annja waved him off. "Go. Find yourself a playmate. After all we've been through, you deserve it."

"What about you?"

"I wasn't the one who died and came back to life." She nodded at the blonde. "Make sure you tell her about the resurrection. Women are suckers for that stuff."

"Will do." Bob slid out of the booth, grabbed his cane and his beer and hobbled over to the bar. In a few seconds he had the blonde laughing and patting him on the arm.

Annja watched him for a few more seconds. It's

so easy for some people. She sighed. It'd be nice to experience that one day myself.

"You all through feeling sorry for yourself?"

Annja looked up, ready to throw her beer in the face of the speaker, but she stopped when she saw who it was. "What are you doing here?"

"I heard there was an amazing woman here feeling down in the dumps over some particularly nasty stuff that happened in Siberia."

"And you decided to swing by and make me feel better?"

"That was part of it." He cleared his throat. "You mind if I sit down?"

Annja shrugged. "Make yourself comfortable."

He slid into the booth, somehow able to squeeze his body into the small confines. As usual, he was clad head to toe in black. The cashmere turtleneck sweater seemed to hug his upper torso, showing off tight muscles and steel-strong ligaments.

He folded his hands in front of him. "Does this place serve a good drink?"

Annja shrugged. "Beer's good."

Garin sighed. "All right, then, I'll have that, although it is a little bourgeois for me."

The waitress hurried over, almost falling over herself when she looked into Garin's eyes. He ordered and sent her on her way giggling.

Annja rolled her eyes. "Was there something you wanted, Garin? I'm not much in the mood to watch you seduce another barmaid."

Garin leaned forward. "I've got something you might be interested in."

"I'm interested in a vacation. You have one of those?"

Garin grinned. "Sun? Tropical environment? Exotic flowers?"

Annja shrugged. "It's a start."

He leaned back and crossed his arms, his eyes twinkling. "Then have I got the perfect trip for you."

Annja looked at him and smiled. From somewhere inside, she started to feel better. Maybe Bob had it right after all. Best to just get back on the horse and keep riding.

She took a sip of beer. "Tell me about it."

As Garin leaned forward and began talking, Annja let her excitement grow until it washed away all of the sadness she'd been feeling.

She was alive.

It felt good.

You've loved the novels, now see the action in **FULL COLOR!**

IDW Publishing presents the first-ever Annja Creed **comic book** adventure:

ROGUE ANGEL

TELLER OF TALL TALES

Story by Barbara Randall Kesel
Art by Renae De Liz and Ray Dillon
Cover art by Rebecca A. Wrigley

Comic Books Available Now
Graphic Novel on Sale September 2008

COMIC SHOP LOCATOR SERVICE
888-COMIC-BOOK
comicshoplocator.com

www.idwpublishing.com

ROOM 59

A nuclear bomb has gone missing. At the same
time Room 59 intercepts a communiqué from
U.S. Border Patrol agent Nathaniel Spencer.
But as Room 59 operatives delve deeper into
Mexico's criminal underworld, it soon becomes
clear that someone is planning a massive attack
against America…one that would render the
entire nation completely defenceless!

Look for

aim AND fire

by

cliff RYDER

*Available July 2008
wherever you buy books.*

**GOLD
EAGLE** ®

GRM593